CHANGELING

ANDREW HASTIE

This edition published by Here be Dragons Limited 2019

ISBN: 978-1-9164747-4-1

5.5

November 2019

A changeling was believed to be a fairy child that had been left in place of a human child stolen by the fairies.

1

RUFIUS

[Summerbridge, Northumbria, England. Date: 953]

The blade splintered his shield and buried itself into his arm. The edge of Hagar's axe had been blunted so as not to sever a limb, but it would leave a scar nonetheless.

Rufius dropped what remained of his shield and, ignoring the throbbing pain in his arm, swung his axe low at his opponent's legs. Hagar performed the 'salmon leap', jumping effortlessly over the sweeping arc of the axehead and bringing his shield down on the now unbalanced Rufius, knocking him to the ground.

'Clumsy,' noted their old tutor, Arnwulf, standing outside of the fighting circle chewing on a stalk of grass.

Hagar grinned smugly as the other boys jeered, stepping back to allow Rufius to get to his feet. His arm was bleeding badly and he had lost the feeling in his left hand, making it difficult to pick up what remained of the small wooden shield. Gritting his teeth, he forced his fingers through the grip of the boss and shook loose the splintered wood. Pushing up on the axe, he got back to his feet. Hagar's blow had winded him badly, but he was not about to yield, taking a deep breath he raised the shield to his chest.

'Enough,' declared Arnwulf, clapping his hands. 'You'll be no good against the King of Dublin with only one good arm.'

Hagar roared and beat his axe against his shield. This was his final test, he had beaten every one of them and proved he was ready to join the Leidang when the raiding season began. A year older than Rufius and a head taller than Arnwulf, he was born to fight. A brute of a man with a thick chest and even thicker skull, he would make a perfect member of Bloodaxe's fyrd.

Rufius handed the old training master his axe and used his good hand to prise the shield out of his unresponsive fingers. He could see the disappointment in the faces of the other boys as Hagar collected his winnings from them. Every week they wagered on how many strikes it would take to defeat him, and once again he had obviously failed to achieve the worst of their guesses.

To them he was a *reklingr* because he was small for his fourteen winters; although no one could be quite sure how old Rufius was, since they had no idea what year he was born — the other boys called him runt all the same.

Rufius didn't care, because he had a secret, one that he hid from all of them, one that kept him awake at night.

He was a *Vixlingr*, a changeling.

His life had begun with a mystery. Rufius was found, abandoned in the woods, by his liege lord, Eric Bloodaxe, whilst out hunting. The King of Northumbria had saved the baby from the jaws of his elkhounds and made a gift of him to the blacksmith Sindri — whose wife had miscarried earlier that summer.

As a foundling, Rufius was welcomed into the smith's family where he was raised listening to the sagas the old women would tell of the Aesir: Odin, Thor, Frigg, Tyr and the mischievous Loki; of Asgard and the nine realms of the world tree Yggdrasil. Rufius loved their tales of magic, treasure and the battles against the giants, but most of all he was enthralled by the elves of Alfheim. His favourite stories were those of Vixlingr, of how the elves would take human form and steal children from their cots and leave demon children in their place.

Rufius would lie awake at night listening to his adopted grandmother, Isolde, as she told her stories, imagining the magical creatures that had left him in the glade, and wondering what his mother would have looked like. He had dreamt of her many times, always with long white hair and wide blue eyes. The clearing would be bathed in moonlight and she would smile as she lay him in the grass, revealing her sharp teeth. He couldn't really say why they had to be pointed, but Isolde's tales always seemed to contain a hidden danger and Rufius liked the idea that his mother would become a fearsome she-wolf — so fangs seemed appropriate.

2

NIGHT TRAINING

Rufius had never really enjoyed Arnwulf's lessons. The axe always felt too clumsy and unwieldy in his hands, and his leaner build made him too weak an opponent for thugs like Hagar.

A sword, however, was a weapon that required agility and balance, and as the apprentice of the blacksmith, he had access to some of the finest blades in Danelaw.

It took weeks for his arm to recover. His stepfather was angry with Arnwulf, not for allowing his son to come to harm, but for disabling his apprentice. The work in the forge was hard, and a one-armed assistant meant more work for him. Further training bouts were forbidden; any talk of becoming a warrior was banished.

But Rufius was not so easily dissuaded. As the winter nights lengthened, he began to borrow his master's swords and venture out into the forest to practice.

It was a serene and magical world beneath the ancient oaks. Their branches stripped of leaves and dusted white with the frost, he imagined himself in Niflheim, the frozen realm. The bite of the cold was soon forgotten, his body warming quickly as he swung the moon-silvered blade at the imaginary creatures of the old legends.

Owls hunted overhead on silent wings. Their hoots, like mournful ghosts, echoing across the valley, until they too became part of his fantasy. He would imagine he was Beowulf, King of the Danes, and the monster, Grendel, was hiding amongst the twisted trunks. In this dream world the rotten, gnarled stumps became trolls or wargs that he would cut down with one mighty blow of *Hrunting*, or *Tyrfing* depending on which saga he was reenacting.

It was harmless fun, a few secret hours to escape the dull monotony of his life as the apprentice of a blacksmith.

Until the night he borrowed the wrong sword.

Everything changed the night he crept into the warm forge and took an old sword from the rack. Usually, the weapons he took were newly forged — to be sold at the next market or made to order for one of the chieftains. Everyone knew that Sindri's steel was the purest in Danelaw and held its edge longer than any blade the Scots or the Irish could produce. Men travelled for days to own a blade stamped with the Mjölnir, Thor's hammer, his stepfather's mark.

He had no idea why he had chosen the relic. Perhaps the gods had placed the magical sword amongst the others as a test. The moment he unwrapped it from the oilcloth, Rufius knew it was enchanted. Holding the leather grip, he felt its power flow through his fingers. It was as if the blade were speaking to him, showing him the battles it had fought in, the men it had slain.

The violent images that came flooding into his mind

were so vivid, so real, that Rufius dropped the weapon as if it had burned him. He had never witnessed such carnage first hand. For a moment, it had felt as though he was the one wielding the sword, slicing off their heads, carving open their guts.

Kneeling beside the sword, he examined his hand in the dim glow of the forge. There were faint marks on his skin, an intricate tattoo of symbols wove over his palm and up his forearm, but they faded before he had time to study them.

Putting on one of Sindri's forging gloves, Rufius tentatively picked up the sword and slid it into a scabbard and walked out into the night.

Climbing the snow-covered hill above his village, Rufius saw the beacon fires of Jorvik glowing orange against the night's sky far off in the distance. In the past he would have stopped to watch them, wondering what it would be like to live in the city. He had always dreamed of leaving like Hagar and fighting the Scottish with Eric Bloodaxe beyond the borders of Danelaw. He longed to leave the mundane life of Summerbridge and the smithy. He wanted to see something of the world.

But not tonight. Turning away from the city, he made his way towards the wood, knowing that there would be no sagas, no fantastical beasts to fight this evening.

Still wearing the glove, he drew the old blade from its sheath. Sindri had taught him how to judge the quality of a sword by feeling its weight and balance. The grip was worn, and the edges bore the notches of many battles. The moonlight caught a line of strange runes that had been etched along its flat, where the fuller should have been.

Holding his breath, he took off the forge glove and held the sword. Once more, he felt the magic flow through his fingers. Lines of light wove out from the grip, snaking up his arm as the images came again.

The screams of dying men echoed in his head. Young and old, soldiers from armies he had never seen fell before the blade. Dark-skinned strangers in armour bearing the insignia of golden eagles fought for their lives, their eyes wide with a manic fear as they came towards him with spear and sword. He was taller in the vision, a great warrior carving through the lines of the enemy as if he were scything a field of wheat. Rufius closed his eyes, but the terrible visions persisted. Their blood painted the blade, filling the runes, blunting its edges. He could feel the blows ring through his arm as if he was executing every deadly strike. The sword was teaching him how to fight, and he couldn't stop himself.

The following morning, he woke to the sounds of his stepfather ransacking the forge. Rufius had overslept, the exertion of the previous night had left him exhausted. Running into the workshop, he found Sindri pumping the bellows his face flushed with rage and cursing Loki, the trickster. When he asked if Rufius had seen the weapon — Rufius lied.

The sword was far too precious to give back, he knew that it had chosen him, it was magical, and he couldn't give it up.

Two days later, the old warrior who had left the sword to

be sharpened, returned. He seemed more than happy to take a shiny new blade in its place. Rufius hid in the stables and listened as Sindri apologised to the shabby-looking man, wondering if it was actually Odin in disguise. He had heard that the Allfather was supposed to walk amongst mortal men as an old wanderer.

His stepfather was not so pleased, his reputation had been damaged, and he blamed Rufius for the loss. Sindri's family was a large one, with three daughters and four sons to feed, giving away a valuable item which had taken weeks of labour was not something that he could let go unpunished. The beating was severe, and it was some time before Rufius was allowed back into the forge unsupervised.

It was not the first thrashing he had taken from Sindri. Just as with his swords, the smith believed in beating the impurities out of a thing. Rufius had learned to take the punishment, knowing that one day he would leave.

3

MARKET

[Road to Jorvik, Northumbria, England. Date: 954]

The winter snows were retreating, and the first green shoots of spring were breaking through when Rufius was finally forgiven and allowed to accompany his stepfather to market.

He had grown tall and strong during the long winter. No longer the gangly, awkward *reklingr*, that had suffered Hagar's beatings. His body was taut and the muscles hardened by his nightly training regime — there were even the beginnings of a beard on his chin.

These changes had not gone unnoticed by his adopted sisters, who began making idle remarks about how the runt was becoming a man. They were all older than Rufius and raised their eyebrows at each other while he stripped down to take the cold bath every Laurdag, or Saturday as the Christians called it.

The dawn was still an hour away.

Pulling his cloak tighter to fend off the pre-dawn chill, Rufius drove the cart along the rutted road towards Jorvik. Sindri was sleeping soundly in the back under a pile of furs; his snoring drowned out by the rattling of swords and shields that made up his bed.

This would be the first market of the new year, and it was always the most extravagant. For a few days, Jorvik would be filled with foreign travellers and traders, some who would have journeyed from the Far East bringing their exotic spices and silks along with their mystical ways.

It was an important event for Sindri. The winter settling was at an end and the raiding would begin soon. Many of the fyrd would be looking to replace their old and damaged weapons, their purses still swollen with coin from the monasteries of the Saxon priests. It was the highpoint in Sindri's year and a chance to catch up with old friends.

They had brought small items too: nails and combs that Rufius would be expected to sell to the womenfolk. Such was the life of an apprentice, while his stepfather would be concentrating on the serious business of selling swords, getting drunk and telling stories, Rufius was expected to sell his own work.

Except he had no talent for ironworking. The trinkets that he made were crude and artless. His fingers were not made for detail, and each of them had been reworked many times over.

His childhood had ended the moment he could hold a hammer and his life as a thrall began. No better than a servant, he was made to work for his keep, sleeping with the animals at the far end of the longhouse. He would always be grateful to Sindri for taking him in — he owed him his life, even if it wasn't the life he wanted.

Rufius wanted the worlds that the sword had shown

him. Every day that had passed since he had found it made his life as an apprentice unbearable. He was convinced that the gods had gifted him the weapon for a reason, that his destiny was bound to it somehow. He would rather have lost a hand than give it up and knowing Sindri, it was highly likely that he would if he ever found out.

The sword was safely hidden in a cave in the rocks above their valley. There had been times when Rufius had thought about telling his stepfather, but he could never think of a logical explanation for why he had taken it, he couldn't think of a non-magical reason that his stepfather would accept.

Sindri was a practical, hard-working man, who had no time for sorcery. In the evenings, when his grandmother told her tales of Fenrir and Vithar around the fire, the smith would take his pipe and go outside 'to study Ymir's skull', sitting alone looking up at the stars.

Like all legendary swords, Rufius had given it a name: *Gunnlogi*. It meant 'Flame of battle' which he thought was fitting considering the fighting techniques it had taught him. Some were similar to those that Arnwulf would show them when he was drunk but refused to repeat when he was sober.

The old warrior's arms were laced with scars: 'Æthelwold's pride', he called them drinking mead by the fire surrounded by his students. They were mementoes of the campaign into Mercia and the Battle of the Holme, which ended with the deaths of Æthelwold and the Eohric, King of East Anglia. Arnwulf had survived more battles than he cared to remember, and still limped in the cold weather — thanks to a Saxon bowman.

Rufius had missed the old man since Sindri had banned him from attending the training. He had considered showing Arnwulf what he had learned. Hagar had left months ago to travel north with Bloodaxe's fyrd, and Rufius knew the other boys would be less spiteful without their ringleader. Yet something stopped him, all the weapons he handled in the forge felt clumsy and useless in comparison to Gunnlogi, they were nothing but cold iron in his hands and without the visions of how to wield it, he felt powerless.

Rufius knew better than to take the sword to Arnwulf. Even though he had carefully cleaned and sharpened the blade, the old warrior would know it wasn't his and there would be questions — especially about the runes. He assumed they were something to do with the magic it held, and he would need a shaman to understand them. Rufius couldn't trust anyone in the village, but there were scribes in Jorvik who would, for a price, decipher their meaning.

Trapping the reins under his feet, Rufius took out the piece of birch bark from his tunic. The runes were carefully copied onto its inner surface, and as dawn broke over the trees, he squinted at the sacred marks, wondering if perhaps they would help him understand the power of the sword. He hadn't any coin, but if he could find some excuse to go into the market, he planned to find himself a scribe and barter for a translation.

4

JORVIK

[Jorvik, Northumbria, England. Date: 954]

The sun was rising over the old Roman walls as they followed the crowds towards the city gates.

Rufius could still remember the first time he saw the walled city; he was nine, and Sindri had taken him with two of his stepbrothers to the midsummer's market. It had been a hard ride through the warm night, but he was so excited that he couldn't sleep and never forgot the view of the old city as they crested the hill. In the glow of the morning light, he thought it was Asgard.

'We've no time for dallying today,' warned Sindri, taking his seat beside Rufius as they approached the tollgate. 'If we're to be home before nightfall.'

'Arnwulf says that Eric Bloodaxe has returned and thrown Archbishop Wulfstan into the stocks,' Rufius said, handing his stepfather the reins.

'King for a day,' grunted the blacksmith, digging a copper coin out of his purse. 'How long until Eadred takes the throne? Heed my word boy, stay out of the business of kings.'

'I wanted to throw something at the Christian.'

Sindri sneered at the idea, handing the coin to the guard before whipping the reins against the flanks of the horse and driving the cart through the gates.

Rufius knew better than to push the matter any further. His stepfather was a man of few words and would grow suspicious if he laboured a point. He would just have to find another reason to go off on his own.

Their progress was slowed by the ramshackle lines of stalls that had sprung up on both sides of the street overnight. Local merchants fought for space alongside the foreign traders, each vying for passing customers. There was amber from the Baltic, walrus tusks and wolf-skins from Scandinavia and beautifully ornate shells from the Persian sea. The air was filled with the scent of roasting meat and spices, reminding Rufius that breakfast had been nothing more than a crust of three-day-old bread and a lump of cheese. Ignoring Sindri's cursing at the people in front of them, he listened to the voices of the merchants as they advertised their wares from far-off lands like Byzantine and Samarkand.

They were late, and Rufius could tell by the way the skin creased on the back of Sindri's bald head how much trouble he was in. The street bazaar was quickly clogging up with an annoying combination of locals and travellers idly browsing stalls in front of them, making it slow going. Frustrated by their progress, Sindri handed the reigns to Rufius and stepped down from the cart, pulling the horse by the nose through the crowds towards the square.

5

SCRIBES

[Jorvik, Northumbria, England. Date: 954]

Despite the late start, it had been a successful morning. Sindri had sold all but two of the swords and taken orders for as many plough-shares as axe heads. The days of the warrior were waning.

'There were more farmers than fighters in the crowd,' he said, 'and their needs are very different.'

Rufius had also worked hard, selling all of his wares by midday. With his chores completed, he was eager to explore the market, but his stepfather shook his head. 'Too many bad men, too much drink,' was all he would say on the subject.

They sat eating lunch together in silence on the back of the cart. Rufius was desperately trying to think of an excuse, brooding over his options as he watched the passers-by.

'Mother needs salt,' he said, hopping down from the cart.

'Does she now?' Sindri replied, cutting another slice from the wheel of cheese.

'Yes, she told me while you were loading up.' It was a small lie, one that would be forgotten once the drinking started.

Sindri wrapped up his cheese and bread in the muslin and stowed it beneath the furs. Clapping his hands, he got down from the cart.

'I'll go. You stay here and keep an eye on the merchandise — see if you can sell that Gokstad.'

'Nobody wants a shield like that anymore,' complained Rufius. 'It's too big.'

Sindri raised his hand as if about to strike him when a group of warriors passed by. They hailed the blacksmith, some calling him by name while others made crude jokes about rusting iron and blunted daggers. He ignored most, only acknowledging those few whom he knew directly.

Rufius saw his opportunity. He had coins from his sales and jangled his purse as if to say, 'I can go if you like.'

Before Sindri had time to object, one of Sindri's oldest customers appeared and asked him about one of the remaining swords. His stepfather took his eyes off the customer for a second and Rufius's heart stopped beating as the blacksmith's eyes narrowed — and then he nodded.

Rufius had to stop himself from running as he made his way out into the crowded market.

The scribes were to be found in the streets around Coppergate, on the southeast side of the market square. On any normal market day it would have taken less than a few minutes to reach, but today was different, the people were like a maze of ever-moving walls.

The greasy scent of roasting boar wafted over the heads of the crowd while Rufius wove his way between them, reminding him how little he had eaten today. Heading towards the smell of the meat, he came across one of the Christian priests locked into a pillory who was being pelted with rotten fruit by a group of Bloodaxe's fyrd.

Rufius spotted Hagar immediately, the boy was very drunk and being goaded into throwing increasing larger vegetables at the man. Rufius was tempted to join in. He had no time for their religion; they spent most of their time preaching about their one true god and telling everyone how they would all burn in hell for following false idols. Rufius wondered how their one god would fair against the might of the Aesir — it would make for an interesting battle. Yet he had to admit these missionaries had courage to cross the borders into Danelaw, most of their order had suffered badly under Norse rule, especially those whose monasteries fell within reach of the raiding parties.

Hagar looked very different since he had nearly broken Rufius's arm. His beard had grown so long that he could braid it and there was a newly-healed scar running down one side of his face. Blood matted his hair — the sign of a recent kill, and there was a vicious-looking double-headed axe strapped to his back.

Rufius turned away before he was seen, walking into the centre of the square where he stumbled onto a caravan of travelling acrobats and dancers performing for the crowds. They were dressed in beautiful, exotic silks. Dark-skinned women writhed to the beat of a goatskin drum, while strongmen stood on each other's shoulders or balanced on one hand on top of a sword. At the centre of their troupe stood a magii. He was tall, with a bald, tattooed head and long flowing robes. His eyes were closed, and Rufius could see his beard twitch as he whispered silent incantations to a blue flame that flickered in the palm of his hand.

It took all of his willpower to turn away from the spectacle — the magic was mesmerising. Isolde had told stories of shamans; how they were supposed to be able to assume the shape of wolves or bears, and could take a man's soul with a single word.

For a moment, he wondered if the magii would be able to tell him the meaning of the sword's runes. The man's head was covered in similar symbols that seemed to glow in the light of the flame as it grew. *Would he steal the sword?* Rufius thought to himself, watching the man throw the fire high into the air. *Could he make me tell him where it was hidden?*

The blue flame transformed into a dragon, its wings spreading out over the awe-struck crowd before dissolving into the air. Rufius couldn't bear the thought of losing Gunnlogi and turned and walked towards the street of scribes.

There were many stalls to choose from: wooden benches and writing desks crammed with pots of quills and a hundred different types of parchment, and they were all busy. Warriors and serving wenches, wives and jilted lovers sat pouring their hearts out to strangers who wrote down their every word. Old men dictated their last will and testament beside weeping mothers learning that their sons would never return. It seemed to Rufius as if the entire population of Jorvik had suddenly got the urge to write a letter.

Eventually, he found a free booth. The scribe was an old man, his skin like paper, thin and stretched over sinewy arms. His heavily lidded eyes hardly opened when Rufius sat down on the stool.

'Three ravens,' the old man croaked, holding out a calloused hand the fingers deeply stained with ink.

'You don't know what I want yet!' Rufius complained, taking the sliver of bark out of his tunic.

'Letters and notices are five. Reading is three.'

'Shouldn't it depend on how many words there are?'

The old man made some kind of noise that could have been a chuckle, or just clearing his throat and held up three fingers of one hand.

'Three.'

Rufius counted out three silver pennies into the outstretched leathery palm. It was more than he expected and his stepfather had taught him never to take the first price, but he had little time and he still had to buy the salt.

The scribe weighed the coins in his hand and then they disappeared inside his robe.

Rufius placed the bark on the low table between them. 'I want you to tell me what this says.'

The scribe examined the bark. 'Interesting material — Birch?'

It seemed to Rufius that the old man had closed his eyes completely as he brought it close to his face, then he took out a large glass lens and moved it across the characters.

'How did you come by this? What book did you copy it from?'

Rufius didn't want to admit that it belonged to a sword; for some reason it still felt like he was confessing to being a thief.

'I saw it on a stone, outside our village.'

'Liar!' spat the old man.

Rufius rose to his feet, trying to hide his fear. 'Just tell me what it says!'

'This is Latin. No one would ascribe this to a rock.' He ran his fingers along the characters. 'It's by Horace, a Roman poet, and it says: "We are but dust and shadow".'

Rufius snatched the bark back out of his hand and turned to leave.

It was only then that he realised there was a man standing behind him, the magii from the market square. His eyes were dark and full of questions.

'Who are you?' Rufius asked.

'My name is Dolovir,' the man said, with an accent that had traces of distant lands.

'What do you want?'

The man smiled and held out his hand. 'May I?'

Rufius couldn't hide his shame. His cheeks burned as he fumbled with the bark.

'Show me.' The man's tone suddenly hardened, and Rufius felt compelled to give it to him.

'I have to get back to my master. He will be wondering where I've got to.'

Dolovir read the inscription silently before looking up at Rufius.

'Pulvis et umbra sumus — a wise sentiment indeed. When did you come by this?'

Rufius ignored the question, grabbing the bark, he bolted into the crowd.

6

SALT

Rufius ran in no particular direction, making random turns in blind panic until he found himself in a dark alley near the river.

He was breathing hard. His lungs felt as if they were going to burst. He could feel his heart hammering against his chest, but the bark was still clamped in his sweating palm.

Studying the strange symbols, he repeated the words of the scribe, trying to understand what they could mean.

'Pulvis et umbra sumus — we are but dust and shadow.'

The sound of the words invoked the same sensation that he felt when holding the sword. The power of the phrase opened memories in his mind that unravelled like a rope, lines of energy twisting around themselves, each one filled with echoes of ancient times.

'And what do we have here,' growled a man unwrapping himself from his cloak and standing up. There was a glint of a dagger in the dim light of the alley.

Rufius put the bark away and stepped backwards into a pair of strong hands.

'*Meyla krafla mikli thur syr*,' said the man behind him in Old Norse. It meant 'a child born of a long-dead sow,' and it was one of Rufius's favourite curses.

Rufius twisted out of his grip and turned towards the other man, finding himself staring into the scarred face of a one-eyed drunk. His breath reeked of rotten teeth and sour mead, and the crude blade shook as he held it out in front of him.

'What've you got in there?' he slurred, waving the rusty blade at Rufius's tunic.

Rufius looked back nervously at the first man who was blocking the only other way out of the alley. He thought about shouting for help but knew that the men would slit his throat before he could raise the alarm. The city watch didn't patrol this part of the city; even they weren't stupid enough to enter the narrow streets near the docks alone.

He took out the bark and held it up to them, showing them the side without the symbols.

The man snatched it from Rufius and examined it with his good eye. 'Runes?' he mumbled to himself when he turned it over.

'What's he got?' demanded the other.

'Runes. Some kind of spell.'

Rufius went to take it back, but the one-eyed man held it out of his reach. 'You some kind of warlock boy? You trying to put a hex on me?'

'Just kill him and take his purse,' growled the cloaked man, walking towards them.

Rufius could see the man weighing up the options; runes were not what he expected.

'I'm a vixlingr,' whispered Rufius, more to himself than his attackers.

'What did he say?'

'Speak up boy.'

The knife was close enough for Rufius to see that it was old, rusted and blunt. Sindri had taught him about the keening on an edge, he could hold it without fear of it cutting himself, but a stabbing thrust could still be deadly.

Rufius cleared his throat and shouted. 'I'm a changeling!' Gripping the blade, he wrenched it out of the man's hand.

The moment his fingers touched the metal, he felt its history open up to him. All the pain and hurt it had inflicted in the hands of the half-blind cut-throat and more. Earlier times when it had been worn in the belt of a warrior; and before that, the quick hands of a Persian assassin who had owned it once and lost it in a fight to the death. Just as with the sword, he immediately absorbed the knowledge it contained, feeling his body learn the graceful moves of its once deadly master.

His hands moved so quickly they were a blur. He executed a rapid series of attacks as though his body were controlled by some unseen puppet-master. In less than a heartbeat, the one-eyed man was on his knees, holding his belly to keep his guts from falling out. The other man was laying on his back, the hilt of the blade sticking out of his chest.

Rufius ran out into the main street and straight into the arms of the magii.

The tattooed man said nothing but looked down at Rufius's hands, which were soaked in blood.

Rufius didn't wait for a response, he barged past the shaman and ran into the crowd.

7

CAVE

Fortunately, by the time Rufius had cleaned himself up and found his way back to the cart, the sun was low and Sindri was very drunk. He had obviously sold everything and gone drinking with some of his friends. Going to market was about more than just selling swords, it was a chance to eat smoked herring, drink mead and trade stories. It was one of the only times of the year that Sindri would drink until he passed out.

The sun was setting when Rufius started out for home. Sindri was snoring soundly under the furs in the back of the cart. The road back to Summerbridge was empty, and he was glad of the peace — it had been an eventful day.

Replaying the fight with the two cut-throats in his mind was like trying to remember a dream. The instant he touched the dagger, his actions were no longer his own, as if he had stepped out of his body and been transported into another time. It was different to when he used Gunnlogi, with his sword there was always a sense of control, of still being part of the action. The knife was less subtle somehow, more eager to kill, perhaps because it had spent its life being used for dark deeds.

The homeward journey went slowly, letting the horse dictate the pace. Rufius was in no hurry to get back.

Listening to the nightjars as evening fell and the moon rose high, he thought about the magii, wondering how long he had been standing at the end of the alley. Had he watched the fight? Did he see what Rufius had done with the knife? Why had he followed him from the scribe? His head swam with questions, and the one that disturbed him the most was why had Dolovir said: 'when' and not 'where did you come by this'.

When they reached the village, only the watchman was awake. He nodded knowingly to Rufius as he passed, this was not the first time Sindri had come back from the market in the back of the cart.

Rufius left his stepfather in the barn. He was too big a man to move when he was in this state, so he covered him with the rest of the furs and put the old mare in her stall.

He was in no mood for sleeping. Instead, he walked out of the village and up into the forest — the scribe's words haunting him along the moonlit path.

'Pulvis et umbra sumus.'

Rising up above the trees, the outcrop of rock stood like an ancient sentinel over the valley. When he was younger, Rufius would imagine it was the head of a Juton, a giant, who had fallen into a deep sleep and let the earth cover its body. There were old symbols carved into its moss-covered sides, the marks of some forgotten tribe that had lived here a long time ago.

There was something about the way the magii had looked at him that was still bothering Rufius. As if he knew his secret and he couldn't shake the idea that the man was going to try and steal the sword — he wouldn't be able to sleep until he knew that it was safe.

The moon was full, lighting the narrow path through the steep-sided walls of the crag, painting it with a silvery, ethereal glow. Rufius knew the way instinctively. He would have been able to navigate the labyrinth blindfolded just using the carved patterns on the rock, they were like sign-posts guiding him towards the cave.

His hiding place was a dark, fern-fringed hollow in the rock that was just large enough for a man to stand in. It was nothing more than a place to weather out a storm, but its walls were carved with ancient hunting scenes that told him people had lived here once.

Sighing with relief, he took Gunnlogi from the darkened recess at the back of the cave. Drawing it out of its scabbard, he felt the familiar tingling sensation spread along his arm.

'What is it that you see?' said a voice from the shadows.

Rufius spun around, instinctively raising the blade, preparing to strike.

'Be calm my young friend. I am not your enemy.'

It was the magii, Dolovir, now dressed in travelling clothes: a long, finely-spun cloak hung on his shoulders, covering a studded leather jerkin. The skin on his head was cleaned of symbols, and Rufius noted that he was carrying a sword but hadn't drawn it, and so he lowered his own.

'Did you follow me?'

Dolovir smiled and shook his head. 'I follow the story.

When someone shows me the words of an old legend, I cannot help but become interested in its origins.'

'This sword has many stories,' Rufius agreed, tilting the blade so the letters glinted in the moonlight.

The magii ignored the threat and continued. 'I have no doubt. It is old and well used, did it belong to one of your ancestors?'

Rufius shook his head.

'Then who told you of its past?'

There was something about the way the man posed the question that made it impossible for Rufius to lie.

'The sword.'

Dolovir's eyes widened fractionally and the tone of his voice deepened.

'Ah, so it's an enchanted sword.'

Rufius sliced the air between them, the blade coming within a few inches of his face. He ended the move in another fighting stance. 'And it taught me how to kill.'

Dolovir never flinched, his gaze still fixed on Rufius. 'Of that, I have no doubt. I saw how you dealt with those cut-throats in the alley. Your technique reminded me of Johannes Liechtenauer.'

'He had a knife. He would have killed me. I had no choice.'

'One always has a choice,' Dolovir said reflectively, 'and did his blade show you how to use it too?'

Rufius nodded.

Dolovir took a silver pendant from around his neck and held it out to Rufius. 'Can you tell me what you see when you hold this?'

Rufius took the pendant in his free hand and rubbed the surface with the tip of his thumb.

The lines of its past unwound around his fingers, and he

gasped at the rich tapestry that unravelled from it. It had once belonged to Azarmidokht, a beautiful Persian princess, given to her by Chosroes II, her father and the last king of the Sassanian dynasty. Rufius witnessed her history unravel, the brutal struggle for the throne of the Persian empire after the death of Chosroes and how she had been blinded and then killed before her sister was restored to the throne.

Rufius handed back the necklace. 'They murdered her.'

'Such is the way of kings.' Dolovir replied, hanging the pendant back around his neck.

'Do you collect magical objects?' Rufius asked, wondering if Dolovir was going to demand the sword.

Dolovir chuckled. 'It is not the object, boy. It is you. There are few that can read an artefact's timeline in the way that you can.'

Rufius looked confused. 'I cannot read.'

'Not words perhaps, but you have a special ability, one that I have been searching the last few centuries to find.'

Isolde had told Rufius that shamans could outlive a normal man, he had assumed the man was no more than forty summers. 'How old are you?'

'Older than I look, but that is another story. Come with me now. My master will explain everything.'

The sky was lightening and dawn was not far away. Rufius realised that he would be missed. 'But what if Sindri wakes and the forge is cold?'

'We will be back before he wakes.' Dolovir smiled, taking out a small book and holding out his other hand.

Tentatively, Rufius lowered his sword and took it.

The world around them twisted away.

8

THE FOUNDER

[Christ Church College, Oxford. Date: 1660]

'Year?' demanded a deep voice.

'Nine hundred and fifty-four,' replied Dolovir.

'Hmm, he appears to have a strong affinity with conflict.'

'Strongest I have seen in a while.'

'You've broken protocol bringing him here.'

'Lord, he's the best candidate I have found. Before the eleventh century it is chaos; they truly were the dark ages,' Dolovir protested.

'Does he have a name?'

Dolovir said nothing.

'Does he know he can weave?'

'No master, he believes the sword is enchanted.'

The older man sighed. 'He's too old. I calculate the odds of success are less than one in thirty. Are you still willing to vouch for him?'

'I will. I'm aware of the risks.'

The sounds of their voices drifted down through a dark,

distant veil as Rufius slowly regained consciousness, it felt like he was surfacing from a deep pond.

Their words were a strange mix of Saxon and another tongue that Rufius couldn't understand. He opened his eyes, blinking until they grew accustomed to the light.

We're not in Danelaw anymore, he thought to himself. He was lying in a room unlike any chamber he had ever seen: the walls were lined with books, the floor was soft and covered in a kind of woven fabric, sunlight shone through coloured glass windows making jewelled patterns on a large map that hung opposite.

At one end of the room was an ornately carved wooden desk, the panels of reliefs were the work of a master carpenter; far more detailed than Eric's throne in the Mead Hall in Jorvik.

Rufius wondered if Dolovir had taken him to the court of some Persian king.

Getting to his knees, he felt his stomach lurch, and a wave of nausea overwhelmed him as he tried to stand.

'Don't,' advised Dolovir in Old Norse, 'don't get up until it passes.'

Rufius took his advice and sat back on his haunches.

He had no idea how they had travelled here. From the angle of the light streaming through the large round window, he could see it was past midday but had no memory of time passing. It felt like only moments ago that they were standing amongst the rocks with the sword.

But the sword was gone. The magii must have stolen it when he passed out.

Rufius cautiously turned towards the owner of the deeper voice, a taller man stood next to Dolovir, holding a strange device: a series of small metal spheres, each rotating around the other.

'This is Lord Dee,' said Dolovir. 'He needs to measure you.'

The older man stared at Rufius. His eyes were a piercing shade of blue, and his beard was threaded with grey. He looked much older than Dolovir and carried himself with the air of a wise man. He wore the long, dark robes of a priest.

The nausea forgotten, Rufius slowly got to his feet and bowed to the man, as his stepfather had taught him.

'Where am I, Lord?'

The wise man's eyes returned to his device, adjusting the orbs until they lined up.

'This is the year sixteen-sixty, not that will mean much to you since you probably have little idea of the century you were in before. In fact, much of what you see here will make no sense, and I expect you will have many questions, those will have to wait. For now, I have only one question for you.'

He nodded to Dolovir, who held out the old sword towards Rufius, hilt first.

The old man held the device out towards Rufius. 'Tell me what you see when you hold that?'

Taking the weapon, Rufius felt the usual sensations coursing through his fingers. Lines of energy unfurled like kelp in water, the fronds of light wrapping around his forearm. He saw the phantoms of the fallen rise up around him.

'I see warriors fighting fierce battles. Many men dying,' he hissed through gritted teeth as if it were a thinly veiled threat.

Lord Dee ignored him, twisting one of the orbs as if he were tightening a screw. 'And these warriors, do you recognise any of them?'

Rufius shook his head, staring at the ghostly soldiers fighting around him. 'They're outlanders and long dead.'

Something about the way the orbs were rotating was disturbing the old man. 'Perhaps, you were right to bring him to me after all,' he said, putting the device down.

'Why *have* you brought me here?' Rufius asked.

Dolovir smiled, he looked much younger now that his hair had grown back, although Rufius couldn't quite understand when that had happened. 'Have you ever thought you were different from the others?'

Rufius was taken aback by the question; it was as if the magii could look into the hidden places in his heart, to the secret that he had held so close all these years. *Yes, I am a changeling!*

'No,' he lied.

'That is a Roman sword, a Gladius,' the master interrupted. 'It's nearly a thousand years old. Where did you come by it?'

'My stepfather was repairing it for an old man,' Rufius replied, hoping to avoid the subject of how he came to have it.

Lord Dee looked unconvinced. 'Did you know this old man?'

Rufius shook his head, unable to meet their gaze in case they asked if he had stolen it. 'Just some traveller, Sindri had to give him a new sword, he wasn't very happy.'

Dolovir's master took the blade and held it in the sunlight, sliding his fingers along the runes.

'Interesting glyphs. Not part of the original design but added later. Someone took great care of this weapon for a very long time. It obviously was of great historical value.'

'Who are the Romans?' asked Rufius.

The air around Lord Dee's fingers began to distort, like the heat haze over a forge. 'Tell me nine-five-four, have you ever actually tried to travel to one of these battles?'

Rufius stared blankly at the old man, trying to make sense of the question.

Dee stared deep into his eyes and the room around them started to shimmer.

'Let me show you.'

9

BATTLE

[Catalaunian Plains, Gaul. Date: June 20th, 451]

Hundreds of men on horseback thundered across the grassy plain towards the shield walls of the Roman army.

Over their heads, dark clouds of arrows fell like black rain, loosed from the bows of the Hun archers riding their mounts towards the lines of Roman infantry. The sound of the horses' hooves drowned out the cries of their riders and those of the dying men who fell beneath the deadly volleys.

They were terrifying scenes when Rufius had watched them remotely, but standing in the thick of battle, surrounded by death, he could feel his bowels loosening, only holding the sword kept him from soiling his breeches.

Rufius felt a cold trickle of blood run down the inside of the armour that Dolovir had strapped to his chest. He had taken it from a dead Visigoth, who, Lord Dee explained, were allies of the Romans. Their king, Theodoric I, had formed an alliance with General Flavius Aetius to defend their lands against the hordes of Attila the Hun.

. . .

Rufius had thrown up the moment they appeared; not because of the scenes of butchery and carnage, but the sense of dislocation from the travelling. He hadn't felt this ill since his stepsister, Agatha, had made him a mushroom stew from the inkcaps which grew on the edge of the wood; it had taken three days before he could eat solid food without bringing it back up.

He assumed that Dolovir's master was a kind of *seiðr*, a powerful sorcerer, one who could transport them into the past. His Grandmother had spoken of shamans who could move between the realms, for whom time was fluid, like a river.

'Drink this,' said Dolovir, offering him a wineskin while he was still on his knees.

The man was already wearing the armour of a fallen soldier. There was a large hole in his breastplate where the spear had pierced it.

The wine was strong and not as sweet as the mead that Sindri would let him drink at Yuletide, but he drank deeply, and the nausea began to ease.

'Thank you,' he said, getting to his feet and handing back the skin.

Dolovir waved it away. 'Keep it,' he said. 'You're going to need it more than I.'

Rufius wiped his mouth with his sleeve and looked around the battlefield. 'Why have you brought me here?'

Lord Dee had wandered off among the dead, carrying a long staff and wearing the red cloak of the Roman army.

'To look for something out of the ordinary,' Dolovir replied.

'Everything looks like that,' Rufius said, watching the archers turn their horses towards them. 'Can they see us?'

Dolovir shaded his eyes. 'Yes, and their arrows will kill you just as effectively as they would in your time.'

They found the old man empty-handed, his face like stone. He sighed deeply. 'Not really a place for a boy, although enough of them will perish this day.'

Turning back to the battle, his eyes narrowed against the glint of the sun on steel. The wind caught his cloak, teasing it back to reveal the dark armour he wore beneath; it was made from a dull metal that Rufius had never seen before.

'The sword has brought us here for a reason, but I cannot say what exactly. There is something in its past which I cannot read. I believe it may have been used to change history — to make an alteration.'

Rufius was confused. 'But the past is the past. Everything has already happened.'

'Not necessarily.'

There was a cry from close by, and a group of Visigoth infantry fell before the axe of a giant warrior. He was no ordinary man, well over seven feet tall. A mass of muscle and fury, he carved through the soldiers as though he were scything through corn.

'Jotun,' said Rufius under his breath, lifting his sword.

Dolovir caught his hand. 'Do not engage. We never interact, there are too many consequences. We're only here to observe.'

No one seemed to be able to stop the giant. He slew anyone who came within the arc of his axe. His skin was painted a deathly blue and covered in strange runes, which seemed to deflect their spears and arrows, while their swords couldn't get close enough to do any damage.

'He's going after their king, Theodoric,' whispered Dee taking out a small leather book and opening it.

Rufius saw a division of heavily armoured men take position around a mounted knight. They were throwing themselves between the warrior and their leader.

'Are they going to kill him?' Rufius asked.

'I'm not sure,' Dee replied, turning to a specific page.

The guards were losing ground, and Rufius could see they had little chance of holding back their attacker. As the men prepared to make their final stand, he realised that it was the scene he had practiced every night in the woods. The sword had shown him a hundred ways to kill the giant, preparing him for this exact moment. His heart was hammering in his chest, feeling the weight of the blade in his hand.

'I know what I have to do.'

Before Dolovir could stop him, Rufius was running towards the fight, leaping over the bodies of the dead, slicing through the Hun that trailed behind the giant until he was close to the brute. Then, leaping off the back of one of the fallen, he travelled high into the air, bringing the sword down on the back of the giant's neck.

10

RECOVERY

[Christ Church College, Oxford. Date: 1660]

When Rufius awoke, he assumed he was in Valhalla.

The room was bright, and there were beautiful women tending to his wounds. It had obviously been a good death, just as he had always imagined it would be: to die in battle with a sword in his hand. He couldn't remember exactly what impulse had inspired him to try and save the Visigoth king. It had just seemed the right thing to do at the time.

Then the shooting pain in his leg brought him back into reality.

'Don't move,' ordered one of the nurses.

A hunchback in black robes entered the room with a vial of liquid the colour of beetle shell.

'Make sure he takes this,' the man said to one of the women. 'Three times a day for the next four days and change the poultice every hour.'

'Yes, Doctor Crooke,' the woman replied with a small curtsey.

Rufius had no idea what a doctor was, but he had no intention of drinking the foul-looking potion. His adopted grandmother had been a healer. She had known the names of all the plants and their medicinal properties, both good and bad. She taught him which mushrooms to eat and which to avoid. She was the oldest person Rufius knew, and with ten sons and five daughters, she was permanently surrounded by grandchildren and had taken in the foundling without complaint.

His earliest memory of Isolde was of her deeply lined face smiling down at him. The taste of warm buttermilk sweetened with honey still brought back the feeling of home. She was the nearest thing he ever had to a mother until she was accused of witchcraft and drowned, then he knew that his childhood was over.

The nurses were not as kind as they appeared, pinching his nose and forcing him to drink large doses of the foul tonic. Rufius had thought that nothing could ever taste as bad as one of Isolde's brews, but he was wrong.

There were flavours that he recognised: peppermint, juniper and elderflower, but none of them had the power to mask the terrible aftertaste. He imagined it was what the sludge scraped off the bottom of a stagnant pond would taste like, trying to spit out the terrible concoction, but the Valkyries held his jaw shut until he swallowed.

This was no way to treat a warrior, he thought to himself as the potion took effect and he fell into a deep, dreamless sleep.

. . .

When he awoke the next day, Rufius found Dolovir reading in the chair beside his bed.

'How are you feeling?' inquired the man, lowering his book.

Rufius winced, pushing himself up into a sitting position. 'I've had worse.'

Dolovir's look of concern transformed into a half-smile. 'I doubt that. Doctor Crooke's medicine is one of the foulest things I have ever tasted.'

They both laughed until one of the nurses walked past and gave them a chastising scowl.

'What's your name boy?' Dolovir asked, taking out a pencil.

'Rufius.'

He wrote a note into his book. 'No father's name, of course. Age?'

'Fourteen,' Rufius replied, examining his leg. It was strapped into a leather harness that was suspended by ropes and pulleys that hung from the ceiling. 'Did the king die?'

'Yes,' Dolovir said without looking up from his notes. 'He fell under his horse.'

Rufius looked disappointed. 'Then it was all for nothing.'

'No, when Theodoric died his son, Thorismund, took command and they turned back Attila's forces. They say that the Visigoth's fought harder because of the death of their king.'

'And the giant?'

'Your attack was truly a sight to behold.' He looked at Rufius's leg. 'Although your landing was rather less elegant.'

Rufius looked pleased with himself. 'The sword showed me how.' Then realising that Gunnlogi was nowhere to be seen. 'Where is it?'

Dolovir closed his book. 'Still buried in the skull of the giant. When you skewered your leg on a spear, we had to move quickly. There was no time.'

'But —'

'When you're fully recovered, we will go back and retrieve it,' Dolovir reassured him. 'One of the benefits of being able to travel through time.'

Rufius wasn't quite sure what had happened over the last few days, it felt like he had stepped into one of Isolde's stories.

'Is your master a *seiðr?*'

'A seer?' Dolovir repeated with questioning eyes. 'Never say that word in his presence.'

'No a *seiðr,* a sorcerer.'

Dolovir laughed. 'No, we are mortals, but with rare and unusual gifts. Like you, we can explore the past.'

'How?'

'I have no idea. Lord Dee found me many years ago, couldn't have been much older than you are now. I was about to be burned as a warlock.'

'Because you could see things?'

Dolovir's eyes twinkled. 'Because I knew things, secret things that a child shouldn't. The priests told my mother I was possessed and tried to exorcise me, but their words made no difference.'

'And he saved you?'

Dolovir nodded. 'Out of the fire and into the frying pan.'

'Can you travel anywhere?'

'There are limitations. You will learn that the past can be an uncharted wilderness.'

'What does your Lord want with me?'

There was a hesitation in his voice before the man answered. 'He is a collector of people rather than things. He is trying to gather together a small band of us to keep watch over the past. I was charged with finding a watchman for your era. Not an easy task by any means, the further back we travel the harder it seems to find anyone with the gift.'

Rufius thought of the watchman that stood guard at the gates of Jorvik. 'What are you protecting?'

'The future, of course!' Dolovir exclaimed. 'What else?'

'But who from?'

The man sighed and held up a page from his book. It was covered in a spider-like web of lines. 'From those who would manipulate the past. Take that battle.' He tapped a finger on a series of interconnecting points. 'Your intentions were honourable, but the consequences of your actions could have been catastrophic. Fortunately for you, Lord Dee believes that the giant was an anomaly; someone had interfered with the timeline. You seemed to have reset the balance, although nearly getting yourself killed was a little reckless — I think you surprised us all with that.'

Rufius frowned. 'Someone sent the *Jotun*?'

'Indeed, and we may be all that stands between them and oblivion.'

11

READING

A few days later, Dolovir returned with a large stack of books and placed them on the table next to Rufius's bed.

'Your sword has disappeared,' he said glumly, sitting down on the side of the bed.

Rufius pushed himself up on the pillows. 'You went back for it?'

Dolovir nodded. 'A couple of hours after the battle, before the corpses were collected, but the giant was gone, and so was your sword.'

'I don't understand, who would have taken the body?'

'To be honest, there weren't many left alive to ask. I took a couple of blades from the fallen, but I know that one was special.'

Magical, Rufius thought to himself, *it was an enchanted sword.*

He looked over at the books. 'Who are they for?'

'You,' he said, happy that the subject had been changed. 'Thought it would cheer you up.'

Rufius frowned. 'You do know I can't read?'

'I had guessed as much.'

Rufius picked up one of the books. 'And you're going to teach me?'

Dolovir laughed. 'No. I'm going to show you.' He placed his hands on the side of Rufius's head and pressed his thumbs onto his temples.

Rufius was confused. 'There's a difference?'

'It's called an intuit. We use it for passing knowledge to each other; mostly for language, but any learned ability could be transferred in theory.'

Rufius pulled away slightly. 'So you have done this before.'

'Yes. Many times.'

'And it doesn't hurt?'

'Not in the slightest.'

Rufius closed his eyes and held his breath while Dolovir's mind integrated with his own. It was a strange sensation to have another consciousness roaming around inside your head, like a forgotten memory or a half-remembered dream, there were flashes of new things, sounds and images flowing between them. Letters formed into words and were given meaning. Rufius could feel his mind absorbing the information, unlocking new areas of knowledge and understanding.

Latin, Greek and English seeded themselves within his speech, growing like the roots of trees among the Old Norse, forming new patterns and linking to concepts and meaning, allowing him to speak as well as read.

When Dolovir took his hands away, Rufius's eyes were wide with wonder. He was no longer the smith's apprentice. Dolovir had changed him, lifting him out of the blind ignorance of the peasant, he realised that this was what he had been missing all his life.

He picked up the first book.

'The Tempest by William Shakespeare.'

'One of his best.'

Rufius opened the pages and began to read.

'Take your time. The memes can take a while to bed in.'

The boy was too caught up in his new ability to take any notice, so Dolovir left him in peace.

12

CAUSALITY

After a week of reading, Rufius was beginning to grow bored.

His leg had healed quickly. The hunchback doctor, Crooke, had come in every day to examine the wound and adjust the leg bracing. There were no more doses of the foul black liquid and regular meals so Rufius should have been happy, but he had never been one for sitting around and was eager to explore this world.

His only company other than the nurses were the daily visits from Dolovir. He would arrive after lunch, carrying a fresh selection of books.

Each time the man arrived, he looked slightly different, his hair had grown back, and a moustache had grown over his top lip.

'A day may pass for you, my friend,' he explained when Rufius asked about the changes, 'but I have spent months in the pursuit of suitable candidates.'

This made little sense to Rufius, who was still struggling to come to terms with the idea of travelling through time. However, his thirst for knowledge was opening so many new doors, creating so many questions, and there was no one to ask other than Dolovir.

'You have the knowledge, but not the experience,' he would say when he couldn't answer a direct question.

Except on this particular day, it wasn't Dolovir who came to see him, but Lord Dee himself.

He leaned upon his silver-topped staff, standing at the end of the bed, his eyes slightly glazed as if searching for the reason he had come.

'Lord?' Rufius prompted, breaking the old man out of his reverie.

'Nine-five-four, you are quite an enigma. Doctor Crooke tells me that you have the constitution of an ox, yet your bones wouldn't set without the strongest medication.'

'My grandmother said I had stubborn bones. I was the smallest in the village.' There were other things that he was called, many of which he chose to forget. The villagers were superstitious people having never warmed to the 'foundling', which was one of the gentler versions of the names that they called him.

One of the nurses appeared and unstrapped the bindings on the leg brace, gently lowering Rufius's leg to the bed.

'Crooke's temporal tonics have accelerated your growth. You may find you're somewhat taller than you were when you arrived.'

Rufius hadn't been able to stand since he had arrived, but as soon as his leg was free of the harness, he swung both of them down and tried to stand. His head swam dizzily as the blood rushed down to his feet.

'Take your time,' warned the old man, 'your body has taken quite a beating.'

Rufius swayed slightly, looking into Dee's piercing blue eyes, realising he was nearly as tall as him.

'Time can be manipulated in many different ways. Doctor Crooke is a master practitioner, and his skills with accelerated healing are beyond compare.'

He handed Rufius the staff and took his arm. 'Walk with me.'

The first few steps were agony. Sharp pains lanced through his injured leg as though he was treading on a thousand bee stings. Clenching his teeth to stop himself crying out in pain, he was determined not to show any weakness in front of Dolovir's master.

The room was part of some larger castle, with long, wide corridors looking out into a courtyard below. Arched windows filled with diamond-shaped glass let in the afternoon sun, warming the air and the flowers that were arranged along the way.

They were lilies, of the genus Lilium. The knowledge that Dolovir had intuited to him awoke in his memory, telling him the names of things. It was a strange sensation to unlock a memory, but wondrous too. To be walking in a new world and yet know it, was an entirely unusual experience.

'Dolovir has told you of our quest?' Lord Dee asked as they walked slowly around the cloister.

'He has Lord.'

'Do you understand what it is we seek to do?'

'You wish to protect the future?'

The old man sighed. 'We do indeed, but did he tell you how?'

Rufius shook his head.

'There are many threats to our future. Some are nothing

more than the foolish mistakes of an adolescent civilisation feeling its way towards adulthood — these are simple to correct. The one that concerns me greatly is the disappearance of knowledge. There are so many parts of the past that have been forgotten. I wish to preserve their learning, use the chronologies of their artefacts to explore their histories.'

'Like you did with the sword?'

'Your sword was a very rare item. Some relics are more dangerous than others. We must ensure that they do not fall into the wrong hands.'

'How can the past change the future?'

'Because I can study its patterns, it helps me to predict what is to come.'

'Like the Vǫlur?'

Lord Dee stopped and turned towards him. 'Who are the Vǫlur?'

Rufius rested against one of the window ledges. 'Seers, fortune-tellers. My grandmother used to say they could see the future.'

'And how exactly did they do that?'

'Mostly in the entrails of goats, I think.'

Dee scoffed. 'Haruspicy. The Babylonians thought they could discover the will of the gods by examining the livers of sheep. I never cease to be surprised by the ludicrous nature of such divination systems.'

'Well, many of the villagers believed in their predictions.'

Dee took out a notebook. It was similar to Dolovir's. 'And are there many of these Vǫlur in your time? And were they always female?'

Rufius thought about this for a while. 'In her stories, they were always women. Odin was said to have consulted one about his future, where he learned of Ragnarök.'

The old man examined one of the flowers, leaning closer to appreciate its fragrance.

'There are many stories about how the world may end. I doubt that it will be due to the earth sinking below the sea and the sun turning black. Although, the flood myth is one I have found in many different cultures.' He tapped his notebook. 'I have my own theories on how we can help the future. Seers like your Vǫlur had little chance of being right. It was more down to luck than any prophetic ability, there was no science to it.'

'Well, many of the farmers were convinced their crops would fail without them.'

Dee laughed. 'Exactly! They were more likely to be skilled meteorologists — weather watchers, than mystics.'

'So how do you predict the future?'

'Probability and causality, I believe by looking into the past, we can deduce the factors that affect the future and in doing so, determine the actions that would produce the best outcome.'

'Change the future?'

Dee frowned. 'Adjust it. Make subtle changes to events that have the greatest influence. My resources are somewhat limited, so we must tread lightly on the past.'

Opening his book, Dee showed Rufius the pages. They were filled with calculations and formula, strange symbols clustered around lines that branched like a tree.

'Populations generally follow a pattern — one that can be calculated — there is a certain science to it.'

'Why not just travel into the future?'

He closed the book. 'We cannot, the future is not yet written.'

'But you have brought me here. This is the future to me — Danelaw is all but forgotten.'

'That is different. The frontier, as we call it; the point where the present meets the future, is currently in the early nineteenth century.'

Rufius realised he had no real concept of time. A century was hard to imagine when you have only seen fourteen winters. Isolde was ancient, at least sixty-years-old when she died, and he couldn't imagine what it was like to have lived that long, let alone nineteen-hundred years.

'What is the nineteenth century like?' he asked.

Lord Dee smiled benevolently. 'We will discuss that when you have recovered. In the meantime, I have a gift for you.'

He took out a small, leather-bound journal with the Latin 'Tempus Fugit' in gold lettering on the front.

'A notebook?' Rufius asked, taking the present.

'An almanac.'

Rufius turned the book over in his hands. It was the first real gift he had ever received, and he experienced a whole new feeling of pride swelling in his chest.

Unwinding the leather thong that held it shut he found that Dee had written a note on the first page.

'Omnia mutantur, nihil interit.'

'Everything changes, but nothing is truly lost,' Rufius translated, using Dolovir's new memories. 'Thank you. Lord.'

'You're most welcome. I've found it quite the only thing to keep track of one's non-linear adventures.'

'What's non-linear?'

'We are. Homo temporalis. We experience time in a non-sequential way.' He lowered his voice as a group of students rushed past them. 'Unlike those who are forced to travel in a more linear direction towards their destiny.'

Rufius looked confused. 'We're not human?'

'On the contrary, we are more than human,' Dee said, patting him on the shoulder. 'There are few who have the gift, perhaps one in a hundred thousand, but when you have the advantage of the whole of time at your disposal, it makes the odds so much greater of finding someone.'

The old man started off along the cloister.

'And how many have you found,' Rufius called after him.

'Not enough.'

13

REASONS

[Christ Church College, Oxford. Date: 1660]

Over the next few days, Rufius began exploring the other sections of the university. After his visit from Lord Dee, he found he could manage short walks around the quadrangle, hobbling along with the staff that the old man had left him.

The Great Hall quickly became one of his favourite destinations. There seemed to be a never-ending supply of food, and its long tables were always filled with students dressed in dark, flowing robes who would rush in with arms full of books. He loved watching the way they would devour their meals while simultaneously having heated arguments with their friends about the meaning of the work of some philosopher or poet. Everyone talked so quickly, switching fluently from Latin to Greek, which Rufius was still finding hard to translate. He would sit in the refectory and listen to them for hours while pretending to read from a book that Dolovir had given him but finding the stories of the students too distracting.

His favourites were about their king, Charles II, whose father had apparently been executed eleven years earlier. It had been an act that many of the college alumni had secretly been opposed to, but who never had the courage to stand up and defend. Rufius deduced that there were many so-called 'Royalists' within the college, all of whom seemed to be relieved at the return of his son to the throne. They called it a 'restoration', and it seemed that many had suffered under another man known as Cromwell.

Rufius had no real idea who these men were. He was still getting used to the idea of a unified England, that the Norsemen were gone and Danelaw was no more.

'Wilkins has gone,' whispered one undergraduate to his friend, sitting down at the table next to Rufius.

'That'll be the end of the Philosophical Club,' replied the other, draining his glass of wine. They both spoke in Latin, as the scholars often did when around the servants and clearly they thought Rufius was below them.

The first produced another bottle and poured them both a large measure. 'He was a good man.' He said, holding up his drink in a toast.

'A man of science,' agreed the other, clinking his glass against his friend's.

'Probably shouldn't have joined the clergy though.'

'Or married Cromwell's sister.'

They both laughed.

'Still, he has Gresham and the twelve.'

His friend leaned in close. 'And the invisible college.'

They noticed Rufius was listening and decided it was better to say no more.

Once they had left, Rufius hobbled quickly to Dee's study.

For some reason, he wanted to be the one to tell him about Reverend Wilkins. He had been the warden of Wadham College, a religious man with a passionate interest in experimental philosophy. Rufius was sure that Dee would be interested to learn about his dismissal and whatever this so-called 'invisible college' might be.

Dee was talking to Dolovir and two strangers when Rufius entered his study. In his eagerness to pass on the news, he had forgotten to knock, the master's look was enough to make him stop in his tracks.

The men were dressed in rather odd-looking clothes. Since Rufius hadn't ventured beyond the walls of the college, he had no real idea of how the townsfolk dressed in these times, but the robes that the visitors wore were finer than any wealthy merchant he had seen at Jorvik market.

Dolovir walked over to him. 'Your leg is recovering well, I see.'

Rufius realised in his haste that he had forgotten his staff. 'I overheard something that I think Lord Dee will want to know.'

'Really?' said Dolovir, his mouth twisting into a half-smile. 'And what is it that you believe my master hasn't heard?'

'Reverend Wilkins has gone to some invisible college. It's a secret, I overheard the students talking about it.'

Dolovir looked concerned. 'When was this?'

'Just this minute, I came as soon as I heard.'

Lord Dee finished his discussion with the strangers, who each took down a book from his shelves and disappeared into thin air. Rufius had seen a few of the master's visitors do this. Dolovir had tried to explain how books were one of the safest ways to navigate the past, but it still came as something of a shock whenever he actually witnessed it.

'Master,' said Dolovir, 'the boy informs me that Wilkins has gone.'

'Indeed,' said Dee, stroking his beard into a point. 'It is logical to assume that those who were associated with Cromwell would be deposed after the interregnum. My latest estimates show that Charles's reinstatement could potentially delay our work by as much as twenty years.'

'And what about the invisible college?' interrupted Rufius, unable to hold back his excitement. 'Will the reverend be safe there?'

The old man folded his arms and smiled. 'And where did you hear such a thing?'

'In the hall.'

'The invisible college is nothing more than a group of natural philosophers, alchemists in search of the essence of life, experimenting with air pumps and gases. They have collected at Gresham College in London. I've been watching them since 1645, they have some interesting members, but none that have shown any significant impact on the future of mankind.'

He went over to his desk and took out a large brass key. 'As for Wilkins, I think it's best if we visit the warden's lodgings, to ensure that certain artefacts don't fall into the wrong hands. You were right to come to me directly.'

Rufius felt the warm glow in his chest again.

14

WARDEN'S LODGINGS

[Wadham College, Oxford. Date: May 29, 1660]

Wilkins's lodgings were located on the west side of the college looking out over his well-tended gardens. Rufius tried to keep up with Dee and Dolovir who were striding through the grounds. His leg twinged as Rufius, quickened his pace, reminding him that it was still only two weeks since he had been impaled on a Visigoth spear.

He wondered what Arnwulf would have made of the battle. It was strange to think that both the training master and Sindri were long dead by this time and yet he could still return and speak to them in a heartbeat if he wanted to. Except he didn't, this era was far too exciting, too full of wonders, making the world that he had left feel backward and dull.

Walking through the neatly clipped gardens, he looked up to the clear blue sky, the sun warming his face. *Even the weather is better here,* he thought to himself, then catching the scent of white jasmine, *smells better too.* It was a stark contrast to the cold, bleak winters they had suffered over the last few years in Northumbria. Rufius guessed it was partly because they were further south, in what he assumed would have been Wessex or the southern reaches of Mercia.

Having never ventured much further than Jorvik, Oxford was like stepping into a new world. It was a fascinating city, filled with beautiful colleges, but it wasn't the capital. King Charles II had returned to London according to the students, where he had just had the body of Oliver Cromwell exhumed and ritually decapitated.

Reaching the warden's apartments, Lord Dee had to force his way through a group of students who were leaving with armfuls of books. It was clear that Wilkins's library was being ransacked and nobody was standing in their way.

'Bar the door!' Dee ordered once they were inside.

Dolovir quickly rounded up the last of the intruders from the rooms and threw them out but not before relieving them of their stolen items.

'The fickle hand of fate,' Dee said to himself, picking up one of the discarded volumes. 'A week ago, this man was one of the most revered thinkers in the country. Now they treat him no better than a vagrant.'

His rooms were filled with a mixture of books and scientific instruments: lenses that magnified the smallest insect, transforming them into giant beasts; a long tube that allowed Rufius to study the moon as if it were as close as his hand; and the most wonderful globe: the entire planet reduced to the size of a ball. Every land and sea were carefully described around a perfect sphere. Rufius asked Dolovir to show him where England and Scandinavia were located, only to find that on this map, the Norse homeland was divided into Sweden, Denmark and Finland. There were hundreds of other countries of all size and shapes, with names like Bohemia and Siam. Dolovir explained how there were still many unknown places in this map of the world, pointing at the illustrations of sea beasts were the mapmakers had simply written 'HIC SUNT DRACONES' or 'Here be dragons', to hide their lack of knowledge.

'Maps are curious things,' he continued. 'Most are copies of older charts, some more accurate than others. The cartographers would combine various maps into one, to try and create the most precise Mappa Mundi. So mistakes were multiplied down the centuries as no one had a precise way of measuring the land, nor the sea.'

Rufius felt the globe move under his fingers, letting its history unwind. He could sense the mapmaker's nib scribing across the parchment, the many hours that had been spent studying the other charts to create this one. He followed the line of its previous owners; academics, astronomers and rich gentleman had all marvelled at the many and distant lands, but to Rufius's disappointment, none had ever travelled to any of the places it illustrated.

'We need somewhere to store this collection,' said Dee, walking into the room with a scientific device under one arm and a stack of books under the other. 'This knowledge must not be lost.'

15

BRITISH MUSEUM

[Montagu House, Bloomsbury, London. Date: January 14, 1759]

Rufius was transfixed by the linen-wrapped bodies that lay mouldering in the long glass cabinets. The cartouches painted onto the preserved figures spoke of priests and priestesses with names like Tamut, Padiamenet and Tjayasetimu.

His new ability to translate the hieroglyphs was just one of the memories that Dolovir had gifted him. They were written in a long-dead language, one whose meaning had been lost for thousands of years until Napoleon's expeditionary forces discovered an inscribed stone near the Egyptian port of Rosetta in 1798. All of this knowledge surfaced in Rufius's mind when his eye caught the inscriptions on the sarcophagi. Every detail of their religious rituals and sacred texts of their dead was instantly available. It was like having another voice in his head, whispering secrets to him while he walked slowly along the rows of display cases.

Stopping at a body which had been partially unwrapped, Rufius studied the desiccated skeleton gaping at him through the glass. He could still see the hair on the dusty scalp, and flaky remnants of skin shrivelled on the bony frame. There was something unreal about these three-thousand-year-old ancestors; they had lost their humanity, becoming relics rather than people. Rufius wondered what it would be like to touch one, would it crumble into dust?

He counted in Coptic, the language of the Egyptians, as he walked. Each glass cabinet contained three mummies carefully laid out on wooden shelves, one on top of the other. There were over sixty and Rufius had heard rumours there were many more waiting to be shipped back from their desert tombs.

He was standing in the Egyptian Room of the British Museum, a grand building that was being prepared to house the collection of a doctor called Hans Sloane. Sloane had spent a lifetime acquiring artefacts from all over the expanding British Empire.

Inspired by Reverend Wilkins's collection of curiosities, Lord Dee had sent Dolovir and Rufius in search of other wealthy archivists. After a few weeks of searching, they came across Doctor Sloane, who, by 1753, had a collection so vast that it was moved to a Manor House in Chelsea once owned by Henry VIII.

Lord Dee was convinced he could persuade the ageing doctor to bequeath his hoard of over seventy thousand items to his grand project. He called it a 'Museum', Rufius had no idea what that meant but was fascinated by Sloane's house of strange and exotic artefacts.

'It is our duty,' Dee reminded them both while they

prepared for the meeting. 'To protect and preserve the knowledge of antiquity.'

They were standing in Dee's dressing room, surrounded by racks of clothes arranged by eras. At first, Rufius laughed at the ridiculously outlandish costumes of the seventeenth and eighteenth centuries, until he saw what Dolovir was selecting for him to wear.

The coat seemed to have unnecessary tails and a long line of buttons that didn't seem to serve any real purpose. The waistcoat was embroidered with golden flowers, and the breeches only came down to his knees, where his stockings were pulled up to meet them.

He flatly refused to wear the wig.

Rufius's hair was long, as was the style of a Dane. Dolovir made him comb it and tie it back with a black bow. The clothes were tight and itchy, making him squirm and fuss at the cravat that was tied around his neck.

'We must blend into the surroundings,' said Lord Dee, looking at them both in the large mirror that hung on the far wall. 'As if we were born in their era.'

We look ridiculous, thought Rufius. *What would Arnwulf say if he could see me now?* It was the second time he had wondered about his old training master since leaving. With the benefit of hindsight, he realised who was really important to him. Arnwulf had been a hard man, but fair too, never showing him any special favours but making sure that the other boys didn't bully him.

There were times whilst he was recovering in the hospital that he considered asking to be returned to his own time, just to see whether they were missing him. But he knew his rapid growth would be difficult to explain. Even if he visited a few years after he had disappeared — there would still be too many questions, and Rufius couldn't think of any answers that Sindri or Arnwulf were likely to believe. They both had an annoying way of being able to see straight through his lies.

Sloane was ninety-two when they went to his home in Chelsea, replacing Isolde as the oldest living human being that Rufius had ever met.

The semi-paralysed doctor smiled genially as Dee described his museum project, sitting amongst the most incredible array of curiosities Rufius had ever seen. The only thing more interesting than the man's collection was the milk chocolate drink the servants gave him, which tasted as if angels had wept in his mouth.

After some negotiation, Sloane agreed to relinquish his collection for a sum of £20,000 and with the caveat that the museum would be freely accessible to the public, a clause that Lord Dee conceded to grudgingly.

That had been six years ago, but less than two days for Rufius.

Standing in a room filled with Egyptian treasures, he was still finding it hard to come to terms with what had happened to him. A few weeks before, he would have been sleeping with the livestock and pumping bellows at the forge, now he was eight hundred years in the future and standing in a house filled with treasures from countries he never even knew existed, and for the first time in his life he didn't feel out of place.

He was beginning to appreciate what Lord Dee was

creating; by storing all of the artefacts in one building, he would have a near-endless source of material with which to travel back into the past.

It was the day before the grand opening of the British Museum. Dee had chosen Montagu House to house Sloane's vast collection. The rooms of the mansion had been lined with cabinets filled with natural history: thousands of specimens lay in velvet-lined drawers, while vast quantities of books were stacked along the shelves.

The museum was complete, all that remained now was to find a curator.

The search for an 'Antiquarian' was not a simple task. Dee insisted on finding someone who would not only help catalogue the current collection but would actively pursue other lost treasures like those of Wilkins and Sloane. This left them with very few candidates, the most qualified subjects tended to be clustered around the eighteenth century, and many of them showed no sign of latent temporal abilities.

Dolovir had left Rufius in the Egyptian room while he went to speak to Daniel Solander, a student of Linneaus who was interested in reclassifying the natural history collection.

'Are you lost?' asked a girl's voice.

Rufius turned to find a beautiful young woman standing behind him. She looked like a princess in her long blue dress.

'I'm looking for Beowulf,' he lied.

She looked puzzled. 'I don't think you'll find it in here amongst the Pharaohs.'

'I don't know. They remind me of Grendel's mother.'

She smiled. 'You seem a little young for such an epic.'

'My grandmother used to read it to me. I was told the museum has one of the last surviving copies.'

'They do, or rather I should say my family did. My father is Sir John Hynde Cotton, we've been invited to a private viewing of the Cottonian library. I'm not sure why, to be honest. We're Landwade, not Connington, but since Sir Robert's line died out when the sixth baronet passed — sorry I'm wittering on. My name is Amelia Cotton, pleased to meet you.'

She held out her hand and he took it, there was an embarrassing silence while he tried to work out what to do with it.

'And you are?'

'Rufius.'

She laughed. 'Just Rufius?'

He had never taken a family name since he had no family and even if he used 'Sindrasson' it didn't sound very English. He looked around the room, and his eye found the label of the cabinetmaker.

'Westinghouse. Rufius Westinghouse.'

Her brow furrowed. 'Not a name I'm familiar with.'

'We make the cabinets,' he said, nodding towards the nearest case.

'Oh, really? How interesting, I've always wondered who did that.'

'So when are you from?' he asked, changing the subject before she could ask any more questions.

'You mean where?' she corrected.

'Yes.'

'Madingley Hall in Cambridge. It's been in the family

since 1543. Papa is the MP, it's all very boring and anyway, would you like me to show you to the library?'

Rufius nodded. He liked her, even if she seemed a little 'touched' as his grandmother would have said. She was the first normal person he had talked to in a while, and he actually did want to see the Beowulf.

16

LIBRARY

'The library is made up of four collections,' Amelia explained, walking up the Grand Staircase. 'Sloane's of course, and ours. Then there's the Harleian — which belonged to the Earls of Oxford and the old Royal Library. It's quite the most eclectic accumulation of manuscripts in existence — they even have the Lindisfarne Gospels, thanks to Sir Robert, he was quite the Antiquarian you know.'

Rufius was distracted by the way her dress seemed to shimmer in the light and was only half-listening until she mentioned the word 'Antiquarian'.

'Although part of the collection was destroyed in the fire, it was a terrible shame.'

'When did Sir Robert die?'

She turned back to look at him, her eyebrows raised. 'What a thoroughly morbid question!'

Rufius shrugged. 'Sorry, I meant when was he born?'

'1571.'

Rufius made a mental note of the date.

She led him past exhibits of stuffed animals: a group of long-necked horses that Amelia called 'giraffes' and a 'rhinoceros' which he had mistaken for an oversized boar until he saw the enormous horn.

'They're from the dark continent,' she explained, while he stood marvelling at the strange beasts.

'Where?'

'Africa, silly. Papa is an abolitionist. He says no man should ever own another. No matter what his colour or creed,' she recited proudly.

Rufius remembered Wilkins's globe. Africa was an enormous continent, greater than any other landmass on the map.

'Do they have more of these creatures?'

'Oh yes, many more, but my absolute favourite is the lion. You can see one at Joshua Brookes's menagerie at the end of Tottenham Court Road, and there's a man on the Strand who has a collection of camels, imagine that?'

Rufius could not, but he was determined to see them before he left.

'Here we are,' she said, pushing open the tall wooden doors. 'Welcome to the British Library.'

The gallery was a long dark room, with walls stacked from floor to ceiling with thousands of books. There was a wooden-railed balcony halfway up the dark mahogany bookshelves, creating a second level.

The smell of old leather and paper was intoxicating, like mouldering leaves in the forest, it reminded him of the nights he had spent fighting off wargs and dragons.

People were sitting at reading desks or clustered around glass display cabinets examining the ancient manuscripts, and one of them caught his eye.

Lord Dee was talking to a round-faced, pale man in a red jacket.

'I want to introduce you to my papa,' said Amelia, scanning the crowd.

'I think I should be going,' whispered Rufius. 'My master told me not to stray.'

She looked confused. 'But don't you want to see the Beowulf?'

'Maybe another time?' he said, watching Lord Dee carefully.

Dolovir suddenly appeared beside him.

'Rufius,' he said, his expression remaining neutral. 'Did we grow bored of Egypt?'

'It's my fault,' Amelia interrupted, 'I insisted he come and see the Beowulf.'

'Indeed,' said Dolovir diplomatically, 'and who might you be?'

She held out her gloved hand. 'Amelia Cotton. Pleased to meet you.'

He took it and bent to kiss the back of her hand. Rufius blushed a little when he realised this was what he was meant to do. Dolovir's attitude changed at the mention of her surname. 'Cotton. Any relation to Sir Robert?'

'No, his line ended, but Papa was invited to lend the occasion some gravitas.'

He cleared his throat. 'We should be going.'

She put her hand out to Rufius. 'Goodbye, Mr Westinghouse it was a pleasure to make your acquaintance.'

Rufius bowed his head and kissed the back of her glove gently.

As they walked out into the hall, Dolovir whispered: 'Westinghouse?'

'I panicked.'

17

ANTIQUARIAN

[Christ Church College, Oxford. Date: 1660]

Lord Dee was not happy when they arrived back at the college later that day. Daniel Solander had proved to be yet another unsuitable candidate. Apparently, his interests lay solely in botany, and he was already making plans for an expedition to the Antipodes with Captain Cook.

'I have an idea,' Rufius said, as the master changed into his usual robes behind an ornately carved screen.

'Nine-five-four, Dolovir informs me that you've been interacting with the linears,' the old man said, throwing a velvet frock coat over the top of the screen for Dolovir to catch.

"Linears" was the name that he used for normal people, those that could only travel in one direction, one second at a time.

'He says you've even given yourself a name, Westinghouse — where the devil did you get that from?'

Rufius glared at Dolovir, who simply shrugged, and then

continued regardless. 'Amelia told me that Sir Robert Cotton was an Antiquarian.'

Lord Dee appeared from behind the screen, adjusting his cloak.

'What do we know about this fellow? Other than his passion for acquiring ancient manuscripts.'

'Not a great deal, the collection was donated to the museum by his grandson,' replied Dolovir, hanging his master's robes on one of the rails.

Rufius opened his new notebook and read his notes aloud. 'He was born in Connington, 1571. Graduated from Jesus College, Cambridge in 1585 and took up law. He supported James VI of Scotland to succeed the throne after Elizabeth I. He was a founder member of the Society of Antiquaries and amassed the largest collection of manuscripts in England until his death in 1631. Although part of his collection was lost in a fire a hundred years later.'

Dee smiled, pleased to see Rufius was putting his gift to good use. 'Well, you are truly the font of all knowledge today. So what do you suggest we do?'

Rufius hadn't thought that far ahead. 'Warn him about the fire, I guess. We could use the Beowulf or the Lindisfarne Gospels, they both survived.'

'A fire that won't occur until a hundred years after his death?' Dee said sternly, his brow furrowing. 'We have rules about that kind of thing. Giving a linear prior knowledge of a future event tends to have very unpredictable consequences.'

'But if he cares about the books as much as Amelia says he does, then he will still want to save them.'

'Assuming we can convince him that we're not madmen. Dolovir, I think our first priority should be to save the books, preferably without raising too much suspicion. We will have to work close to the time of the fire.'

Dolovir nodded and left.

Lord Dee turned to Rufius. 'As for you, Master Westinghouse, are you feeling up to another adventure? Can I trust you not to go running off and taking matters into your own hands?'

Rufius bowed his head. 'Yes, Lord.'

18

THE FIRE

[Ashburnham House, Westminster, London. Date: October 23, 1731]

There was already a faint smell of burning when they appeared in the library. Dolovir and Dee took different ends of the stacks and began to search through the unburned books. Three other men appeared, one of whom Rufius recognised from the college.

'What are you looking for?' asked Rufius, trying to ignore the nagging feeling of nausea. The feeling of disorientation was lessening with every jump, but it still made his stomach churn.

The strangers paid him no attention but continued searching through the manuscripts until they found a specific document which they opened before disappearing into thin air.

Dolovir handed Rufius a book. 'We don't have much time. The deputy librarian will arrive soon. Take this and read its timeline, check to see if it was supposed to end tonight and then take it back to Montagu House if it does.'

Rufius wondered why they didn't just put the fire out, but knew better than to question his elders, so did as he was told.

The lettering on the pages danced as its chronology unravelled. Unlike the sword, the timeline of the book Dolovir had given him was simple. The line wound back to a Welsh scholar by the name of Asser, it was his biography of Alfred, King of Wessex, and it was destined to perish that night.

He took hold of the silver key that was hanging from a leather thong around his neck. Dolovir had given it to him while they were dressing for the mission. It was a homing key, he explained, something that was linked to the museum in 1759 and it was the only way for him to travel back from the past alone. He closed his eyes and focussed on the vault in the basement of Montagu House, pushing his mind into the moment.

It was the first time he had travelled without assistance, and he felt a small moment of pride as he stood in line behind the others to hand the book to the waiting curator.

The real skill was returning within a minute of when you had left. It was hard work, the chances of meeting yourself were high, and Dolovir had warned him to leave at least 60 seconds safety margin between jumps.

The temperature in Cotton's library was increasing with every visit. Soon they had to wear wet scarves over their mouths to filter the air as thick, acrid smoke gathered like thunder clouds across the ceiling.

By the time the deputy librarian arrived with his assistants, flames were licking up the shelves, and over a quarter of the collection had been moved to the museum.

. . .

Lord Dee took a final book down from the shelf. It was a thick volume with an engraved leather cover. He opened it to the first page where the name *Laurence Nowell* was inscribed in a thin, spidery script.

'The Nowell Codex,' noted the old man, handing it to Rufius. 'I believe we have found your Beowulf.'

The book was warm, and the edges of the pages were already charred, but the main body of the text was still legible and running his fingers over the text, Rufius could feel the scratch of the nib from the scribe's pen as he copied down the letters.

'I'm afraid it will have to stay here,' Dee said, taking it out of Rufius's hands. 'This will survive the fire. The continuum must not be altered.'

As he slid it back into the stacks, the old man's finger lingered on its spine. 'Although it may have one last use,' he said, offering Rufius his hand. 'Shall we visit Sir Robert? See if he has what it takes to be our Antiquarian?'

Rufius nodded and placed his hand in the outstretched palm.

19

SIR ROBERT

[Westminster, London. Date: 1600]

Rufius was fascinated by the large portrait of Sir Robert that hung on the end wall of his library. He wondered if the artist had captured the true likeness of the man. He had a thin, elongated face, which was made even longer by his dark brown beard that came to a point. It was painted against a dark background, making the ghostly, pale face, and the white lacy ruff below it, feel almost as if the man had been beheaded.

His library was small compared to that of Montagu House. Measuring only six feet wide and twenty-six feet long, Rufius could stretch his arms and almost touch both sides of the room.

Further along the chamber, Lord Dee was admiring the white marble busts of famous people from antiquity who were staring blindly down at them from the top of each bookcase.

'Julius, Augustus and Cleopatra,' he said, walking past

the first three of the fourteen figureheads. 'Certainly an interesting organising principle.'

Sir Robert appeared out of thin air just before Dee got to the fourth head.

If he was surprised to see two strangers standing in his private library, he hid it well, but there was a slight air of apprehension about him as if he were worried about what they may have just witnessed — that he too was a traveller.

Rufius was relieved to find that Cotton's face was not quite as long as the artist had drawn.

'Sir Robert, it seems we haven't had a wasted journey after all,' remarked Lord Dee.

'Who the devil are you?' demanded the Antiquarian, drawing a dagger and holding it out before him. 'Explain yourself! Are you the villains that have been taking my books?'

Rufius noticed a slight tremor in the way he held the blade, Arnwulf had always taught them to look for signs of weakness in their opponent, and the wavering point told him that this was not a man used to combat.

'My name is John Dee, Astrologer Royal to her majesty Queen Elizabeth I,' said Dee, bowing deeply.

'You think I wouldn't notice? That I have too many manuscripts to miss one or two, eh?' Sir Robert asked, his eyes searching the shelves. 'I have lost too many ancient texts to time bandits. This collection seems to draw you like moths to a candle.'

Dee glanced over at Rufius. 'Someone is stealing your books?'

The Antiquarian held up the book in his other hand. 'Don't act so innocent. I know you're using them to plunder the past. I've never managed to catch one until today.' He waved the dagger at them.

Dee waved one of his hands. 'I can assure you we are simply interested in joining your Society of Antiquaries. We have quite an extensive collection of our own. One that has been accumulating over many centuries.'

The man eyed them both suspiciously. 'So you profess to being fellow collectors. Then what, may I ask, brings you into my library unannounced?'

'We came to warn you about a fire —' Rufius began.

'I would advise your squire to hold his tongue. Lest he wishes me to relieve him of it.' Sir Robert said, spinning the knife around in his hand. The man was obviously more adept with the blade than Rufius had first assumed.

Lord Dee stepped protectively in front of Rufius. 'I believe we both have a common interest in the preservation of knowledge.' He nodded to the book that Sir Robert held in his hand. 'Is that not a copy of Euclid's Elements? I assisted Billingsley in translating it from the Greek. I think you'll find I wrote the preface.'

Sir Robert flicked open the cover and glanced over the first page. Then, lowering the dagger, he put the book back onto the shelf. 'You will have to excuse my scepticism. These are difficult times for an archivist. There are those who would slit my throat for a single page of Bede's Historia ecclesiastica gentis Anglorum.'

'I believe that together we may be able to protect them,' said Dee.

The Antiquarian sighed. 'It has been a burden that I have carried for most of my life.'

'Tell me more about these time thieves.'

Sir Robert sheathed his dagger and walked along to one of the other cases.

'It began with the medieval chronicles and a number of Roman coins. At first, I couldn't detect a pattern. Some would return, but misplaced in the index. They seem to be searching for something, going further back in time.'

Dee took out his journal and handed it to him. 'I'm curious to know how far you have travelled into the past?'

Cotton opened the book and studied the thousands of small maps and charts that covered its pages. He smiled, handing back the journal and took out a notebook of his own, showing them a similar set of charts and times across its sheets.

'It seems we have a similar philosophy,' he said, 'although you appear to have a wider range compared to my limited experiments.'

'We have much to discuss,' agreed Dee, his eyes brightening.

'Where should we begin?'

'Seventeen fifty-nine. I have a wonderful library to show you.'

20

ACCESSION REGISTERS

[Montagu House, Bloomsbury, London. Date: 14th January 1759]

The following weeks were spent helping Sir Robert to establish his headquarters at Montagu House. The Antiquarian was delighted to discover that they had managed to save his collection from the fire in 1731. Although Lord Dee cautioned him that certain books could never be allowed back into the general population. The Antiquarian's disappointment was short-lived once he was introduced to the collections of Sir Hans Sloane and the impressive array of books that had joined his own to create the British Library.

The two men spent many hours together, and Dolovir was twice as busy as before serving two masters. Left to his own devices, Rufius was free to explore the other parts of the museum.

The building was like a giant treasure chest, full of strange and wonderful artefacts that Sloane had gathered from all over the world. Inspired by Sir Robert's tales of time thieves, Rufius spent his days investigating different periods in time, using random objects from the collection to take him to curious and exotic places.

Some of the most interesting documents were Sloane's handwritten accession registers; nineteen leather-bound volumes of specimens collected from his travels across Jamaica, Barbados and the West Indies. Each page filled Rufius with visions of warm, tropical islands with azure seas, verdant jungles and brightly coloured birds — sights so contrary to the dun hills of Northumbria, that Rufius found it near impossible to resist. It was made even more tempting by the beautiful sailing ships that Sloane chartered for his journey.

When Rufius discovered that the good doctor had once treated a dying pirate by the name of Henry Morgan, he scoured the library for any mention of the man and discovered a book called *About the Buccaneers of America,* published in English in 1684.

He spent hours reading about Captain Morgan's adventures: his bold attack on Panama and Porto Bello, as well as the numerous sea battles with Spanish warships. The islands of the Caribbean were lawless places attracting all manner of brigands seeking to make their fortunes from the conquests of the Spanish. They reminded Rufius of the tales Isolde told of her grandfather and his raids along the coast of the North Sea.

Buccaneers was a first-hand account, written by Morgan's barber-surgeon, Alexandre Exquemelin, who had sailed with him until 1674. One of the librarians had told Rufius that the book was rare because it had been used in a famous libel case where the enigmatic Morgan had contested the depiction of him as a ruthless, violent pirate and sued the publishers, winning £200 in damages and had the book retracted.

Rufius knew then that he had to meet the man.

But the copy of *Buccaneers* was a reproduction, and he didn't have the skills to navigate through the tangled web of linkages to reach the original manuscript.

So he concentrated on Sloane's journals.

Morgan had died in Jamaica, a wealthy man with plantations and slaves. The pirate had been a friend of the Lieutenant Governor, the Duke of Albemarle, who was concerned with Morgan's health and asked his private physician, a young Hans Sloane, to attend to him. Through the timeline stored in the journals, Rufius witnessed the last days of the bloated old buccaneer that Sloane had treated. He was nothing like the pirate adventurer that he was expecting.

No one appeared to notice when Rufius began to make expeditions back into Sloane's past. He began with small jumps, testing his abilities, moving slowly backwards through the journals, using the homing key that Dolovir had given him for his return journey.

As his confidence grew, he reached further back into the past: leaving England altogether and appearing in more exotic places, following Sloane on his travels around the West Indies.

Tentative minutes turned into hours, and before long Rufius was spending days in the sunny climates, wandering the beachheads, collecting shells and swimming with green sea turtles in the azure waters of Barbados before returning to the museum just moments after he had left.

It was the best game he had ever played, made even more exciting by the fact that no one seemed to notice, at least not for the first two weeks.

Until one lunch with Dolovir.

'Where have you been hiding?' he asked with a quizzical glint in his eye. The man looked completely different from the shaman Rufius had met in the market square in Jorvik. His hair had grown long, and he was sporting a cavalier-style beard, Rufius could only guess that he had been working in the seventeenth century.

'Studying,' Rufius replied between mouthfuls. Doctor Crooke's tonic had strengthened his appetite as well as his bones.

Dolovir laughed. 'Well, you must be the most sun-tanned student I've ever seen! One generally avoids daylight when reading books. Especially when under strict instructions about taking them out of the library.'

Rufius looked down at his arms. His pale skin was now a dark brown. He looked as if he had been working in the fields all summer.

'I've been spending some time in Sloane's past,' he admitted, 'watching him collect the plants.'

Dolovir smiled, dabbing the corners of his moustache with a napkin. 'I think that still constitutes studying but be careful that you don't interact.'

Rufius had been expecting punishment. Sindri would have taken his belt to him for much less. He was not used to such a relaxed way of teaching; unlike Arnwulf, there were no real lessons or hours of repetitive training. It was as if Dolovir was actively encouraging him to try new things, to experiment and discover for himself. He was beginning to enjoy this new freedom, for the first time he didn't feel like a thrall — he couldn't imagine going back to his old life now.

'How's the museum project going?' he asked, changing the subject.

Dolovir pushed back his plate and began to slice an apple with his knife. 'Very well. The Antiquarians have already filled Montagu house, and they're talking about moving the natural history collection out to create more space for the books.'

'Antiquarians?'

'That's what they've decided to call themselves. Lord Dee wants them to focus their efforts on saving other endangered artefacts and becoming the custodians of lost knowledge. Sir Robert has recruited quite a number of curators over the last few weeks. There is even talk of formalising them into a guild — all thanks to you.'

Rufius felt his cheeks flush with pride. No one had ever told him that he was good at anything. It was a strange sensation to know that he had been partly responsible for creating something so important.

'I'm conscious that I've been ignoring your training,' added Dolovir more sternly, carving off a piece of apple and offering it to Rufius. 'I think it would be wise to apprentice you to someone while the master and I are so busy.'

Rufius refused the fruit. This was the last thing he wanted, but before he could protest, Dolovir held up a hand to silence him.

'The past is a dangerous place. I can't have you galivanting unchecked all over the last two hundred years unaccompanied. I will find you a tutor, one who will ensure that you don't get into too much trouble.'

21

HARRISON

[Christ Church College, Oxford. Date: 1759]

John Harrison was an intelligent young carpenter whose love of clocks was only eclipsed by his obsession with the calculation of longitude. He was recruited by Dolovir in 1713 when Harrison was still in his twenties. Apparently, Lord Dee had been impressed with his later work on marine clocks and was keen to see if Harrison could create a timepiece that would mark time across a significantly longer period.

Walking down the corridor towards the horological collection, Dolovir tried to explain his master's plans: he needed a chronological system that could accurately measure the last ten thousand years to the nearest tenth of a second. But it fell on deaf ears; Rufius was still sulking over the loss of his freedom. All he could think about was how his wings were being clipped, and worst still, he was being handed off to some stranger.

. . .

The room was filled with all manner of clocks. Many were silent, their mechanisms still from lack of winding, but there was still one longcase clock ticking rhythmically in one corner. Dolovir walked over and opened the slender wooden door to reveal a series of metal rods and a swinging pendulum. The face of the clock was engraved into a silver plate, and Rufius could make out the words 'John Harrison Barrow' engraved into its metal.

'Why do we need to measure time anyway?' he asked, staring at the slowly moving hands.

'That is a very good question,' said Dolovir, taking a key from inside the cabinet and winding the mechanism. 'Some believe it is an illusion, that all events, both past, present and future occur all at once. While others believe that everything is preordained, that our fates are already cast and that nothing we can do will change them. There are even some who think that without our observation of time, it doesn't actually exist.'

'Tell that to my grandmother.'

Dolovir laughed. 'Yes, the passage of time does eventually take its toll.'

'But not for Lord Dee?'

'He does seem to be blessed in that regard. It wears less on him than the linears.'

'How old is he?'

'I couldn't say, and I find it wiser not to ask.' Dolovir grasped the pendulum and stopped the clock.

[Christ Church College, Oxford. Date: 1713]

The shelves were lined with intricate devices: fine clockwork gearing and mechanisms were carefully arranged around the watchmaker's workshop. The aroma of oil and brass brought back memories of his days in the forge. The smell of ground metal and the wide array of tools spread across the bench made Rufius feel slightly homesick.

'This is Westinghouse,' Dolovir said as a way of introduction.

Harrison looked up from his work, his eyes enlarged by a complex array of magnifying lenses attached to a pair of brass spectacles.

'Pleased to meet you,' he said, holding out his hand. 'Call me John.'

'Rufius,' replied Rufius, shaking the hand and finding the man's grip was stronger than he expected.

The watchmaker held up a sketch of an unusual-looking timepiece: it was round, like a pocket watch but with concentric rings instead of a normal clock face. 'I would value your opinion,' he said with a glint in his eye. 'I'm basing it on a Jefferys watch.'

Dolovir examined it closely.

'I'm favouring five rings,' Harrison explained, 'each one denoting a part of the temporal notation.' He pointed at the outer ring. 'Assuming that we are all agreed that the best way to represent a ten-thousand-year timespan is to use the Holocene Calendar of course.'

Dolovir nodded demurely. 'Very impressive. I'll leave you to explain the details to young Rufius here.'

And with that, he touched the homing key around his neck and disappeared.

'I don't think I'll ever get used to that,' muttered Harrison, staring at the space where Dolovir had been standing a moment before.

'What's a Holocene Calendar?' Rufius asked.

'Ah. You're newer than I thought. How far back have you gone so far?'

'I'm from 954. Does that count?'

Harrison smiled. 'Of course it does old chap. Makes you positively ancient. Now see how the outer rings are orientated to create five digits. Your origination date would be — '

'0.0.9.5.4'

'Er no, not quite. We're using a system that begins ten thousand years before Dionysius's Anno Domini. Lord Dee has requested a device that can measure a much longer date format. So your point of origin would be something more like 1.0.9.5.0. It helps if you think about the first year of our lord as 1.0.0.0.0 or ten thousand.' He wrote the numbers down on the drawing.

'Why ten thousand?'

Harrison beamed, his whole face seeming to light up. 'I do love an enquiring mind! The Holocene epoch is something I like to define as the beginning of the human era. It is an arbitrary value that allows us to measure the past in positive numbers rather than having to think into the negative for the years before Christ, although it does align with the end of the Pleistocene and the last ice age.'

'There was an age of ice?' asked Rufius — thinking back to the stories of Niflheim, the oldest of the nine realms.

'Oh, indeed there was. Although the debate about it is still being hotly disputed up in 1837. Many believe that it marks the beginning of human civilisation, settlements and the like.'

Rufius couldn't imagine what a thousand of something would look like, let alone ten thousand.

Harrison saw his confusion and motioned to the boy to sit down on a stool beside the bench. 'It's a hard concept to grasp, but an interesting challenge nonetheless. I've been working on a temporal coordinate system that factors the hours, months and days into a series of smaller dials, but once again this will require an abstraction and a touch of symbolic logic — the universe doesn't run on clockwork after all.'

Rufius studied the drawings. There were hundreds of tiny details and diagrams all carefully annotated in Harrison's flowing script. He had never seen anything quite so complex, the smallest items that he had ever been able to forge were nails and combs, and the finesse and finishing that they required were beyond his skills. The blacksmith used to say that Rufius's hands were 'made for hammers and shovels, not nicknacks and baubles'.

'Dolovir says you are to be my mentor,' Rufius added, worrying that he would have to spend the next ten years learning how to make watches. 'I was apprenticed to a smith back in my old life.'

Harrison smiled. 'I believe he wishes me to teach you the more practical side of the gift. Although I'm sorely tempted to teach you a little horology if time permits — excuse the terrible pun.'

Rufius smiled, his fears forgotten. Harrison was a good man, and there was a gentle, kind way about him. 'A man who sought to measure the world,' Dolovir had told him. 'One who would make it possible to sail around the globe without fear of losing your way.'

Isolde used to talk about sailing west into the unknown, of grand raids that took many years before the dragon boats returned. Rufius thought of all the places in history, all the forgotten corners of the past that he could explore and began to understand what it must have felt like to leave the shores of home, to venture out into the wide, open seas.

He was about to embark on his own great adventure.

'What will you call it?' Rufius said, pointing at the drawing of the watch.

Harrison looked down at the blueprint once more and thought for a moment. 'I was thinking along the lines of a tachyometer. Although I haven't yet found the man who could manufacture it.'

22

LONGITUDE PRIZE

The next few weeks went quickly. Harrison kept Rufius busy, using him to collect information about the work of his competitors in the race to solve the longitudinal issue. Since he was forbidden from knowing his destiny or interfering with his own timeline, the watchmaker would send Rufius on various missions to report on the activities of his rivals. It was essentially cheating, but Harrison referred to it as research. Rufius wasn't quite sure this was what Dolovir had intended him to learn when he apprenticed him to the engineer.

He began by sending Rufius to 1714, the year that the Longitude Act had been passed in Parliament in an effort to find a simple, practical method for long, transatlantic voyages. Harrison explained the difficulties of navigating by 'dead reckoning', a process that had caused so many ships to lose their way once they lost sight of land. The Act established the Board of Longitude and monetary rewards were offered to try and find a solution that would end disasters like the one in 1707 when four Royal Navy warships had perished off the Isles of Scilly because of navigation errors — claiming the lives of fifteen-hundred-and-fifty men.

Rufius had no idea what longitude was. His experience with boats had been limited to fishing trips along the River Ouse in small, round coracles — nothing like the dragon boats that his ancestors had sailed across the sea from Hordaland. Those days were long gone, as were the men who built the ships.

'Latitude can be calculated by the position of the sun at noon, indicating how far north or south you had travelled,' Harrison explained. 'Finding a way to calculate how far east or west required knowing the difference between the time at your current location and that of a fixed point, such as Greenwich.'

Rufius learned that in Harrison's time, there was something of a race to try a find a way of keeping time accurately onboard ship. The cumbersome casement clocks were not good in pitching, yawing seas and other methods such as measuring the lunar distance could take hours.

The Longitude Prize offered a series of rewards depending on the accuracy of the solution. Harrison was adamant that his watches would be the answer.

On his final mission, he made Rufius follow the soon-to-be Astronomer Royal, Nevil Maskelyne, on the HMS *Tartar*, who was testing the lunar distances method during the second sea trial of H4, Harrison's sea watch. It was 1765 and Maskelyne was obviously not impressed with the accuracy of the chronometer even though it was three times more accurate than his own calculations.

'He said what?'

'That the going rate was due to inaccuracies cancelling themselves out,' Rufius repeated verbatim.

Harrison's face turned bright pink at the news. Rufius had considered not telling him that when Maskelyne had returned from Barbados, he had been given a position on the Board of Longitude and seemed determined to deny Harrison the £20,000 prize.

'So, what happened next?'

'Are you sure you want to know?' Rufius asked, reminding his mentor that he was supposed to be teaching him about the dangers of foresight.

Harrison shook his head. 'No. You're quite correct young Westinghouse. One should never try to change one's destiny. Still,' he said, with a glint in his eye. 'If I were me, which I am, I would go to see the king, petition George to test H4 for himself.'

Rufius gave a subtle nod. This was exactly what the watchmaker had done, convincing the king to take his side against the board and forcing them to pay.

A sly smile twisted Harrison's lips, and he clapped his hands. 'We shall say no more on the subject? I do believe it is time for tea.'

Progress on his tachyometer was painfully slow, and Lord Dee was finding it hard to hide his frustration whenever he came to visit. The two men would sit for hours and discuss the problems with travelling long distances. Rufius would always find some excuse to linger in the workshop when Dee arrived. From what he overheard, there were issues when travelling back further than two thousand years — somehow it became hazardous beyond that point, and the few that ventured into the deeper parts of history never returned.

Dee was losing experienced men and women, and the search missions were taking up valuable resources as well as endangering the rescue teams. Just like the Board of Longitude, it was becoming obvious that they needed a better solution than the homing keys that they had been using.

'I need some way to return them to a fixed point,' concluded Dee after another long discussion. 'One that can be worn without being cumbersome, and is not reliant on modern materials.'

Harrison believed that he could make the tachyometer both a chronometer and a homing device, as he called it, promising he would have a working prototype in under a year.

'We'll need more help,' he muttered to himself after Dee had left.

'I can learn,' offered Rufius.

Harrison shook his head. 'I need someone like John Jefferys or Kendall.'

'Or Graham?'

'George Graham died in 1751.'

Rufius smiled as he watched the realisation dawn across Harrison's face. 'Of course! Why didn't I think of that, you're a bloody genius!'

He grabbed his drawings and his coat and disappeared before Rufius had a chance to ask what exactly he was going to do.

The idea was simple: go back in time and have the old watchmaker build the device earlier, as a private commission. It would literally be ready by the time Harrison returned from the trip.

Rufius waited for over an hour, but Harrison didn't return.

Assuming that the watchmaker had got side-tracked, Rufius went up into the library.

It was one of his favourite parts of the museum. Mainly because of the exotic locations it gave him access to, but also because it was peaceful and quiet.

Books were still a novelty, and reading them gave him no end of joy. Even without opening their timelines, he could still be transported to the worlds they described through the words of the author.

He wandered along the stacks until he found Sloane's accession registers, and took the seventh volume carefully from the shelf.

It had been weeks since he'd visited Sloane's past. As Harrison was otherwise engaged and there was at least another hour until dinner, he allowed himself a small indulgence.

23

PORT ROYAL

[Port Royal, Jamaica Date: 1688]

The funeral of Henry Morgan was an extravagant affair. An amnesty had been declared between the governor and the privateers so that both could pay their respects without fear of retaliation. An uneasy truce lay over the town as some of the most notorious 'Brethren of the Coast' wandered through the town under the watchful eye of the Royal Navy Marines.

Since reading the *Buccaneers*, Rufius had become fascinated by pirates. The similarities to the Viking raids of his own people were indisputable: they both used their ships for plundering and were accomplished sailors feared by all that met them. Although in the case of Morgan and his company, their victims were the settlements and ships of the Spanish Empire for which they were paid handsomely by the British Government under something called a 'letter of marque'.

Walking down a sun-drenched lane called 'Thames Street', Rufius marvelled at the shantytown that had sprung up around the pirate harbour. The buildings were a jumbled mixture of canvas-walled hovels and wooden shacks lashed together from pieces of flotsam and driftwood. Taller, three-storey buildings loomed over the others, their shingled roofs sporting the flags of captured ships.

Rufius flinched at the resounding boom of cannons. A twenty-two gun salute exploded from the ships moored out in the bay, sending a flock of brightly-coloured birds out of the trees and wheeling over the town, squawking their protests as they turned for the mainland.

In response, a volley of shots issued from a nearby tavern. The ramshackle grog shop was filled with drunken pirates shooting their pistols into the air and singing bawdy songs to the passing prostitutes.

They were a mean-looking bunch of men. Their faces were scarred or burned, and some were missing hands or legs, replaced with hooks or finely carved pegs that they used to tap along to the songs. Rufius could tell by the state of their swords which were the men to avoid. Cutlasses and daggers hung from wide leather belts, some more cared for than others, but all had seen action, and those that showed the sharpest edge were the ones to watch.

'A warrior is only as good as his weapon,' Sindri would remind him, quenching another glowing blade in the cold water to harden it. 'Beware the ones who keep their blade keen.'

The Spanish steel of their swords may have been far superior to anything he had ever seen Sindri forge, but Rufius hardly noticed, his eyes were on the flintlocks.

. . .

Harrison had warned him about this new kind of weapon; one that could kill a man at a distance with far more accuracy than any arrow. Much smaller than a cannon, but just as deadly, the pistol could send a ball of lead shot through a man's skull over a hundred feet away.

The watchmaker had explained how Chinese alchemists had discovered the explosive properties of a black powder while searching for the elixir of life. It took Rufius less than an hour to discover an alchemical book in the library that described the process of creating gunpowder: *De scientia experimentalis*, in the Opus Majus by Bacon, or Doctor Mirabilis as Harrison called him.

The secret of the explosive black powder had been kept in China until the twelfth century, and it had revolutionised warfare. No longer did a man have to learn how to swing a blade or defend himself with a shield. He could simply point and fire. Assuming he could aim well enough, there was no other skill required.

And it seemed that everyone in Port Royal was carrying one. They came in all shapes and sizes: from tiny pistols that could be hidden beneath a woman's skirts — which he saw more than once while he walked along the street, to heavy two-handed cannons whose stocks were chased in silver with butts that looked as if they could stove in a man's skull.

The patrolling marines carried longer muskets over their shoulders, their bright red coats a stark contrast to the flamboyant clothes of the pirates they walked amongst.

Port Royal was built on a sand bar, a promontory that curved out from Kingston to create a natural harbour. Looking out over the bay, Rufius counted more than fifty boats: Brigantines, Men o' War and Spanish ships-of-the-line, floating in the calm sea like resting birds-of-prey.

Their sails were furled and flags set to half-mast as a sign of respect, but the gun ports were open and every one of their heavy iron cannons was trained on Fort Charles. It felt as if the entire island was holding its breath in an uneasy peace, both sides waiting for the other to make a wrong move, like the night before a battle.

Rufius wandered down to the quayside, unable to resist taking a closer look at the magnificent craft. They were far larger than the fishing boats he used to see sailing up the River Ouse. These were true ocean-going vessels: tri-masted galleons that towered over the small quay, touching one of the thick mooring lines, he wondered how far they had travelled across the world.

Leaning on a mooring post at the end of the dock was a one-eyed man in a weathered old coat, one of his legs had a metal brace around the knee and most of his teeth were missing.

'You looking for a ship boy?' he asked, spitting a large brown lump onto the sand.

Rufius shook his head. 'Just admiring them.'

The old man scratched his chin. 'Royal's not a place to be frequenting without a reason,' he warned, taking out a leather pouch and shovelling a wad of shredded tobacco leaf into his mouth.

Rufius could see where his lips were permanently stained yellow.

'Which is Morgan's?'

The old man nodded to a fierce-looking warship wallowing in the deep waters, its sails made of black cloth.

'That's the *Concord*, she's a fine ship, but she'll never replace the *Satisfaction*. She was a real beauty, lost her off the

Lajas Reef in seventy-one when we took Panama. Now that was a raid I'll never forget.'

'You were with him?'

'I was a bosun,' the old man said proudly. 'We took thirty ships and eighteen-hundred men into the Chagres. It was the largest fleet Morgan every raised. Just shows you the kind of power the man had. God rest his soul.' He made the sign of the cross over his chest.

'And was it full of treasure?'

The old bosun shook his head and spat out another wad. 'Worst haul we ever had. Damned Governor burned the city before we got there, but the Spanish will never forget that day; three forts and over five hundred men died, while we lost no more than fifteen men.'

'And his ship.'

The old pirate took out a bottle of rum and raised it to the sea before drinking deeply.

'Went down with ten good men, all because of that damned *Bruja*. I told Morgan we should never have let a woman aboard!'

'A Bruja?'

'A witch — Morgan was enchanted by her. I swore she'd cast a spell on him. Still, at least she drowned when they hit the reef. Good riddance.' He spat and crossed himself again. 'May the saints protect us.'

Rufius was intrigued by the mention of the witch, but before he could ask more questions, a rough-looking group of men approached the old man.

'You found us a new mate?' asked a short, round man with tattoos all the way up his thick arms.

The old bosun laughed. 'I was beginning to wonder when you'd pull your sorry arse out of that whore's bed and get back to business.'

'Some of us need longer than five minutes,' the round man said, winking lecherously at Rufius.

The rest of his group went over to a small boat and began to haul it into the water. The old bosun stood up and flexed his leg, his eyes narrowing as he looked back up the street.

'Any sign of the watch?'

'No, there'll be tailing Mansvelt or Brasiliano around Royal for the rest of the night.'

'Then let's be on our way.' He made a gesture towards Rufius and someone grabbed him from behind. Before he had time to react, they had thrown a rough sack over his head and then someone punched him hard in the stomach.

24

BRETHREN OF THE COAST

[Bradley's Mayflower. Date: 1688]

Rufius woke to the sound of waves slapping against the hull. His hands and legs were bound with rope, and his jaw ached where someone had wedged a wooden bit between his teeth.

He was lying in the hold of a ship, his clothes soaked through with cold, foul-smelling water. A throbbing pain in his skull reminded him of the hard landing he made when they threw him through the hatch. There was a faint memory of being manhandled into a jolly boat, and being beaten whenever he struggled to get free.

Isolde had warned them many times about strangers: in her younger days, children were always being stolen and sold or used as slaves by other clans. Rufius used to wonder if that was how he came to be separated from his parents; that he was stolen, not by elves, but by some raiding party from another village.

He certainly never imagined that he would be taken twice in one lifetime.

The bindings chaffed his wrists when Rufius tried to free himself. They were tied with knots that seemed to tighten as he strained at them. His mouth was parched, and the wooden bit was rammed in so hard that it made his teeth ache.

Bracing his feet against a joist, he pushed himself into a sitting position. The hold smelled like the animal pen Sindri used to make him sleep in. The beasts were kept at the far end of the longhouse during the winter, and their body heat had kept him warm through many a cold night. As a thrall, he was treated slightly better than one of the cattle, at least until he proved his worth in the forge.

His eyes slowly adjusted to the darkness until he could see the shapes of bodies lying half-submerged in the bilge water. He was surrounded by slaves, dark-skinned men and women were staring at him with pleading eyes, their hands and feet manacled together. No one spoke, the expressions of fear on their battered faces was enough to convey the brutality that they had already suffered at the hands of the crew.

Weak beams of sunlight filtered through a grille in the deck above them, creating chequered squares across the filthy planks and their thin, emaciated limbs.

Rufius could hear the tap of the bosun's leg as he walked overhead barking orders at the crew. They were heading for somewhere along the coast that he called 'Montego Bay'.

Slowly, and with a great deal of pain, he managed to free one of his hands and pull the gag out of his mouth. The others shook their heads, trying to warn him that it would make things worse. He ignored them and untied his legs.

Rubbing his wrists, Rufius felt for the homing key around his neck, only to find that it was gone.

There were barrels and sacks stacked into the stern. Rufius waded through the bilge water to them, hoping that the cargo might have some kind of history, but it was organic material: wood, sugar cane and molasses. He knew that it would be too difficult to use to escape, the only obvious way out was through the deck hatch.

Everyone shrank back as he stood beneath it, surveying the lock. It was nothing more than a metal bolt threaded through a hasp, but he guessed than anyone foolish enough to put their hand through would come back with fewer fingers.

The boat groaned and lurched to one side as the wind caught it, throwing Rufius across the hold and onto the chains of the nearest slave. Picking himself up, he accidentally touched the metal of their manacles and instantly felt a connection with its history. The timeline unwound around his hand, lines of energy rippling across his skin, revealing hundreds of journeys and thousands of slaves who had passed through them.

He forced himself to look back through the terrible moments of suffering until he found one event that looked safe, and he shifted into it.

25

PANAMA

[Chagres, Isthmus of Panama. Date: January 6, 1671]

The hold was empty.

Holding his breath, Rufius listened closely for any sounds from the deck. There was nothing but the creak of the rigging and the flap of loose sail canvas in the breeze. He placed the empty manacle carefully on the floor and hoisted himself through the open hatch.

Some of the crew were gathered at the bow, leaning over the gunwale, watching the landing party rowing towards the shore in small canoes.

Rufius quickly ducked out of sight and crept slowly towards the stern, before climbing to the quarterdeck.

The air was humid and full of small biting insects. It smelled differently from Port Royal. They were anchored in the bay of some strange island, with a long sandy coastline that wound away into the distance, the beach like a golden edge to a luxuriant green jungle that swept back inland as far as the eye could see.

The ship's wheel creaked, turning gently back and forth

as the currents twisted the rudder. Rufius couldn't resist the temptation to take hold of the handles, feeling its timeline open at his touch. The wood was awkward, and its chronology wound randomly like the roots of an old tree, there was hardly any sense of order to it. Through the callused hands of the helmsman, he caught glimpses of the terrible storms the crew had weathered while crossing the Caribbean Sea.

Using their route from Jamaica, he guessed that this must be Chagres, the port where ships were loaded with treasure to be sent back to Spain.

A stone fortress stood at the mouth of the river. Rufius remembered from the *Buccaneers* that it was called San Lorenzo. Its walls were bristling with men and cannons. Watching the men row towards the shore, he saw smoke blossom from the battlements and ducked below the gunwale just as the first barrage hit the sea directly in front of the ship — they were only just out of range.

He ran down below decks, ducking instinctively as the crash of another near miss shook the timbers of the hull. Finding the captain's cabin, he went to the charts that were spread across the table. The ship's voyages around the Gulf of Mexico were plotted out across it, with notes marked against various islands — like a treasure map. In the fluid copperplate were the names of places and times, his eyes were drawn to one particular location that had been underlined three times: 'El Dorado'.

The lamps rattled from the impact of two more salvos, reminding Rufius of the need to find a way out.

A pair of dividers, a rule and an engraved brass disc lay where the captain had left them. They were finely crafted instruments, the disc was inscribed with numbers and dates, and there were levers and smaller rings that could be rotated to calculate the time.

Holding it up to the light, Rufius could sense the navigator standing out on the deck at night, calibrating his position by the stars and knew then that it was called a Nocturlabe.

It reminded him of Harrison's devices.

A cannonball struck the side of the ship, ripping a hole through the planking and sending splinters of wood across the room. Rufius was knocked down by the force of the blast.

His ears were ringing as he got back to his feet. Pulling thin darts of oak out of his arm, Rufius realised he was in real danger now. He needed to find something with a useable history.

Stumbling around in the smoke, he snatched up random objects: bottles, swords, trinkets from the captain's travels, testing each of their timelines. They were all useless, nothing in the cabin was connected to anything that could move him forward, and nothing that could take him anywhere near Oxford.

He stumbled on the ship's log where it lay open on the floor. The last entry was dated January 6, 1671, and signed by Joseph Bradley. Rufius remembered the name from Exquemelin's stories. Bradley would be killed taking the fort, one of many who would perish that day. It felt odd to know that the man would die today and that Rufius could, if he wished, prevent it.

The details of the attack were nothing more than a few lines on the yellowing pages of a rare book hidden away on the shelves of the British Library. Exquemelin had written that the assault would succeed after heavy losses and that

Bradley would perish from his wounds before Morgan's fleet arrived.

Tucked within the pages of the log like a bookmark were a set of orders written in the hand of Admiral Morgan himself. Rufius opened the letter, his fingers sensing the scratch of the old pirate's quill, sitting in his cabin on the *Satisfaction*. As he focussed on the moment, he could smell the rum on the Admiral's breath and was tempted to jump, but stopped himself. Morgan's ship was going to crash and sink on the reef in less than three days. If he shifted onto it, he would need to find a way off before the wrecking.

But his only link to Sloane was through Morgan. Rufius knew that his best chance of getting back to the museum was to find a way to use the pirate. He had no idea how he was going to get close enough to the man, but he had to try.

26

MORGAN

[Caribbean. Date: January 4th, 1671]

The *Satisfaction* was a magnificent ship. Morgan's cabin was a sumptuous room, fit for a king: decorated with finely carved furniture, gilt-framed paintings, velvet curtains and soft Turkish rugs.

The pirate sat at his desk, staring directly at Rufius, his eyes wide.

The admiral had a mane of long, dark hair and a beard whose moustache was oiled into points that turned upward as a wide grin spread over his face.

'Hecate told me you would come,' he said, his words slurring a little. 'I have to say I had my doubts.'

Rufius was lost for words. He wasn't quite sure how he screwed up the jump, the timeline of the note was simple enough — there shouldn't have been anyone in the room when he arrived.

'Master Exquemelin!' Morgan barked.

A man opened the door and stepped into the cabin. He was wearing a leather apron and a white shirt whose sleeves were stained with blood. 'Sir!' he said, deferentially dropping his eyes to the floor.

'Is Maman Brigitte still aboard?'

'Aye, sir. She's with the quartermaster.'

'Bring —'

'I is already 'ere,' a deep female voice interrupted.

The woman who walked in behind Exquemelin took Rufius's breath away. Her black hair was bound in long beaded dreadlocks with silver charms woven into the ends. The brown skin of her face and arms was patterned with tribal tattoos, and her eyes were like clear blue pools that drew Rufius in. Bright white teeth shone beneath her full red lips as she studied him, ringed fingers caressing his face. He could smell jasmine and other exotic oils radiating off her body.

Around her neck, she wore strings of bones, the skulls of tiny creatures and carved knuckles were threaded on fine silver chains that hung between her breasts.

'He be 'ere long?' she asked, taking something out of her leather skirt. Rufius saw the glint of steel and knew it was a knife.

'A matter of a minute or so,' replied Morgan. 'Just popped into existence, there on me carpet, as you predicted.'

Brigitte shook her head and the charms chimed against one another. 'No! Just as the spirits predicted, but they never told me he would be so pretty.' Her tongue swept along her teeth as if she were about to devour him.

She took one of Rufius's hands and turned the soft palm upwards.

'So, Maman, what does this mean for the mission? Will we be successful. Shall we take Panama?'

She closed her dark-lidded eyes and in one quick motion, slashed the blade across his open hand, holding the cut up to her mouth, tasting the blood as it ran down his arm.

Rufius bit his lip to stifle the cry, his eyes never leaving the woman's face. She sucked at the cut, and he felt his face growing hot, his pulse pounding heavily in his ears. The feel of her mouth on his hand was stirring powerful new feelings in him, and he couldn't help but enjoy it.

She looked up. 'Panama will burn,' she said with a smile, her teeth still stained with his blood. 'But you must take another ship. This one be bad luck.'

'She's my best ship!'

'I will ride her, you take another,' the woman said with a wave of her hand. 'I keep the boy too,' she added with a wicked smile. 'He interests me.'

'Do what you like with him,' Morgan said dismissively. 'Alexander, seems we'll be taking the *Concord*. Tell the bosun I'll be assuming command.'

The man nodded and left. Morgan stood up from behind his desk and walked over to Rufius. The wound on his palm was nothing more than a pink scar when the admiral examined it.

'She told me you would be from the future.' He leaned in close and whispered. 'Tell me, will I die tomorrow?'

Rufius looked at him blankly.

'Hush!' hissed the witch, moving between them. 'No one can know this thing! It is forbidden.'

'Shame,' said the pirate with a chuckle. 'Would've made things a little easy to plan for.'

'Or avoid,' the woman added. 'Death is for Papa Ghede.'

Morgan pulled her closer to him. 'What do you say to a going away present?' He asked, his hand groping between her skirts.

She put the blade to his neck and pushed him away with

her other hand. 'I say, adieu! Bon voyage. *Lè ou mouri se mouch kap vinn bay nouvèl.*' Her teeth flashed from between tightly drawn lips, and Rufius could see her eyes were cold and hard.

Morgan's face paled, and he crossed himself as though he had been cursed. 'I'll save you a share, nonetheless.'

'See that you do.'

She took Rufius by the hand and led him out of the cabin.

27

MAMAN BRIGITTE

Her quarters were towards the bow. Following her through the narrow passageways, Rufius noticed several of the crew crossing themselves when she passed. He could see fear in their faces; they were scared of her.

She had taken a small space behind the galley. It was warm, and smelled of stews and boiled bones. Makeshift shelves had been wedged into the curved wooden joists of the hull. They were stacked with boxes of dried herbs and glass jars filled with dead birds pickled in alcohol. The glass-eyed specimens watched him silently as she rummaged amongst the curios squirrelled away in her cubby holes.

Maman Brigitte lit a small oil lamp. Hanging it from a bent nail in the beam above her bunk, she motioned for him to sit down. Then, drawing up her skirts, she squatted down on her haunches and cast a handful of stones onto the floor.

When she spoke, there was hardly a trace of the Jamaican patois accent.

'How long have you been here? And don't lie to me, boy. I have tasted you, so I'll know.'

'No more than a day,' he replied, wondering why she needed his blood to see the future.

Her eyes narrowed as she studied the stones, placing her finger on one and then another. 'And before, when you were in Port Royal?'

Rufius paused for a moment, unsure of what to say, her expression left him in no doubt that it was wiser to tell the truth. 'I've been there a few times, but never stayed more than a couple of hours.'

'And how do you travel?' she asked, picking up the stones in a specific order before throwing them down on the floor once more.

He watched as they scattered into a rough circle. Isolde had used something similar to read the villager's fortunes, telling them the details of their future husbands. It was just for fun, and no one took it seriously. Brigitte's stones were different. They looked like they had been carved from bone, with runes and symbols on each of their eight sides. She spoke to herself as she read their meaning.

'I use the timelines of objects,' Rufius replied reluctantly as if he were giving up a secret.

Maman Brigitte made a tutting noise with her tongue and scooped up the stones in one swift movement of her hand. This time she closed her eyes and whispered something over them, before casting them down again.

'Hah!' she exclaimed, clapping her hands together. 'You're a Dubh-Gall! One of the Ashmen of the North.'

'A Norseman?' he asked, not quite understanding her terms.

'Yes, see how your lines cross back and forward through time.' She moved her hands between the stones as if connecting them with invisible twine. 'You have come a long way from your home.'

Eight hundred years, Rufius thought, but simply nodded and asked. 'And who are you?'

She sucked air through her teeth, raising her eyes to the ceiling. 'To them, I am Maman Brigitte, the *Bruja*. They believe I consort with devils, among other things, and they would slit my throat in my sleep if it weren't for the captain.'

Satisfied with her reading, she began to pick up the stones. 'But you may call me Maebh.' She spoke the name like a child admitting to a guilty secret. Dolovir's memories told him that it was an old Irish name that meant "enchanting one".

Maebh kissed each stone before putting them carefully back into a leather purse.

'Why did you cut me?' Rufius asked, rubbing the thin line of a scar on his palm. 'And how did it heal so quickly?'

Maebh laughed, making the charms in her hair chime like silver bells. 'I am of the Tuatha. I can see things in people, in their blood — events that may happen.'

She went over to a small basin wedged into the bulkhead and poured water into it. 'And time is a great healer.'

She slipped out of her dress, and Rufius turned away. She laughed at his shyness but said nothing. He caught sight of her body in the reflection of a broken mirror stored on one of the shelves. She gently washed away the symbols that covered her arms and her face, revealing a beautiful young woman.

'My grandmother was a völva — a seer, but the Christians called her a witch.'

'Men of faith!' she snapped. 'Fools who kill what they don't understand, and all in the name of a god they cannot see.'

Rufius tried to hold down the emotions that were welling up. He could still see Isolde's serene face as the priests held her by the banks of the river while they tied sacks of stones to her feet. 'They told her she would burn in hell for her beliefs, but she laughed. "Hell is a cold place", she said, "no fire could ever be kindled there".'

'Fire has great power,' Maebh agreed. 'Its paths lead to both destruction and creation — it is chaos incarnate.'

'We burned her body after they left. Everyone from the village came to pay their respects.'

'Your grandmother was a brave woman.'

Rufius felt his throat tightening. 'She wasn't my real grandmother. I never knew my ancestors.'

'Ah, you were a foundling?'

'I thought you could see that?'

Maebh threw the cloth into the bowl and pulled on her dress. 'You think I'm nothing more than a bone-conjurer? The stones are nothing more than tools, they show me dates and places, but your blood allows me into your future. I can see the roads ahead, the paths yet untaken. I know nothing of your beginnings, but I could tell you how you will end, do you want to learn of how you die?'

He shook his head. The thought of his death had always seemed so far away, and he liked it that way. All Rufius really wanted to do right now was go back to the museum. He'd had enough of this part of history, it was dangerous, and he was beginning to understand why Dolovir was so insistent about a mentor.

Seeing the fear in his face, her expression softened. 'We are two sides of the same coin you and I. Both caught up in the web of destiny. Our fates are not like theirs,' she flicked her eyes towards the curtain. 'They walk towards their death like a blind man searching with his stick. We see the way of things, things that may never come to pass. The mysteries of tomorrow can be glimpsed, like starlight on a lake. If you know how to look.' She pointed to a symbol on her arm that had not been washed away. It was three spirals made from one continuous line, a Triskele.

'What does that mean?' he asked, pointing at another particularly complex sigil.

'A Hamsa — a warding glyph. Protects me from the sea.'

'Are you afraid of drowning?'

She laughed, her smooth shoulders rising and falling with the sound. 'Show me a sailor who isn't, and I'll show you a fool. But it's not so much the water, more the things that live within it.'

'Fish?'

Maebh shook her head. 'No, much older things. Ancient creatures that have slept for eternity, ones that can take a ship like this and snap it in two.' She clicked her fingers.

Rufius had heard many stories of boats being taken by Kraken, giant sea monsters that could drag a ship to the bottom of the ocean.

'Are we going to die?'

Maebh sat down beside him on the bunk, her dress clinging to her body where the water had run down between the swell of her breasts. She put her hand on his arm, her lips close to his ear so that he could feel her breathing on his neck.

'It is dangerous to be wandering through the timelines alone. There are other travellers who would see you dead rather than let you live to tell their tales. My work here is almost over. If you stay and help me, I can show you a way back to your own time.'

She stroked the hair away from his face, pushing him down on the bed. 'We have a few days before this ship will crash onto the reef. I think it would be better if you stayed with me,' she said, taking off her dress again.

28

SPANISH SECRETS

Rufius woke from a dreamless sleep. Smiling to himself as he felt her body pressed against his.

The ship was rocking gently and he could hear the sounds of the crew moving above them. Morgan was giving orders, to the skeleton crew that he was leaving behind to man the ship, reminding Rufius that in less than three days it was going to sink below the waves.

'I know you're awake,' she whispered softly in his ear, making the hairs on his neck stand on end.

'How?' he asked.

The lamp had burned down, and their cabin was cloaked in darkness. Her hand moved under his arm and her fingers curled into the hairs on his chest.

'Your breathing changes and you stop snoring,' she giggled.

'What are you doing here?' he whispered, finally asking the question that had been on his mind since he arrived.

'Helping the good captain look for something.'

Rufius remembered the treasure map he had seen on the last ship.

'You're looking for El Dorado?'

He felt her tense slightly as he said the words, her fingers ceased their stroking. 'You know of the city of gold?'

'No,' he assured her. 'I saw it on a map on one of the ships. Is it really an entire city made of gold?'

She laughed, her breasts rubbing gently against his back. 'So the Spanish believe, as does our beloved Captain. There is a tribe, whose chief is supposed to be covered in gold before being submerged into a lake. El Dorado means "golden one", but over the last hundred years, men's greed has created a fabled city. Morgan believes my powers will lead him to it, but it is something far more rare that I seek.'

'Diamond?' Rufius wondered aloud. It was the rarest thing he could think of.

She moved closer, her leg wrapping around his.

'No, rarer still, a metal that has fallen from the stars.' She bit his ear. 'Enough talking.'

29

WRECKING

[Chagres, Panama. Date: January 8th, 1671]

The ship was pitching so violently that it threw Rufius out of the bunk. The deck was awash with seawater sluicing up and down the planks as the boat yawed from side to side.

Singing to herself, Maebh calmly painted symbols back onto her skin. Her hand was steady, even with the motion of the sea.

'I've been a wild rover for many's the year
And I've spent all me money on whiskey and beer
But now I'm returning with gold in great store
And I never will play the wild rover no more'

Rufius crawled back onto the bunk. He was soaked to the skin, and the constant movement was making him feel sick. The nausea was worse than anything he had experienced when shifting through time. He fought back the urge to throw up, not wanting to embarrass himself in front of her.

She sat down beside him on the bed. He could smell tobacco on her hair. It reminded him of the old bosun he'd met in Port Royal. The old man had warned that five ships would be lost against the reef today.

'Drink this,' said Maebh, passing him a small brown bottle. 'Rum with a little Maman magic.'

Rufius drank deeply, feeling the warming liquor slide down his throat, calming his churning stomach. He had forgotten about the impending storm, the last few days with her had been a sweaty blur of sleep, sex and food — one that he didn't want to end. They had been shut away from the rest of the world, and she had been a kind and gentle lover. This was the first time she had resumed the role of Maman Brigitte.

'The storm will throw us onto the reef. We need to be leaving,' she said, taking off one of her bone necklaces and placing it over his head. 'This path is ending.'

Rufius took off his wet shirt and pulled on a pair of breeches. 'What about the crew?'

'Damned, my dear,' she sneered and kissed his cheek. 'Wouldn't listen to a woman. Especially a *Bruja*!'

'Shouldn't we at least warn them?' he said, wringing the water from the shirt before putting it back on.

She laughed. 'They will be coming for me soon. Trying to appease their superstitions — they'll give me to the sea.'

The ship's hull groaned under the pressure of the waves as if the wood was screaming. Maebh placed her hand on one of the joists and closed her dark-lined eyes.

'She knows her end is coming,' she muttered, stroking the wood. 'The water is calling to her.'

They heard the crew moving along the passageway; clumsy footsteps and the scrape of swords being drawn from scabbards announced their intentions.

Rufius looked for a weapon amongst her treasures but found none.

'Calm yourself, boy, this isn't how you end,' she said, placing her dagger into the back of her belt.

They burst through the curtain and pinned them both down. Rufius could smell the sour rum on their breath as thick, greasy fingers wrapped around his throat and rough cord was wound around his wrists. There was no point in trying to fight them in such a small space, and he caught her eye as they were dragged out of the cabin, even with the wooden gag between her teeth, she still seemed to be smiling.

Water poured through the hatches, soaking them both to the skin. Cold leached into his bones and the salt stung his eyes. The deck was under two feet of water as they were pushed up the ladders and into the grey world above.

The waves were like white-tipped mountains, rising and falling around them, driving the ship against the wind. The sails were torn, ripped from their shrouds they flapped uselessly in the gale. Some of the crew had lashed themselves to the masts, while others tried bravely to gain control of the canvas from high up in the rigging.

'Chuck 'em off before they end us all,' barked one of the crew from the quarterdeck. His voice nearly lost against the howl of the wind.

They were pushed roughly towards the gunwale. The deck was slippery and treacherous, half-submerged debris washed across their path as the relentless onslaught of the storm rocked the ship. While the men holding Maebh clung frantically onto the guide ropes with their free hands, she seemed to be unshaken. Like the queen of the sea, moving gracefully between two drunken guards, she walked to the edge of the ship. An enormous wave crashed over the side and Rufius watched it engulf both Maebh and her escorts.

The boat lurched under the impact, his captors lost their grip and were swept away into the boiling sea. Rufius used his legs to brace himself against a capstan and felt his bonds loosen slightly, enough to get his hands free.

A man screamed from somewhere high above him as the ship went into freefall. The bow dipped, and suddenly they were plummeting down the slope of an enormous wave. He felt his back lift away from the deck as the ship went almost vertical. He watched men sliding past him desperately clawing at any kind of handhold and failing.

Rufius closed his eyes, trying to ignore what Maebh had told him: that the sea was full of ancient beasts, but his imagination took hold, conjuring tentacles below the surface of the rising waves.

The ship was close to the bottom of the swell and dark walls of water rose around them on all sides. Rufius could feel the sea preparing to claim them.

Holding his breath, he let go.

There was a moment of weightlessness as his body was lifted from the deck, then carried away on invisible forces he flew towards the water. He struck the surface and was sucked down into the deep. The cold numbed his body, pushing the air from his lungs as he sank into oblivion.

Rufius looked up, catching flashes of the storm above him, but they were like distant moments from another world. In the tomb-like stillness of the water, he saw the outlines of other things, shapes shifting in the depths below him. He tried to tell himself they were just the bodies of the crewmen, but his mind was starved of air and he began to conjure other, darker monsters. He made a feeble attempt to swim for the surface, but his clothes were too heavy, and he was too weak to make any headway.

Sinking quickly into the dark, his lungs aching with the urge to breathe, to suck in the water, he remembered something she had said: 'This is not how you end.'

Like a sleek, graceful fish Maebh appeared through the grey-green waters. Her body was glowing as she swam towards him, the symbols on her skin burning with luminescent blue light.

'Time to be gone,' her voice whispered inside his head as she wrapped her arms around him and placed her lips on his.

Her air was sweet and filled his lungs. When their lips parted, he felt sharp teeth, and pulling away, he noticed her eyes had changed too. She was less human than before; the water had altered her.

A bubble began to form around them as the water seemed to harden and retreat, becoming a solid, mirror-like wall.

'What do you see?' The question seemed to appear in his thoughts. Somehow she was able to speak to him without using sound.

They were surrounded by many paths, as if standing at a crossroads, with trails leading off to other worlds. He saw the outline of trees and a path into a moonlit valley. It reminded him of home, another seemed to lead to an ancient stone castle high on a rocky promontory.

Rufius ignored both and chose the one that led back to the college.

30

REPRIEVE

[Christ Church College, Oxford. Date: 1713]

Harrison was hunched over his worktable when Rufius stepped out from the mirror. For a moment, the engineer looked startled through the multiple lenses of his eyeglasses, and then breathed a sigh of relief.

'Well, where the devil have you been?' he exclaimed, taking off his spectacles and frowning at the small puddle that was forming at his apprentice's feet.

Rufius was soaked to the skin and shivering uncontrollably. The simple act of breathing was still painful as if his lungs had forgotten how.

'I got a bit lost,' he said weakly, looking down at the expanding pool of seawater.

'When?'

'1671. I mean 11.671,' Rufius stuttered, unable to stop his teeth from chattering.

Harrison grabbed a blanket and wrapped it around his shivering shoulders. 'Come, warm yourself by the fire before you catch your death!'

. . .

Rufius slept by the fire for hours, letting the warmth slowly take the chill from his bones. Harrison returned with warm broth and plied him with hot toddies until the taste of the sea was nothing more than a memory. He tended to the rope burns on his hands with one of Dr Crooke's more pungent remedies, but Rufius didn't care about the smell, this was the closest thing he had to a home, and he swore to himself that he would never leave it again.

'And this woman conjured paths through water to send you back here?' Harrison asked when Rufius had recovered enough to answer questions.

Rufius nodded. 'She did something to the sea.'

'An ability to weave with water is a rare talent indeed,' Harrison noted thoughtfully, looking back at the mirror still surrounded by seawater.

'She said she was of the Tuatha Dé, but the bosun called her a witch — the crew were scared of her powers.'

'Did she say why she was on the ship?'

Rufius nodded. 'She was searching for some kind of rare metal. One that had fallen from the stars, I think it was in a place called El Dorado.'

'Ah, yes the legendary city of gold, I don't suppose she'd located it?'

Rufius shook his head. 'No, Morgan was looking for it, and so were the Spanish. She was using the pirates to find it.'

'And yet she saved you?'

He blushed a little, changing the subject before he had

to explain why she had come to his aid. 'There were creatures below the waves. I thought it was the Kraken.'

'Ah, the mythical cephalopod. I don't suppose you actually saw one?'

'I was too busy trying not to drown.'

'Pity. They're part of the squid family, I have heard reports that some have grown to over fifty feet in length.'

'She wasn't talking about a giant squid, but something far older.'

Harrison lit a pipe and sat down in the chair opposite.

'And you say she could swim unaided, without the need for air?'

Rufius thought she looked more like a kelpie, a water sprite. 'She swam like a fish. I guess she could breathe like one too.'

The watchmaker blew a cloud of smoke out of his nostrils as he laughed. 'My dear boy, do they teach you nothing in your time? A fish has no lungs, but simply gills,' he said, putting his hand to the side of his neck and fanning out his fingers. 'One cannot grow a pair on command.'

'She breathed air into me when I was all but dead.'

'Then she may be a very rare creature indeed!'

Rufius stared into the fire for so long that Harrison thought he might have gone back to sleep.

'I don't think she's the only one.'

Harrison shifted uneasily in his chair. 'Really, what makes you say that?'

'She talks in her sleep,' Rufius answered, his cheeks flushing.

The watchmaker folded his arms. 'Ah, I see.'

'She mentioned someone called Dun Sgathaich.'

'Never heard of him.'

'It's not a person, but a place,' came Lord Dee's deep

voice from the other side of the room. 'It means "Fortress of shadows".'

'My Lord,' Harrison said, standing and bowing to his master.

The old man's face looked strained as he came closer. His eyes had lost their fire and there were dark shadows beneath them. 'You've lost your homing key I see,' Dee observed.

Rufius started to apologise, but Dee held up his hand to silence him. 'You of all people should know how dangerous the past can be, not just because of the consequences your actions might have on the timeline. It is a wild and lawless place where violence and disease are rife.' Dee took out his almanac, opening it on a long list of names. 'Not to mention the other temporal factions. Sir Robert was right to suspect there were thieves stealing his books. There is significant evidence of those exploiting the past for their own gain.'

'Like the Tuatha Dé?'

The old man shook his head. 'They are nothing more than an old Irish myth.'

'She told me they could weave stone to follow ancient paths.'

'There are many such legends, the pagans erected stone temples, monolithic constructions that were supposed to harness the powers of the elements, but the chronology of stone is too complex and unpredictable, it would take you into the deep past, and strand you there.'

'And what of this woman weaving with water?' Harrison asked.

'Rufius is clearly enamoured with her. I would assume she tricked him with some hidden artefact. The boy has been raised on tales of elves and trolls after all.'

'But she claimed she could see the future!' Rufius protested.

Lord Dee seemed to be slightly taken aback by this; his eyes narrowing a little. 'No one can see beyond the frontier.'

'Well, at least we have Rufius back in one piece,' Harrison said, trying to lighten the mood.

Rufius went to speak, but the Lord Dee raised his hand once more.

'He disobeyed an order and endangered himself as well as those that came looking for him. We must abide by our own rules or else we risk falling into chaos.'

Rufius had no idea that others had come in search of him. He wondered how long he had been away — it seemed like no more than a week.

Lord Dee closed his book, his mouth set in a thin, hard line. 'You're squandering your gift with these foolish games,' he said. 'I have a mind to send you back to your own time until you learn that there will always be consequences to your actions.'

Rufius didn't know what to say. He could see the disappointment in the old man's face.

Harrison looked at him sternly, clearly agreeing with his master.

'Yet I have lost too many men to cast off the ones that do return. Harrison has nothing but good things to say about you, and I have to consider your contribution to the Antiquarians. So, I am willing to overlook this misdemeanour on the understanding that there will be no more of these impetuous acts or solo adventures and no more fairy tales!'

Rufius nodded his head and assured him that there would not.

31

RAPHUS CUCULLATUS

[Montagu House, Bloomsbury, London. Date: 1759]

A month had passed since the reprimand from Lord Dee. Harrison had advised Rufius to keep a low profile. The old man had stopped visiting the workshop and Rufius was quite glad to stay out of his way.

He had tried his best to forget about Maebh, yet she still haunted his dreams. He would wake in the night, drenched in sweat, with the feeling of her cold lips still lingering on his, and wonder where she was now.

Unable to settle back to sleep, he had taken to exploring the museum in the middle of the night. Dee's project was becoming something of an attraction, and during the day, the once quiet corridors of Montagu House were crowded with Antiquarians, academics and the general public.

There was an eerie quiet to the darkened halls during the hours before dawn. He loved wandering amongst the cases of glassy-eyed specimens, wondering which distant land they had walked upon, resisting the urge to reach in and find out for himself. Instead, Rufius restricted himself to learning the various names of the exotic collection.

On one particular night, he was standing before the skeleton of a large bird-like creature, practising the Latin name whilst trying to imagine what the creature would have looked like with flesh and feathers.

'Raphus cucullatus', he recited to himself, letting Dolovir's Latin roll over his tongue.

'*Raphus* cucull*atus*,' corrected the skeleton.

Rufius stared in amazement at the giant bird, which glared mutely back at him through empty eye sockets, and then he noticed the figure of a girl standing on the other side of the cabinet.

'It's from the sub-family of Raphinae. The same family as pigeons and doves. I believe they were most prevalent on the island of Mauritius, east of Madagascar in the Indian Ocean.'

A dark-haired young woman walked around the cabinet and stood beside him. She was only half his height and was wearing a dark velvet dress. 'The last sighting of one was in 1662. Sir Thomas Herbert wrote that the Portuguese called them dodos, from the dutch "Dodoor" for sluggard, but I prefer "Dodaars" which means fat-arsed,' she added with a giggle.

For a moment, Rufius wondered if she could be an older version of Amelia Cotton. But this girl spoke with a strong accent, like Dolovir, one that he couldn't place exactly.

'My name is Alixia, what's yours?' she asked, holding out a gloved hand. It was made from fine leather, with what appeared to be a mythical creature stitched into the back.

'Rufius,' he said politely, taking her dainty hand in his.

'And when do you hail from?' she continued, gripping his hand tightly.

Unsure of who she was, Rufius decided to play the innocent. 'Here,' he replied. 'Where else?'

She let go of his hand. 'No, silly. I'm from 1838. I've travelled back here to save this ridiculous bird from extinction.'

'954,' Rufius admitted. It was the name that Lord Dee had given him when he first arrived. A Christian date that meant nothing to him until Harrison explained the measurement of time.

Her eyes widened slightly. 'Interesting. Saxon or Viking?'

'Dane,' he said proudly, pushing out his chest.

She folded her arms. 'I've never ventured back that far, but the chronicles of Winchester are quite fascinating.'

Rufius scoffed. 'Stories for old women and children.'

'Quite,' she said, her lips pursing together. They made a cute bow shape, and Rufius found himself wondering what it would be like to kiss them.

'What year is this?' she asked, looking around the other exhibits.

'1759.'

She took out a small notebook and leafed through it. 'According to my research, there should be a way to reach the Tradescant collection from here. I believe it was bought by one Elias Ashmole in 1659. I should be able to follow his records back to find one of the last surviving specimens.'

Rufius knew the name only too well.

Two days ago, Harrison sent him to fetch a book from Duke Humphrey's library in the Bodleian. Many of the rare manuscripts had been moved there from Montagu house as the collection had grown significantly thanks to Sir Robert's Antiquarians. Security was becoming an increasingly significant issue. Rufius could no longer simply walk in and take a book. They had begun to fasten the books to the shelves by long, thin metal chains which required a key to remove. Since this meant the spines to be turned inward, no one but the librarians knew the location of a book, and he was forced to make his request on a slip of paper. This was diligently copied down into a register before novices were sent off into the stacks with large rings of keys jangling on their belts.

A tall young man was standing at the desk waiting impatiently for his books. He looked at Rufius with disdain, the same way Hagar would do before a fight as if he were nothing more than dirt on the bottom of his boot.

'Can I help you?' asked the librarian that sat behind the desk.

Rufius handed the slip over without a word, and the man's eyebrows arched as he read the title. 'It'll take a while. This one's being stored in the sixteen-sixties.'

Rufius shrugged, he was in no real hurry, he liked the library — it was quiet and smelled of old leather.

The other boy made a tutting sound with his mouth.

The librarian turned towards him. 'Master Ashmole, your request is being dealt with. As I've already explained, we cannot allow you to access the repository.'

'Perhaps if your indexing were more logical,' the boy said arrogantly, 'you'd have found it by now.'

Rufius winced, he knew better than to criticise the indexing of the library. It was a contentious issue within the Antiquarians; no one could agree on a singular system of cataloguing the artefacts and books. He had heard that actual fights had broken out in the stacks between the various factions. Ashmole obviously didn't realise how dangerous the ground was on which he was treading. It was like poking a bear with a stick.

'Master Ashmole...' began the librarian.

Rufius walked away, leaving them to their debate.

'I know Ashmole,' he said to Alixia, 'and I know how to reach Oxford in 1660.'

Alixia looked up from her notebook, her dark eyes wide with excitement. 'You do? I would be very grateful if you would introduce me to him.'

Rufius scowled. 'I don't think he will be much help.'

'Why ever not?'

'He doesn't strike me as the kind of man that wants to save an extinct species.'

While he had been waiting for the novice to return with his book, Rufius had wandered into one of the reading rooms. It was filled with students from the last two centuries. The Bodleian was like a magnet for time travellers. There was no longer any need for Dolovir to go looking for recruits, the library drew them like bees to a honey pot.

Distracted by a woman wearing the strangest set of purple robes, Rufius watched as she scanned a page of an ancient text with a magnifying glass, muttering quietly to herself while analysed the text. The words were making strange shapes on her thin lips, and when she reached a specific phrase, she let out a high-pitched shriek and pulled off one of her gloves with her teeth. Running her fingers along the gothic script, she disappeared into thin air.

Two other readers, who had been standing on the opposite side of the desk, placed their hands on the page and followed her. The library acted as a staging post for all types of traveller, the books creating a safe passage to a specific part of history.

Harrison had warned Rufius that visitors were made to swear an oath before they were allowed into the libraries, and at last count, there were now over a hundred members of the 'Order' as Dee called it.

With more members joining, two distinct types of Antiquarians were emerging: those who preferred to work with the physical artefacts like Wilkins's astrological equipment or the curiosities collected by Sloane, and the more academic types who favoured the library and the preservation of manuscripts. The separate factions had adopted different coloured robes, and Rufius had overheard some of the more bookish Antiquarians refer to themselves as "Scriptorians".

Ashmole broke the silence with a loud 'Finally' when he was handed his book, before storming away like a spoiled child.

Until then, Rufius had assumed he was the youngest member of Dee's Order. Everyone else seemed to be much older. Ashmole was the first youth he had met since Dolovir had recruited him.

His stomach groaned, reminding him it was nearly time for lunch. If they didn't find his book soon, he would miss his chance to visit the Great Hall. No matter what period of history he explored, there was nothing more delicious than the roast suckling pig they served every day at midday. Dolovir always used to joke that the pig was probably a boar from Carpathia and more than likely over a thousand years old. Rufius didn't care; the thought of the apple sauce alone was making his mouth water.

A few minutes later, a rather sweaty librarian returned to

the desk with Rufius's book. He thanked him and was on his way to the hall when he found Ashmole standing outside on the wooden staircase, talking to another boy.

'Who are you?' Ashmole asked, blocking Rufius's path. They were nearly the same height, though Ashmole wore a wig that made his head a few inches taller.

'Rufius Westinghouse.'

Ashmole mouth twisted into a slight sneer. 'Oh, and there was me thinking you were someone important, have we met?'

'No.'

'Elias Ashmole,' he said, holding out his hand limply. 'This is Bodley, he's a dolt but has his uses.'

Rufius gripped his hand and then let go. It was like holding a dead fish.

'Aren't you apprenticed to Harrison?' Bodley asked with a look of genuine interest.

Rufius nodded and held up the book. 'He's waiting for this.' Hoping that it would be enough to signal the end of the conversation.

'What do we have here?' Ashmole said, snatching the book out of Rufius's grip. 'Novum Organum Scientiarum,' he read the frontispiece aloud. 'What does the watchmaker need from Master Bacon?'

'He needs something from 11.620,' Rufius explained.

'Don't you mean 1620?' Ashmole said, pointing to the date printed on the page.

'It's a new numbering system that Harrison is developing,' Rufius replied, unsure if he should actually be telling anyone about it.

'Many will travel and knowledge will be increased.' Ashmole sneered, translating the Latin under the illustration. 'And how did you come to be so privileged?'

Rufius could tell that they were both a little jealous. 'I don't know, Dolovir assigned me to him.'

Alixia smiled and pulled a stone from a leather purse. 'He may not be a good man, but nevertheless, I have found that with the right incentive, most collectors can be persuaded. I need him to introduce me to Tradescant the Elder. Once I have a connection, it should be a simple case of following this unfortunate creature's journey back across the Indian Ocean.'

She held an object up so that it caught in a beam of moonlight.

The crystal glowed violet and inside Rufius could see a creature entombed within a luminescent glass.

'What is it?'

'Blue amber. Ancient, crystallised tree sap from *Hymenaea protera*. The insect was caught in the sticky resin many millions of years ago. I haven't met a natural philosopher yet who isn't fascinated by such an artefact, and I'm sure that Master Ashmole would be only too happy to assist us.'

Us? Thought Rufius, not quite sure what he had agreed to exactly, but whatever it was, he knew it would probably land him in trouble with Lord Dee.

She put the gemstone back in her purse and took his hand. 'So, Oxford 1660 if you wouldn't mind?'

32

NATURALIA

[Musaeum Tradescantianum, Vauxhall. Date: 1652]

Alixia and Rufius appeared amongst piles of dusty books and stacks of boxes. They were surrounded by all manner of unusual artefacts: elaborate feather cloaks and headdresses, weapons, coins and books lined the shelves of the room.

She groaned. 'We're in the wrong part of the collection.' Shaking her head and opening her notebook. 'This is *Artificialia*. We need to find *Naturalia*.'

It had taken Alixia less than half an hour to persuade Ashmole to help her. She had begun by appealing to his sense of duty as a natural philosopher, his moral obligation to preserve the past and help avert the extinction of the innocent and rather gullible dodo.

Ashmole sat nonchalantly behind a desk in his rooms at Brasenose College listening intently to her pleas. For a brief moment, Rufius had thought she was actually on the point of convincing him. The man nodded in all the right places and even smiled once or twice during her argument.

'I would like nothing better than to help you, my dear,' he said condescendingly when she had made her case. 'But the simple fact is that the collection was bequeathed to me. I've little enough time and less money to go about looking for bills of sale or letters of provenance! Who knows where the Tradescants managed to acquire half of the things in their collection, I hardly think one bird is going to be missed in the grand scheme of things.'

When she took the blue amber out of her purse, Rufius saw the greed ignite in his eyes.

'Of course, there is nothing to stop you two from visiting the Ark and having a look around for yourselves,' he said, taking a large iron key from one of his desk drawers and offering it in exchange for the gem. 'Assuming that you're willing to part with such a fascinating bauble.'

Alixia handed over the amber with a knowing smile and took the key.

Rufius could see why they called it the Ark. The second room, which bore the words *Naturalia* over the door, was a shrine to animal bones. Carefully labelled and displayed on the walls were the skeletal remains of hundreds of different species. The air smelled of death and dust, the bones were bleached, picked clean of flesh and fur. Rufius recognised various skulls and jawbones, but some, like the bony carapaces of giant sea creatures, looked unworldly and alien. There were some that looked like the teeth of dragons.

Alixia pulled out a battered ledger that was wedged between the dried husk of a beehive and a jar of browning butterfly wings.

'The Tradescants were naturalists and collectors who travelled as far as Arctic Russia. On one expedition against the Barbary Pirates, the son collected many rare specimens of plants from the Levant and Algiers.'

Rufius winced at the word. He'd had quite enough of pirates for one lifetime.

She opened the book and placed it on a table. 'What we need to find is a link to the dodo.'

'Why are you doing this?' Rufius asked, looking at the fossils pinned to the walls of the small room. 'There must be many thousands of creatures you could choose to revive?'

Alixia sighed and looked up from the ledger.

'Because, unlike some of the other extinct species, the eradication of the dodo was the direct result of contact with humanity. They were hunted out of existence. The woolly mammoth may have perished because of changes in its climate, but the dodo was guilty of nothing but its own stupidity.'

There were tears welling in the corners of her eyes and Rufius could tell that this was going to end badly if she didn't find a way to reach a living specimen.

'What do you need?'

She took a deep breath and composed herself. 'A clutch of eggs would be best. The chances of survival are higher when they are still in embryo.'

He took the ledger in both hands, feeling the timelines unwind around his fingers. 'Let's go and find your giant pigeon.'

33

DODO

[Mauritius. Date: 1638]

They followed the chronology of the Trascendants' documents across the Indian Ocean back to Mauritius. The island was a lush jungle, full of the most diverse range of flora and fauna. The Dutch traders had built a port, and their ships wallowed in the natural harbour created by its deep clear waters.

Mauritius was a beautiful place, reminding Rufius of some of his early trips to Jamaica and the West Indies. Alixia was eager to leave the trading post. The sight of captured animals being transported in small wooden boxes made her weep. Along the quayside, there were hundreds of cages stacked with specimens bound for the West. Finely dressed merchant captains, who were obviously growing rich plundering the resources of the island, stood watching from their decks as cargoes were hauled aboard.

Once they were clear of the port, Alixia relaxed. Rufius could tell by the way she navigated through the dense undergrowth that this was not her first venture into the jungle. She moved like a cat stalking her prey, somehow managing to walk silently between the vines and fallen trees. He, on the other hand, sounded like a lumbering bear: treading on every other branch and twig, scaring flocks of birds from the trees and causing her to turn around and glare at him more than once.

Luckily, the dodo was not hard to track. They seemed unconcerned about the noise and within an hour they had discovered a nest with a clutch of eggs and some very friendly parents.

'It's no wonder they died out,' she said, stroking the head of the mother, who clucked in appreciation. 'They've never known a predator.'

'No wolves here?' Rufius asked, looking down at the large speckled shells.

'No, Mauritius and Madagascar are interesting environments. After the breakup of the supercontinent of Gondwana in the Cretaceous period, eighty-eight million years ago, the native wildlife diversified — ninety per cent of the species on these islands are found nowhere else on earth.'

'The islands moved?'

'It's known as plate tectonics. Continents have shifted away from each over millions of years. Along fault lines, where you usually find volcanoes.'

Rufius frowned, searching his Dolovir's memories for the meaning. 'What is a volcano?'

Alixia laughed and pointed to a large mountain rising out of the jungle. 'A mountain that spouts fire? They are quite a sight to behold.'

Rufius looked up to the ragged peaks that rose up out of the jungle and could not help but think of Muspelheim, the land of fire, wondering if Surtr, the fire giant, was waiting in the caves beneath with his flaming sword.

. . .

They spent the rest of the day exploring the south side of the island. Alixia would stop every so often to make a sketch of a plant in her journal or collect seeds in the old leather bag she wore at her hip.

The sun was beginning to set when she finally stopped and picked up one of the eggs from a ground nest. The parents were nowhere to be seen.

'How do you know it will survive?' Rufius asked as she handed it to him.

'I've been doing this for a while. Eggs and seeds seem to survive the temporal dislocation where adults do not.'

There was a loud screech from the bushes as something broke through the foliage.

Rufius jumped at the sound and dropped the egg.

34

BODLEY

[Christ Church College, Oxford. Date: 1660]

A few days later, Bodley approached Rufius while he was crossing the quad. He had tried to keep his head down so as to avoid catching his eye, but the boy made a detour towards him.

'Sorry about Ashmole, he's a complete arse.'

Rufius smiled weakly, unsure as to whether this was some kind of trick. His eyes quickly scanned the cloisters in case Ashmole was watching from the shadows.

Bodley fell in step beside him, walking back in the direction he had come. 'He's absolutely obsessed with starting his own collection. I've heard he's going for a position coming up in Broad Street. That will make him the youngest curator in the Order.'

'Broad Street?'

Bodley looked confused. 'Haven't you heard? The collection has grown exponentially under Sir Robert, the Antiquarians have started creating new repositories in different parts of time.'

Rufius had heard rumours about the expansion, but no details. There was a matter of pride at stake, the Order was growing, and he was beginning to feel like Lord Dee had forgotten he existed.

'Oh that,' he said, 'I'm not really interested in books — I'm more of an explorer.'

'When were you born?'

'10.940. You?'

Bodley paused, using his fingers to calculate the date. '11.545. I was studying under Calvin in Geneva until Elizabeth took the throne, then we moved to England, and I joined Magdalen college under Humphrey. Dolovir recruited me in 11.563.'

Rufius made a quick mental calculation, Bodley was eighteen years old — three years older than him. They were nearly the same height and build, thanks to Doctor Crooke's tonic, and Bodley obviously assumed they were the same age.

'I heard that you got a little lost,' Bodley added, slightly ashamed at listening to gossip. 'Or so the rumour goes.'

Rufius was hoping that the entire incident would have been forgotten, but the Order was small enough that word could spread like a fire through dry bracken. The search and rescue team were notorious drunkards, and there is nothing better than a tale of pirates and sunken ships to help pass the time when the wine is flowing.

The fact that the rescue team hadn't been able to locate him had been just as newsworthy as the actual adventure itself. No one knew the exact details of what transpired, which saved him some blushes, but there was a new look of respect from many members that passed him in the corridors of the museum.

Lord Dee called them his 'Dragons', a handpicked group

of individuals who were more practical than academic. Good with their hands and able to think on their feet, warriors who weren't afraid to go into the dark, forgotten places in the past. Rufius had tried to find them to apologise, but they were hard to track down.

'What are they saying?'

Bodley slowed down as they reached the pond in the centre of the quad, standing in the shadow of the statue of Mercury.

'That you nearly died onboard Captain Morgan's ship, and that you were rescued by a sea witch.'

'Not a witch. She was different.'

Bodley frowned. 'Different how?'

Rufius nodded. He didn't want to say too much, he hardly knew Bodley, and the last thing he wanted was Ashmole to learn about his secrets.

'She could weave with stone and water.'

Bodley's eyes widened. 'An elemental? I'd heard there were some that could, but never thought they were real. Did you learn how she did it?'

'No,' said Rufius, shaking his head. *She taught me many things but not that,* he thought to himself.

'They're saying that the founder nearly banished you for disobedience, that Harrison had to step in and vouch for you.'

'The founder?'

'Lord Dee, that's what they're calling him in Antiquarian circles. As in "the founder of the Order".'

Rufius could still see the disappointment in Dee's face when he stepped out of the shadows. Banishment would have been a kinder punishment than to suffer that look again.

A group of students appeared through the arch under

Tom Tower and made their way towards them. Rufius turned away from them and started towards the Canterbury gate.

Bodley, realising he had overstepped the mark, caught up to him.

'Sorry, apart from one disastrous expedition into the Flavian dynasty, I've spent most of my time in the sixteenth century, nothing too adventurous. How far back have you travelled?'

'I've watched Attila take on the Romans on the Catalaunian Plains of Gaul,' Rufius said, as he stepped out onto Merton Street. Carts and horses rattled past, throwing clods of mud and dust into the air.

Bodley coughed. 'You've met the Visigoths! I've only read about that. What did you use to get back there?'

Walking into the narrow confines of Oriel Street, Rufius thought about Gunnlogi. In all the excitement of the last few months, it had slipped his mind.

'An old Roman sword.'

'Do you still have it?' Bodley asked eagerly.

Rufius sighed, his fingers clenched as if he could still feel the grip in his hand. 'Lost it in the battle.'

'Shame. I would have loved to have heard them speak.'

'Why?'

'I'm something of a collector of languages,' Bodley said with a grin. 'I can speak French, Italian, Spanish and Greek, amongst others.'

Rufius came to the door of the Bodleian. Heraldic shields were painted on the front of the wood panelling.

'That's my coat of arms,' said Bodley proudly pointing at one of the shields. It was white with five black birds and three gold crowns on a blue band. 'We're part of the Dunscombe line. Not that it will mean much to you — I'm guessing Devon didn't even exist in your time. It was all part of Wessex.'

'Have you been given a position too?' Rufius asked.

Bodley's chest puffed out a little. 'I have actually, well in one sense at least. They want me to go back and rebuild the University's library after the reformation in 1598.'

35

HARRISON'S EXPERIMENTS

[Christ Church College, Oxford. Date: 1713]

Harrison kept a close eye on Rufius after the incident with *Satisfaction*, keeping him occupied with the tasks on his tachyon project.

Going back in time to have George Graham build the device had accelerated the process to the point where they now had a working prototype.

Rufius was his ranger, Harrison explained, he would be sent back to specific points in history to calibrate the device. At first, Rufius was happy to put the prototype through its paces, until he realised that every trip resulted in a long list of modifications and refinements which his mentor would expect him to document methodically. Sitting in the study until late into the evening writing up his notes, it soon began to feel like a form of punishment.

The latest prototype felt heavier than the previous versions and half the size, neatly fitting in his palm. Harrison made some remark about miniaturisation that Rufius didn't understand; he was just happy to have something that didn't require two hands to hold.

The benches in the workshop had been pushed back to create more space, and his mentor had drawn a chalk circle onto the stone floor, its circumference marked with a number of unusual symbols at regular intervals.

'These are temporal coordinates,' Harrison instructed, pointing towards the marks. 'Each one coincides to a specific date and time that I need you to go to.' He placed a small object on top of each one as he walked around the circle. 'When you reach the designated time, I want you to align the dials and press the second button.' He pointed to the brass knob on the side of the large watch.

The face of the tachyon was constructed of concentric rings just as Rufius had seen in the original plans. This was the first time he'd been able to move them. Harrison slapped his hand away as he went to touch them.

'Not yet! They've been carefully calibrated. The slightest touch could ruin the experiment. Only change them when you get there, not a second before. The next iteration should be able to do this automatically, but Graham's engineers are having trouble finding an alloy sensitive enough for the movement of the tourbillon escapement.'

In one of the early trials, the tachyon had been nothing more than a blank-faced brass box with a button that returned him to the workshop a few seconds after he had left. It was so heavy that they used a leather harness strapped to his chest to make it less cumbersome, which became something of a problem on the trial that dropped him into the middle of a lake. Having nearly drowned while freeing himself, it took the rescue team two weeks before they found him working in the kitchens of Urquhart Castle. Rufius learned later that he had landed in Loch Ness just before Edward I of England captured it in 11.296.

The watchmaker was obsessed with perfecting his 'longitude of time' — a temporal coordinate system for time travellers, one that had already improved the accuracy of Rufius's returns to a matter of a few seconds.

It was already proving to be a powerful tool, but Harrison knew he could make it better, make it more than just a homing device.

The tachyon, as they had both come to call it, could be used to remember where you'd been. Unlike other artefacts that had a fixed linear chronology, Harrison wanted his device to store temporal locations, like bookmarks. It was far more practical than carrying around a return object, like the homing key he'd lost to the pirates of Port Royal.

There had been a number of setbacks during their experiments but only one serious issue: the time that Rufius returned before even setting off. This had led to the implementation of the 'Closed Loop' safety margin.

The fabric of the room appeared to ripple, like water on a pond and Rufius felt an invisible force pushing him away from the workshop. He woke to find himself on the roof of the college in the middle of the night with the rain pouring down on him.

Harrison theorised that the electrical storm that raged through most of that week was a direct result of the temporal accident, but made Rufius swear never to tell anyone else about it.

'I think you'll enjoy this one,' Harrison said, placing objects around the circle. 'I was inspired by your mention of El Dorado. Thought you might like to see the Spanish conquistadors in action.'

The first coordinates were attached to a compass, one that had once belonged to an Italian explorer by the name of Christopher Columbus.

The timeline that unwound around him was extensive. The compass had travelled widely with the navigator. There were four voyages between Spain and the Americas. Rufius was sorely tempted to investigate, but Harrison was watching him too closely and so he resisted the urge to jump onto the *Santa Maria* in 1492.

Instead, he wove through the timeline until he found the mission dates.

[Pinta. North of Hispaniola. January 6, 11.493]

Rufius executed a perfect landing on the quarterdeck of the *Pinta*, taking a deep breath of the sharp sea air, letting it fill his lungs.

Taking a moment to acclimatise, he was pleased to see that the clothes that Harrison insisted he wore were still intact. There had been a number of missions where the first hours were spent trying to find something to wear before his nakedness drew too much attention.

No one seemed to have noticed his arrival. The crew were all too busy attending to another ship, the *Nina*, that lay alongside. He watched the men moving back and forth between the two boats which had been lashed together while cargoes were transferred by block and tackle.

Rufius had never seen so much gold in his life. The gleam of the yellow metal lit up their faces as the sun caught it. A vast hoard of treasure was being moved from the *Pinta* to her sister ship, but he had no time to find out where it had come from as the tachyon began to vibrate in his hand as the internal timer reached its end.

He quickly set the dials as Harrison had instructed before leaping back into the workshop.

[<<]

'What was Columbus doing with all that gold?' Rufius asked, handing back the tachyon to Harrison.

The watchmaker ignored him, chewing his lip while he inspected the dials. 'Are you sure this was right?'

Rufius nodded. 'I'd say it was pretty close.'

Harrison went over to his desk, strapped on his array of head lenses and began to take the device apart with a tiny screwdriver. 'Close can get you dead.'

'Or rich, based on what I saw.'

Harrison sighed. 'What you witnessed was the conquests of the Pinzon brothers. Their agenda was not so much exploration as exploitation. At that time, Spain needed gold and land, and the brothers had their eyes on the Aztecs of Mesoamerica.'

'It looked more like the treasure of Andvari.'

Harrison looked up and smiled. 'Another one of your Norse legends?'

Sitting down opposite his mentor, Rufius picked up one of the spare gear wheels and placed it over his finger. 'He was a dwarf who lived beneath a waterfall with a magical ring called Andvaranaut, and it made Andvari rich until Loki caught him and forced him to give it up. But the dwarf cursed the gold so that it destroyed anyone who possessed it.'

'As it so often does. Although in the case of the Spanish, their lust for riches proved fatal for many of the indigenous tribes of the new world.'

'Did they kill them?'

Harrison took off his headset. 'They brought epidemics with them that the native population had no defence against — millions of people died.'

Rufius frowned. 'What are epidemics?'

'Pestilence, sickness, poxes. Diseases that accompanied the conquistadors in their American conquest were mostly smallpox and typhus — diseases that have never crossed the Atlantic and to which they had no immunity.'

Harrison could see that Rufius was struggling to understand and put down the tachyon.

'Sorry I forget when you're from. In 1768 an English physician by the name of John Fewster realised that a prior infection of cowpox rendered a person immune to smallpox, a far more deadly variant. His work was improved upon by Edward Jenner, who used the pus from milkmaids infected with cowpox to immunise test subjects and prove that it prevented the smallpox infection.'

'They used one disease to fight another.'

'In a manner of speaking, yes. They used a less deadly version of a disease to train the body to fight the other.'

Rufius smiled. 'So disease is like an evil spirit.'

Harrison sighed. 'We still don't know exactly what

causes smallpox, but there are doctors working at the frontier trying to understand that very thing.'

'Have you ever been to the frontier?'

'Once. Terrible place, one never knows what's going to happen next!'

Rufius had heard others talking about it. The frontier was always whispered about in hushed conversations. It was the point where the present met the future and a place that most of their kind avoided. The uncertainty of not knowing what tomorrow would bring made most of them nervous, but Rufius relished the idea — there was something thrilling about standing at the precipice of time.

'Since you're so impressed with their gold,' Harrison said, picking up the compass. 'Let me show you some of the other wonders of the New World.'

36

THE NIGHT OF SORROWS

[Chichen Itza, Yucatán Península, Mexico. Date: 1531]

From the top of the stone pyramid, they could see for miles across the flat peninsula to the sparkling seas that surrounded them. Flocks of turquoise-blue jays swooped over the dense forest, chasing clouds of flies above the trees.

Harrison slapped the side of his neck as another insect sampled his blood.

'Damned mosquitoes,' he swore. 'The tropics are rife with them.'

They were standing on the Temple of Kukulcan, a step-pyramid dedicated to their serpent god of war. Sculptures of serpent heads gaped at the base of the stairs that rose up towards the square temple at its apex. Harrison said that the Spanish would rename it 'El Castillo' and station a garrison here within the next three years.

'The Spanish first encountered the Maya in 1502, on Columbus's fourth voyage, but it wasn't until 1517 when an expedition landed on the peninsula that the bloodshed began. The rumours of Aztec riches to the West came to the attention of Hernán Cortés, and so began the Spanish conquests.'

The plateau surrounding the pyramid was crowded with warriors in brightly-coloured feathered headdresses and cloaks. News of the conquistadors' arrival had travelled fast, and the men were preparing for war. Rufius spotted a number of elderly shamans making their way towards the base of the pyramid, a small procession of young men in tow, each one naked and painted bright blue.

'Sacrifices,' whispered Harrison, walking inside the temple. 'We don't have long. I wanted to show you this.'

Inside the stone structure, the air was cool. The stone provided shade from the worst of the sun.

'Thanks to the Spanish, there are hardly any surviving documents from the Mayan culture. They obliterated most of the written record, the only remaining texts are mostly carved in stone,' he said, tapping on the east wall. In the semi-darkness, Rufius could make out a large circular carving. 'This is the Haab, one of three Mayan calendars. The one that you would recognise, it's closest to our Gregorian calendar with three hundred and sixty-five days, the same number of steps which we have just climbed. But this — ' He moved to the other wall and another more complex disc. 'Is the long calendar, meant to keep track of the world cycle. It predicts that the world will end in 2012.'

Rufius stared at the series of interconnected dials, each with their own rings of glyphs. 'How does it end?'

'It doesn't say.'

'Are they travellers?'

Harrison smiled. 'No, they are cosmologists. They study the stars and the planets, they found Venus long before Galileo pointed his telescope at it. Their calculations of time were the greatest achievement since the Babylonians divided the circle into three hundred and sixty degrees which led to the invention of time.'

'What?'

Harrison held up his tachyon. 'The Babylonians used a numerical system based on sixty, which they inherited from the Sumerians. Medieval astronomers went on to apply sexagesimal values to time. It harks back to the observation of the sun and the stars.'

Rufius ran his fingers over the carved symbols, feeling the stonemason's chisel cutting into the surface.

'According to the Dresden Codex,' Harrison began. 'Their world would end with a great deluge and the sky falling. It's also part of their creation story, a very popular theme in this part of the world.'

Harrison stumbled and nearly dropped his watch.

'I feel a little dizzy,' he said. 'Must be the damn heat.'

Rufius could see the man had turned very pale. 'I think we should leave,' he suggested, taking Harrison by the arm.

37

MALARIA

[Christ Church College, Oxford. Date: 1713]

Harrison was sweating. His skin was pale and clammy when they returned to the workshop.

'Is the fire lit?' he asked, collapsing into his favourite chair.

'No master, would you like one?' said Rufius, helping Harrison take off his boots.

The watchmaker shook his head. 'No! Just a glass of water?' he said, loosening his collar and trying to take off his jacket.

Rufius saw the bite on his neck, an angry-looking red carbuncle stood proud on the white skin.

'Perhaps I should summon the Doctor,'

'Not old Crooke,' protested Harrison deliriously. 'He'll have my head off!' He made a cutting motion with one hand and passed out.

. . .

'Malaria, most likely,' Doctor Crooke declared an hour later. 'You were right to call for me.'

He examined the bite mark carefully, placing a leech on the boil.

'I would prefer it if I could treat him in the Medica.'

Harrison's breathing was shallow, and he shuddered as if he were cold.

'I can look after him,' Rufius insisted.

The doctor stared at the boy over his glasses. 'Do you know the first thing about this condition?'

Rufius shook his head.

'*Mal-aria* was a term the Italians coined for the disease. They believed it could be caught from bad air. Others have called it Marsh fever or Tertian Ague. The parasite enters the bloodstream from a biting insect such as a mosquito. Then goes to the liver and begins to reproduce, it multiplies in your blood cells, bursting them. Hence the fever.'

'Will he die?'

The doctor grunted as he prepared a brass syringe. 'This is Quinine, a toxic plant alkaloid from the Cinchona, or fever tree. He will need regular injections, or I can give you a powdered form to mix with water, once he wakes.'

He pushed the needle into his arm.

'The shaking will pass soon. Make sure he takes lots of liquids and keep the fire burning. If he worsens, I will have no choice but to admit him.' He picked the leech from Harrison's neck with a pair of brass forceps and dropped it into a glass vial. 'I will test the blood to determine which type of parasite he has. Until the fever passes, he must have complete rest.'

38

FOUNDER

It was two days before the shivering abated.

Rufius never left his side, sleeping in the chair beside his mentor, and attending to his every need as Harrison drifted in and out of his delirium.

On the third day, his eyes cleared and he complained at the bitter taste of the water, a sure sign that he was back to his old self.

The doctor had returned each day to check on his progress and seemed impressed with the care he was receiving. The leech had been examined and the parasite identified as *plasmodium vivax*, a variety that was known to cause relapses.

Harrison was more concerned about the tachyon's progress than his own condition and refused to rest any longer once the doctor left on the fourth day.

The founder held the tachyon in his hand, weighing it like it was made of gold.

'How accurate is it?'

Harrison smiled like a proud father. 'To within a minute of your departure. Our tests have shown that it was safest to leave a sixty-second margin to avoid a causal loop.'

Dee nodded, his blue eyes turned to Rufius. 'Yes, I heard the storm was quite spectacular. Dolovir tells me that all the birds in Oxford lost their bearings.'

'There was a magnetic disturbance that would have affected them.'

'And how far back have you tested it.'

'Over a thousand years, but there is no reason to believe it would fail at ten thousand. The principle is the same if you apply my Holocene numbering system.'

Rufius could tell that the founder was impressed. It was the first time he had seen Dee since the incident in the Caribbean and was hoping that this would prove to him that he could be trusted.

'Good. How quickly can you fashion five of these?'

'In the blink of an eye,' said Harrison, taking out a mahogany case from beneath his workbench. The highly polished lid was inlaid with a circle of silver in the shape of a serpent eating its own tail.

'Ouroboros,' noted the founder.

'The alchemical symbol of renewal, I thought it was rather appropriate.' Harrison said, opening the lid to reveal ten brass tachyons nestling in a velvet lining.

The founder's eyes widened slightly at the sight of the gleaming objects.

'I thought that it would be best to let Rufius show the rescue team how to use them — since he's had the most experience,' added the watchmaker, nodding to his apprentice.

The old man seemed to be lost in his thoughts for a moment, and Rufius wasn't sure he'd heard his request.

'Fine,' he said absent-mindedly. 'As long as he's not required here.'

'Oh, I think I can spare him for a few days,' Harrison said, with a subtle wink. 'Just while they get used to them.' He lowered the lid of the case and handed it over to Rufius.

'I will inform Drake to expect you,' the founder said, tapping the case. 'They're an interesting bunch, so be prepared for a challenge.'

He shook Harrison's hand. 'Thank you, John. I suppose you would like to be returned to your own time?'

Harrison laughed, and Rufius heard the rattle of a cough beneath it. 'No, I think I'll rest here a while longer. Doctor Crooke has some new remedies he wishes to try on me.'

'As you wish.' The founder nodded and turned to leave.

'Master?' Rufius asked, holding up the case. 'Where should I take this?'

The founder smiled and took out a small key, handing it to him. 'To the Dragons.'

39

DRAGONS

[Pendennis Castle. Cornwall. Date: 1558]

Rufius was so excited that even the rain that hammered down on him, soaking his clothes, couldn't spoil the walk towards the castle. He wiped the water from his eyes with his free hand, the other holding tightly onto the mahogany case under his cloak to keep it dry.

Harrison had given him strict instructions on how he was to deliver the demonstration; nothing too complicated, stick to the basic functions and don't try to explain the Holocene date system. It was a simple enough task, show them how to use the device and leave.

The founder was pleased with their work, and that alone should have made Rufius happy after the months of worrying about whether he would ever be able to regain his approval. But that wasn't what had put a spring in his step this morning; it was the fact that he was about to meet the most interesting group of renegades within the Order — the Dragons.

The round, stone fortress stood on the edge of the cliff, brooding over the stormy seas and the distant shores of France beyond. Ringed with stone ramparts and bristling with cannon, it was a menacing deterrent to any ship that came too close to the English coast.

Approaching the keep, Rufius saw a dark-skinned man in leather armour sheltering from the rain beneath the arch of a large wooden door, smoking a pipe.

'Welcome,' he said with a broad smile that exposed a golden tooth amongst the pearly white. 'We've been expecting you.'

Rufius bowed slightly, his eyes remaining on the man, whose free hand was never far from the hilt of his sword. He held out the box, but the man waved it away with the stem of his clay pipe. 'Not me, boy. Bring them inside. Drake and Carstairs will be very interested to see them.'

Rufius followed the man through the gatehouse and into the main keep. It took a moment for his eyes to adjust to the dim light, just in time to duck below the heavy oak beams that were hung with all manner of weapons.

'We leave our swords at the door,' instructed the man, unbuckling his belt and hanging it on an empty peg. He looked at Rufius, realising then that he was unarmed. 'Only a fool or a priest travels these times without any protection.'

Rufius looked at him blankly.

'Let's hope your god is watching over you.'

The keep had little natural light. Tallow candles burned in the soot-stained lamps arranged along the long wooden beams, their weak glow diminished by the open fire that roared in the hearth in the middle of the circular room. Rufius caught the scent of roasting meat and saw a wild boar being slowly turned on a spit by a round-looking man with a red face.

'Tarrend,' called the dark-skinned man. 'Another mouth to feed.'

The cook took a swig from an odd-shaped bottle and raised it to them. 'Less for you then, Selephin!'

On the far side of the room, beyond the fire, two men were discussing something over a table. As Rufius came nearer, he could see that there was a map laid out upon it and they were pointing at various lines that were drawn across it.

Selephin put his hand on Rufius's shoulder.

'Gentlemen, I bring you the watchmaker's apprentice. Master — damn boy, what was your name?'

'Rufius, Rufius Westinghouse,' his voice sounded thin and weak in comparison to the deep baritone of the man standing beside him.

'Master Westinghouse has brought us a present.'

The shorter of the two men sneered.

'About time.'

The other smiled benevolently, he had a proud bearing with a neatly trimmed beard that came to a point.

'Welcome to the Draconians,' he said, walking towards Rufius. 'Please excuse my rude friend. Carstairs is having a little trouble with his manners. My name is Francis Drake.' He bowed.

Carstairs scowled and went back to studying the map.

Drake took the case from Rufius and placed it on top of the chart table. 'Shall we take a peek at our new toys? I've heard they may one day put us out of a job!'

Opening the box, Drake took out one of the tachyons and held it up for them all to see. 'Smaller than I expected, not quite small enough to wear, but still has a weight to it. What are they made of?'

'Mostly brass, mixed with tin and aluminium oxide — the surface is self-healing,' explained Rufius.

'Brass eh? So not affected by magnetism, nor liable to corrode. A wise choice.'

'The mechanism has to be synchronised with your local time,' explained Rufius taking another watch from the case and showing Drake the mechanism. 'Once you have a reference point, it will be able to calculate how far you have travelled and act as a homing device should you need to leave in a hurry.'

Drake looked at Selephin and grinned. 'Could have used that a few times over.'

Selephin chuckled. 'Indeed.' He scratched at an old scar that ran down one side of his face. 'Although the ladies tell me that my lines make me more interesting.'

Carstairs tutted, pushing the case out of the way of his work. It was obvious he wasn't impressed by Harrison's inventions. 'There's nothing better than an artefact, what's wrong with a homing key?'

'It can be configured to remember multiple locations,' answered Rufius before the others could speak. 'And adjusted to work with any timeframe.'

'And what do you call it?' asked Drake.

'A tachyon.'

Their conversation was interrupted by the sudden appearance of two women in the middle of the room. One leaned heavily on the other as if she were drunk, the side of her head was covered in blood.

'Selephin,' gasped the injured woman.

'Tarrend, some hot water if you please,' ordered Selephin, taking the woman in his arms before she collapsed.

He laid her gently on a table and began to examine her head.

'What happened?' asked Drake.

The other woman took a long drink from one of Tarrend's flagons before answering. 'Bloody bandits. Caught us off guard.'

Rufius stared at the wound as Selephin carefully moved her hair aside and began to clean away the blood with the warm water.

The uninjured woman was called Valeria and as Selephin tended to her friend, she told them how they had gone back to rescue an Antiquarian.

The man had been stranded in Moscow looking for the Golden Library of the Tsars. It was a rare collection of ancient Greek, Egyptian and Latin texts from the libraries of Constantinople and Alexandria which Ivan IV had hidden during his reign. Valeria said that when they found the Antiquarian in the archives, he was half-mad, gibbering on about a hidden chamber beneath the Kremlin. They had tried to persuade him to leave, but he was obsessed with finding the location of the texts and refused to go with them.

Before they had a chance to reason with him, they were attacked by a group of time thieves. Valeria killed one, but two more appeared and wounded her friend Kasia before they could escape.

'Head wounds always bleed badly,' Selephin observed, stitching the cut with a small fishhook needle. Rufius watched the man as he delicately closed the wound. 'She'll live. Which is more than I can say for those brigands when I catch them.'

Drake took Valeria to one side and spoke quietly to her.

Selephin lifted Kasia and placed her gently into a chair by the fire. The cook, Tarrend, handed him a small bowl of steaming broth. He blew gently on each spoonful before feeding it to her.

'Are there many thieves?' Rufius asked.

'Bane of our lives,' the cook replied. 'We first encountered them in the late fourteenth. They seemed to have the opposite agenda to ours, they're stealing anything of historical value.'

'Looking for talismans,' Kasia murmured. 'Fetch a higher price.'

Selephin frowned and shushed her with another spoonful, she shook her head and nodded to the bottle of brandy. 'Enough! Give me a damned drink!'

He did as he was told.

She held the bottle to her lips, draining every drop.

'Better,' she said hoarsely. She was a dark-eyed woman, not much older than Rufius's stepsister, Elin. He could tell from the way Selephin was doting on her that they were lovers. She reluctantly took the bowl he offered her and began to eat.

'Talismans?' Rufius asked the cook.

Tarrend handed Rufius a large metal dish and began to carve meat from the side of the boar, laying thick slabs of greasy pork on to the plate.

'Seriously ancient artefacts from pre-history,' he explained, sucking the meat juices from his fingers. 'They're supposed to possess magical properties or at least powerful histories. Certain collectors will pay anything to get their hands on them.'

'Sick bastards,' hissed Kasia.

Rufius thought back to his sword, wondering if it had been stolen because of its past.

Drake brought the case of tachyons over to the fire.

'Talismans are a powerful tool,' he agreed, 'and incredibly rare. As to whether they have special powers, no one can say for sure.' He glared at Tarrend and opened the case. 'In the meantime, I want all of you to take one of these. Master Westinghouse will show you how they work. If this experiment is successful, every member of the Order will be given one.'

'And we'll be out of a job,' Carstairs moaned, still bent over his charts.

'So we can concentrate on more important things than locating lost Antiquarians,' corrected Drake.

They each took a watch and turned them over, inspecting the finely-detailed dials. Selephin tried to prise his open with the end of his knife.

'I wouldn't do that if I were you,' warned Rufius. 'The internal mechanism is quite fragile.'

'Will they work underwater?' Carstairs asked, smirking as he dropped his into his tankard.

'They've been tested to a depth of six-hundred feet,' Rufius replied. Harrison had made him go back and retrieve the one he left at the bottom of Loch Lomond using a diving bell made out of an old barrel.

'Ah, yes. I knew we'd met before!' exclaimed Tarrend. 'You were the squirt we pulled out of Urquhart Castle.'

Rufius tried not to blush and continued with his demonstration. 'You can track your travel with these dials,' he said, ignoring the chuckling cook. 'Each digit of the Holocene date can be encoded and stored in memory by using this button.'

'Holocene?' scoffed Carstairs.

Drake scowled at him. 'And what exactly is this Holocene date?'

Rufius had forgotten about Harrison's instructions and began to explain how his mentor had devised a temporal coordinate system based on the year zero being set at the beginning of the Holocene geological epoch, 10,001 BC. By the puzzled looks on their faces, he wasn't too sure that he did that good a job of educating them.

Trying to ignore their confusion, he pushed on, showing them how to set their current location on the dials and store it. Inviting each of them to pick a random artefact to test it with.

Tarrend picked up a bottle and held it above his head. His round face broke into a wide grin as he released it and disappeared. Time slowed as the bottle hung in space, everyone held their breath, watching it fall to the ground and smash over the floor. The cook reappeared thirty seconds later and attempted to catch the already broken bottle, causing everyone to laugh, even Carstairs.

Rufius went on to explain about the built-in safety margin.

Everyone took a turn. Carstairs dried off his tachyon and selected one of the many confiscated artefacts to jump back over a thousand years, returning seconds later with a look of amazement on his face. The mood lifted, and Rufius was slapped on the back by Drake and Selephin, the cook ruffled his hair before going off to find a broom.

It felt wrong to take all the credit for Harrison's invention, but no one seemed to care — they had obviously been through a tough time.

40

SEVENTEENTH

Harrison's instructions were: 'to remain with the Dragons until they had become fully acquainted with their devices.' Which Rufius took as a coded way of saying he could stick around and spend some time with them.

Kasia had finally fallen asleep after the meal, and Selephin gently picked her up and took her to their quarters.

Carstairs went back to his books. He was researching something important that no one wanted to discuss and Rufius could tell that he was one of those people that preferred his own company.

Tarrend returned with more wood for the fire and began to peel potatoes and carrots for another stew. His nose glowed bright red in the firelight, and he kept fumbling the vegetables and dropping them into the bucket with the peelings, making Rufius laugh every time.

An awkward calm fell over the company, and Rufius took

the opportunity to explore the keep, wandering up through its many floors until he found Drake on the battlements looking out to sea. A fire was burning in the brazier and the commander stood smoking a pipe and warming himself. The storm had calmed and the night air had cooled, clouding his breath when he spoke.

'You know Henry VIII built this as a defence against invasion from France. A severe deterrent for a threat that never came, at least not for another ten years.'

'He wasn't to know.'

Drake sighed. 'No, that I suppose is our curse, to know what may come but not act.'

Rufius thought back to the war, and how he had failed to save the king, fate or destiny had reasserted itself all the same — Isolde would have called it the *Wyrd*.

'I take it you've recovered from your Caribbean adventure? Contemplating the life of a privateer I take it?' Drake asked with a glint in his eye.

Rufius shook his head. 'No, it was a mistake.'

'An educational one no doubt. Captain Morgan was an interesting character. Never met him, a bit after my time, but from what I've heard, he was quite the buccaneer.'

'I only met him once,' Rufius said, 'before Chagres.'

'Ah yes, the routing of Panama. Not one of his most profitable missions. Not like the *Cagafuego,* she was a beauty, full of Spanish gold and silver.'

'You fought the Spanish too?'

'Yes, it's actually part of the reason I ended up working for the Order.'

'How?'

Drake drew deeply on his pipe. 'It was the strangest thing. Some of the treasure was Mayan, golden idols of their gods and other ritual items. One moment I was assaying the weight of a statue of Itzamná, and the next I was standing in the middle of a temple. Dolovir turned up just before they had a chance to disembowel me.'

'He knew you were there?'

Drake pointed up to the stars with the end of his pipe. 'Lord Dee had seen it in his predictions. Fate was truly on my side that day.'

A flash of lightning lit up the distant clouds, illuminating a wide strip of silvery water and a fleet of ships that were battling the white-tipped waves.

Rufius shuddered at the thought of what his life would have been like if Dolovir had missed him at the Jorvik market.

'Do you think the future can be changed?'

'I think it's constantly changing, ebbing and flowing just like the tide. Yet it still moves in the same general direction, the arrow of time moves ever forward. Unlike this damned weather,' he said, stamping his boots. 'Feels colder than the last ice age. Time to get inside.'

When they returned downstairs, they found Valeria and Carstairs poring over a large book, called the 'Register', which, Rufius quickly learned, contained the last known location of every member of the Order.

Scanning down the rows of names Valeria would call out the ones that had not been seen in the last two or three days, and Carstairs would check against a tally in his journal.

'Magellan, McAllister, Morgan...' the list seemed to go on forever, there were many names Rufius didn't recognise, he had no idea what the purpose of this ritual was until they came to 'Wallace' and Carstairs suddenly sprang out of his chair.

'Fifth day,' he said, holding up his book.

'Last known location?' asked Selephin.

'Somewhere in the seventeenth, close to the assassination of James I,' Carstairs added, swinging a pair of compasses across the temporal map.

41

A LETTER

'Wallace was supposed to be watching for any potential interventions,' Selephin explained, adjusting the straps on Rufius's armour. 'One that might have caused a serious deviation in the timeline, changing the outcome of a single event.'

'Like the assassination of a king?'

'Exactly, James I wasn't supposed to die on November 5, 1605. The explosion wiped out the English Government and most of the noble families as well as decimating a larger part of London. They say the fires burned for days.'

'Do you think Wallace died in the attack?'

'No way to know without going there. Drake thinks it's the perfect opportunity to try out your contraption.'

Walking down the narrow stairs to the 'ready room', Rufius still couldn't believe he was going on a mission. He could feel the excitement coursing through his veins as if he were about to go into battle. Finally, he knew this was what he was meant to do, who he was meant to be.

They found the others waiting in full battle dress. Tarrend gave him a wink while the rest focused on the briefing that Carstairs was giving in front of a large map of London.

'In the last report, Wallace said he had identified several conspirators whom he believed were involved in the scheme. Robert Catesby, being the main instigator and the man who recruited a number of other disaffected Catholic aristocrats to their cause.' Carstairs tapped on an area near the centre. 'During this period the parliament was based in a warren of buildings clustered around the medieval chambers, chapels, and halls of the Palace of Westminster — the impact radius of the blast tore the heart out of England.'

Valeria pinned up a large chart of branching lines that looked to Rufius like a tree on its side, which reminded him of Yggdrasil.

'The perpetrator, Fawkes should have been arrested on the fourth of November by Thomas Knyvet,' she said, running her finger along one line. 'King James was supposed to order a search of the undercroft beneath the House of Lords, after being shown an anonymous letter sent to Baron Monteagle. The note should have warned him to stay away from the opening of parliament on the twenty-sixth of October.'

Drake scratched his beard. 'So, Wallace never delivered the letter?'

'And James I died,' Carstairs concluded, pointing to a set of lines that ended abruptly. 'Along with his heir, Charles I, who would have been four years old at the time, not to mention a host of powerful protestant nobles. Henry Percy is crowned king, then allies himself with Philip III of Spain and marries Anne, his eldest daughter, and a member of the House of Hapsburg. Anne should have ruled France with Louis XIII. England suffers for many years under the influence of the Spanish and of the Holy Roman Empire.'

'So one letter is all that it takes to bring down a country?' Rufius asked Selephin, slightly confused.

'That and thirty-six barrels of gunpowder,' whispered Selephin.

[Hoxton, London. Date: Saturday, October 26, 1605]

A grey curtain of rain swept over the streets of Hoxton, flooding the gutters and turning the roads into a quagmire of mud and sewage. There was no sound apart from the bell of the body collector's cart as they trudged through the mud, their cargo of dead jostling along behind.

The garrets of the houses loomed over them on either side, their leaded windows shuttered and the doors bolted. Each was painted with a white cross.

'Plague,' muttered Selephin, walking beneath the eaves of the houses, trying to stay out of the rain.

'What is it?'

'The Black Death,' said Kasia, cursing under her breath. 'Thirty thousand die in this one, but it's not the worst. That's still to come.'

They made their way towards the home of William Parker, 4th Baron Monteagle. It was getting late, and the light was fading. Rufius was ordered to wait in a nearby alley while Drake and Selephin each took a team, one approaching from the front, the other covering the rear.

Rufius didn't complain, he knew how much of an honour it was to just be allowed to accompany them on this mission. The armour they made him wear was heavy and cumbersome, but it made him feel like a warrior.

He was ordered to watch the road, keeping lookout for any sign of a courier or carriage. Wallace was supposed to ensure that the letter arrived safely, but it hadn't, and they had no choice but to start their search at the home of Monteagle. Carstairs had calculated that their agent had probably been intercepted further back in the timeline, but Drake insisted they follow protocol.

Kasia returned, her mouth set in a thin line of determination. 'We have to go,' she shouted, the rain running down her face. 'There's no sign of Wallace.'

'Do you know who he was following?'

She shook her head. 'No one knows, that's the reason he was here.'

'How far back?' Rufius asked.

'Not back. Forward,' she said, pointing in the general direction of Westminster. 'Drake wants to go nearer to the event.'

[Palace of Westminster. Date: Tuesday, November 5, 1605]

The undercroft was a vast network of vaulted chambers that ran beneath the palace. Moving quietly through the darkened basement, Rufius could hear the shuffling footsteps of the nobility above them, gathering for the state opening. It was strange to think that the king was standing just a few feet above his head.

'Why have we come here?' he asked Kasia in a low whisper.

'It's the last known location of the conspirator known as Fawkes. If we can find him before he lights the fuse, we can at least stop the detonation, and then use him to go back and find out who was supposed to warn Monteagle.'

'But don't you know who else was involved?'

Kasia gave him a look that said she wasn't about to question her commander and moved off into the dark.

Rufius's hand found the tachyon in his pocket and stroked its case, instinctively feeling for the milled edges of the homing button and twisted it clockwise, marking the moment.

Drake had ordered this to be a black-lantern mission. No naked flames were allowed in case of an accident. Rufius followed the sound of their footsteps through the undercroft. No one spoke, they moved as one unit, keenly aware of each other's movements, as they searched each area thoroughly.

'This is going to take too long,' said Drake bringing them to a halt at a junction. 'We'll split into three teams. Selephin you take the boy and go left, Tarrend and Carstairs the right, and Kasia you're with me. Remember we have less than ten minutes to find him.'

With a silent nod, they paired up and moved off.

Rufius felt Selephin grab his arm and allowed himself to be pulled into the tunnel.

They weren't more than ten paces along the corridor before they heard the sounds of someone praying.

It was a man's voice, deep and solemn, repeating the same few lines over and over to himself.

'Credo in Deum Patrem omnipotentem, Creatorem caeli et terrae, et in Iesum Christum, Filium Eius unicum, Dominum nostrum, qui conceptus est de Spiritu Sancto, natus ex Maria Virgine...'

Approaching the entrance to the chamber, Selephin drew

his sword. At first, Rufius thought the sound was the steel leaving the scabbard, but his partner had smothered it with his gloved hand. When he heard it again, he knew it was the sound of iron on flint as someone tried to light a fuse.

'Stay here,' Selephin growled, moving forward towards the archway.

Watching the shape of Selephin run into the room, time seemed to slow. A moment later, Rufius felt the wall of pressure as the blast hit him squarely in the chest. An orange fireball exploded through the brick wall, firing splinters of wood and stone in every direction.

As the tongues of flame leapt out to engulf him, his finger slid across the button and pushed down hard.

[<<]

He was running behind Selephin once more, weaving through the corridors.

'Wait!' hissed Rufius.

'No time,' replied Selephin without looking back.

'I know where he is!'

Selephin stopped in his tracks.

'I don't have time to explain,' he grabbed the man by the arm and activated the homing button.

[>>]

Over the next few minutes, the respective teams arrived back in the kitchen, by the scorch marks burned into their armour, some had left if far too close to jump out.

Carstairs arrived last, his hair still smoking. The entire team looked bemused.

Drake walked over to Selephin.

'Did you see who it was?'

Selephin looked at his feet. 'No, the boy pulled me out before I could get close enough.'

'So we have nothing from the actual event?'

'No, sire.'

'But I saved you!' protested Rufius, 'you would have died.'

Drake turned. 'Give my thanks to Master Harrison boy,' he said, holding up his tachyon. 'I think it's time you left us to resolve this particular situation.'

42

MASTERPIECE

[Christ Church College, Oxford. Date: 1713]

When Rufius returned to Harrison's workshop, he found the man reading in his favourite chair with his feet up, smoking a pipe.

'Well?' he asked, an expectant gleam in his eye.

Rufius put down the empty case and tried to hide his disappointment at being sent home. 'They seemed to like it.'

'Seemed!' Harrison bellowed, sitting upright. 'What do they want? Blood?'

Rufius smiled. 'Drake said it was the most significant scientific advancement since Copernicus's model of the universe.'

Harrison's eyes widened. 'Did he now? That's quite a compliment from El Draque.'

'Why do they call him the Dragon?'

'It's the name the Spanish gave him. I hear they're calling themselves Draconians in his honour.' He waved to the empty chair. 'Come sit by the fire and tell me all about it.

Did they try and break them? I bet Selephin had his knife into it the very second you gave it to him. What did Drake think of the Holocene calibration?'

Rufius avoided the awkward questions, focusing on the ways it had saved them from disaster without going into the details of how it resulted in him getting sent home.

As they talked, he realised how haggard Harrison had become. The shadows under his eyes were darker than usual and his breathing wheezed like a hollow reed. There was no doubt that his condition was worsening, but Rufius knew better than to mention it, there was an unspoken agreement between them. A future that was to be ignored until it arrived.

Satisfied that he had wrung every detail from him, Harrison sat back in his chair and lit another pipe. The stench of the smoke was foul, like a thousand roasted beetles, but whatever it contained seemed to ease his breathing.

'Crooke's latest potion,' the watchmaker said, holding up the pipe and blowing out a smoke ring. 'Eucalyptus, a native of the antipodes. Reeks worse than a burning pile of rotting things, but it does seem to open up the airways.'

Rufius hadn't met that many sick people in his short life. In his time, they didn't tend to last too long. Unless Isolde's herbal remedies could heal them, it was down to the gods as to whether they recovered — and many didn't. Sindri had lost a young son to a fever just before they had found Rufius, and he'd always wondered if the boy hadn't died whether the blacksmith would have been so keen to take him on.

When they first recruited him, Dolovir had explained that

there would be plenty of time to go back and visit his family. That time was fluid, and although weeks would pass for Rufius, he could still return within minutes of his leaving. But that was before Crooke's medicine had accelerated his growth. He couldn't walk back into the forge and resume his old life now, not with the body of a grown man. Although he relished his new physique, the well-defined muscles and the way his voice was deepening, it would be difficult to explain how he could have aged overnight.

'So, now that you've completed your apprenticeship have you any thoughts on what you'll do next?' Harrison asked.

Rufius had thought of nothing else since he'd visited the Draconians. They were so different from the academic Antiquarians, their lives seemed to be one long adventure into the unknown. He didn't want to hurt Harrison's feelings, but there was a sense of danger about their work that intrigued him.

'I thought I would join Drake and his team,' he said, phrasing it in a way that made it sound more like a question.

Harrison nodded. 'I assumed you would. You're a wild spirit Rufius, this world of dry books and artefacts doesn't suit your wandering mind. You need adventure.'

'How do I become one?'

'Joining the Draconians is by invitation only. They are hand-picked by Drake, under the direct command of the founder. Not something I can help you with I'm afraid, but Dolovir may have more influence.'

Rufius hated the idea of leaving the watchmaker. The man had been so kind and patient with him, no one had ever shown him that much attention since he was a child. But he knew it was time to move on. There were so many other things to learn, and he was eager to find out more about the Tuatha Dé.

Harrison took a long pull on the pipe and blew out a large smoke ring.

'I wonder if you could demonstrate your prowess with search and recovery. There are a number of artefacts that the Antiquarians are keen to find. Ones that have significant timelines for their research. It won't be as exciting as the Draconians, but still something of a treasure hunt which I think you will find quite challenging. Which reminds me...' He put down the pipe and took something from his coat pocket and handed it to Rufius. 'You will need this.'

It was a golden tachyon. The casement was beautifully inscribed with his name. 'Prove to them what a resourceful young man you really are.'

Rufius turned the watch over in his hand. It was the most beautiful object he'd ever seen. The gold shone in the firelight, tracing the fine detail that Harrison had etched into every facet of its design. It truly was a masterpiece. But something was different, there was a second button.

'Thank you, Master. But may I ask what this second button is for?'

There was a gleam in Harrison's eye when he spoke. 'My latest improvement: the Mark II has the ability to calculate a reverse temporal coordinate of one hundred and twenty-five seconds. I like to think of it as an emergency procedure, should you find yourself in a tricky situation.'

Rufius placed it carefully into one of the pockets of his robes and bowed.

'Now, now, no need to stand on ceremony,' he said with a cough. 'You've been a fine apprentice, if a little impulsive. Without you, the tachyon would be naught but a lump of unfashioned brass. Go and stake your claim in this wonderful world and if you should find yourself anywhere near Red Lion Square before the twenty-fourth of March, 11,776 be so good as to drop in and have supper with your old friend.

Rufius had no idea why the date was so important but promised he would. Then shook the man's hand and left.

43

THE LIST OF IMPOSSIBLE FINDS

[Montagu House, Bloomsbury, London. Date: 1759]

Walking through the corridors, Rufius could feel the tachyon bounce against his chest. He desperately wanted to take it out and examine it. It was one of a kind, smaller and more advanced than any of the others, and the most valuable thing anyone had ever given him. But it would have raised too much suspicion amongst the general public who were milling about the exhibits, closely watched by the more junior keepers of the museum.

Under Sir Robert's stewardship, the collection had expanded enormously, outgrowing Montagu house and the Antiquarians had branched out into several other large museums. Bodley had taken charge of the restoration of the Oxford library, while Ashmole was already boasting about various cabinets of curiosities that he had managed to secure for his own small collection on Broad Street.

Everyone seemed to have a job except for Rufius.

There were over a hundred Antiquarians now, virtually every student in Christ Church College was affiliated to the Order or served in some ancillary role. They were becoming a hierarchical organisation under Lord Dee. The founder had created rules and strictures on how they should behave and there were grades and codes of conduct. Roles like 'Curator' and 'Keeper' were created; Harrison was referred to as an "Engineer First Class".

Rufius would become a Draconian, he just had to prove to Drake that he was worthy.

Although many of the expeditions were now planned and prepared in infinite detail before any object was 'requisitioned', there were still objects that remained out of their reach. Displaced items which had been lost in history with no safe route to retrieve them. For the Antiquarians, 'safe' required some kind of linking artefact that could be used to reach the last known temporal location. The difficulty with the safe option was that things were generally lost in fires or sank to the bottom of the sea. No one was stupid or crazy enough to try and take something off a sinking ship.

Except for Rufius.

The list of impossible finds was pinned on the notice board outside Sir Robert's office. Amongst other notices about music tutoring and joining the Astronomical Society, was a long slip of paper with each of the 'Dangerous goods' written out in a fluid copperplate. Beside each item was a date and the names of the individuals who'd been brave enough to try and retrieve it. Ashmole had put his mark against three objects on the list, two of which had been scratched out, indicating that they had been successfully retrieved. Rufius wondered if this was how he had earned his place as a Curator, the second most respected position in the Antiquarians, the man was obviously ambitious enough to risk his life to further his career.

Rufius eyed the irretrievable, searching for one that could earn him similar merit.

Ashmole was still searching for the alchemical texts of Arthur Dee and Rufius was tempted to go after it himself, just to prove he was the better man, but it wasn't the most challenging thing on the board. His eyes drifted down until he found it.

Babylonian astrolabe, 1100 BC.

It stood out because it was the only item that no one had tried to claim. Rufius took the pencil hanging by a string from the board and scribbled his name against it. A small group had gathered behind him, eager to see what he had opted for. They muttered to each other as he walked away, a self-assured smile lingering on his lips. He knew what they were calling him, and he didn't care, he'd been called a lot worse by Arnwulf. No one could curse better than a Dane, especially one who had lived as long as that old goat.

44

ASTROLABE

[Bodleian Library, Oxford. Date: 1606]

Rufius waited until the flickering light in the night porter's window dimmed — a sure sign that he had fallen asleep and the candle was burning low. He crept barefoot across the moonlit quad, keeping to the shadows and away from the shingle paths. Bats flickered silently across the silver rooftops, their chirps and tweets serenading their prey.

Beyond the gates, Oxford was sleeping. A cool night breeze brushed through his hair as he moved silently along the darkened alleys that ran beside Oriel College, careful to avoid the drunks and whores of Gropecrotch Lane.

The door to the Bodleian was closed, but never locked and Rufius opened it slowly, grimacing at the sound of the iron hinges straining under the weight of the oak. Shutting the door with an equal amount of restraint, he lit a small greasy stub of his candle and walked into the stacks.

Bodley was standing a few feet away, his face a mixture of concern and disbelief.

'You of all people should know better than to bring a naked flame into my library!' he bellowed.

Rufius snuffed out the candle with his thumb and forefinger. 'How —' he began as Bodley turned up the oil lamp he had been hiding under his cloak.

'When I heard you'd been stupid enough to put yourself down for the astrolabe — I knew you'd come looking for a suitable vestige — the British Museum's too well guarded, so it had to be something from my collection.'

Rufius shrugged. 'All the others were taken.'

Bodley sighed. 'You know it's one of the longest jumps back in time ever attempted? To the reign of Nebuchadnezzar?'

Rufius smirked, he'd already done the calculations. 'Two-thousand-seven-hundred years. And it won't be one jump, probably three or four.'

The librarian looked impressed. 'Well, at least you've actually thought it through. I assumed it was some stupid attempt to prove you were better than Ashmole.'

'Now why would you think that?' Rufius smiled and walked past him into the darkened building.

Bodley came after him. 'Wait! You may not have to go that far back — I think I know where it might have been stored.'

Rufius had no idea what a Babylonian astrolabe was when he'd signed up for it. It was the date that had caught his eye. Bodley was right, no one had ever gone back that far — except perhaps the founder. Many of the younger Antiquarians thought the astrolabe was nothing more than a practical joke, added to the list by one of the students in Sir Robert's hand as a way to dupe the new recruits. The furthest most of them had ventured was back into the twelfth century. Books were by far the safest way to travel into the past and manuscripts before the eleven-hundreds were hard to come by.

Moonlight was streaming through the large arched window of Duke Humphrey's reading room. Bodley had done an incredible job of restoring the collection to its former glory. The wooden galleries and oak-panelled bays held the second largest library after the British Museum, but it also was home to some of the most curious artefacts. Ones whose historical timeline Rufius knew he could use to begin his journey back to the Babylonian Empire.

'You know that Ashmole has already made the most outrageous wager on your failure, don't you?'

'Have you taken it?'

Bodley shook his head. 'I'm waiting for the odds to settle. They're fluctuating too rapidly.'

They reached the first of the artefacts, which was a simple metal lantern with a conical lid and a crudely riveted door.

'What's that?' asked Rufius.

'The lantern of Guido Fawkes.'

He had heard Drake mention the name. 'The man who killed James I?'

'The Catholic conspirator who *tried* to blow up parliament in 1605.'

The Draconians changed the timeline, Rufius thought, knowing better than to mention it. They had obviously managed to correct the timeline after he left.

He went to touch the lid, but Bodley stopped him. 'You'll be wanting something much older than that,' he said, aiming the beam of his lantern towards the back of the room, it glinted off hundreds of fine metal chains.

'I believe you'll be able to find the astrolabe in the Great Library of Alexandria. It was reported to be the single greatest repository of antiquities of its day. But we'll need something to get us there — maps would probably be the best option. They've been copied down through the ages and survived better than any papyrus scroll. Although you may have to follow it back through the cartographers' reproductions.'

Bodley handed Rufius his lantern and walked over to the stacks, carefully pulling out a large leather volume as if he were handling a baby and placed it on the nearest reading desk.

'Of course, the further back you go, the less likely they are to have used any form of paper. With the Babylonians you'll be working with clay tablets and cuneiform unless you can find yourself a Codex Vaticanus Urbinas Graecus,' he said, turning the pages with a small metal blade.

The chart was drawn across two pages, the ocean painted in a vibrant blue and the continents marked out in a broad curving grid.

'This was recreated in 1300 by the monks of the Chora Monastery in Constantinople. It's recreated from the works of Ptolemy — his Geographies. The projection is conical and describes everything they knew of the world at the time. Quite amazing to think how much was still to be discovered.'

Rufius thought back to the globe in the founder's office, and how little he knew of the world then. 'So where is Babylon?'

Bodley pointed to an area. 'Mesopotamia, just down and to the right of the Ottoman Empire, and here is Constantinople.'

Rufius ran his fingers over the map, feeling the timelines sliding beneath the surface of the page.

'I suggest you change into something more appropriate before attempting that.' Bodley interrupted. 'Ravenscroft has been working with a material that should be able to survive that far back.'

45

PLANUDES

[Chora Monastery, Constantinople. 1300]

The first leg of his journey had taken him back more than three hundred years in the blink of an eye, but it left him feeling as though Hagar had knocked him down with his shield.

Rufius had used the timeline from Bodley's chart to travel back to the monastery in Constantinople where he was relieved to find that Ravenscroft's robe survived intact. It was made from a kind of homespun material, similar to the tunics Rufius had worn in his own time. There were small pockets sewn into the inner lining of the cloak, one of which was a perfect fit for his new tachyon.

The scriptorium was unoccupied when he appeared beside the half-finished map. The desk was one of many, crammed into the hall. It was covered in notes, translations and calculations based on Ptolemy's coordinates as well as an assortment of quills, inkpots and fine sable brushes.

The air was heavy with incense. It wafted down from a gently swinging thurible that hung in the high-domed ceiling above his head. The walls of the chamber were covered in Byzantine mosaics of Christian scenes: Magii bowing down before Christ; the Virgin mother and child, and a whole host of saints whose golden haloes reflected the light from the amber glow of the oil lamps.

Bodley had told him to look for the original Greek text of Ptolemy's *Geographies*, which he should be able to use to get back to Alexandria around 150 AD, but none of the books on the scribe's bench were much older than a few hundred years. The original Greek text was nowhere to be seen.

Rufius sat down on the wooden stool and studied the unfinished chart. He picked up the quill of the monk and let the latent energies of its timeline flow around his hand. He could feel the man's hand as it worked meticulously across the parchment, the tiny marks he made with its nib on the conical grid as he followed the translation of Ptolemy's instructions. He dropped the quill, realising that the book had never been here, someone had already translated it.

'I've just thought of something,' whispered Bodley, appearing suddenly beside the desk and causing Rufius to nearly fall off his seat. 'Maximus Planudes would probably have translated the original Greek into Latin for the cartographer, there's a very good chance that the book won't be here.'

'I worked that out for myself, thanks. Do you know where he would have kept it?'

Bodley was staring at the chart. 'Hmm? Sorry, what?'

'Where would Planudes have kept Ptolemy's original?'

'In his chambers most probably, it's rather rare. Notice how there are none of the Americas.'

Rufius shook his head. 'Americas?'

'I thought you Vikings had discovered it. Perhaps not. There is another continent, Terra Nova, on the other side of Oceanus Occidentalis.'

Rufius picked up the Latin translation and felt the words as they were written onto the page. He could see the small cell of Planudes and the original Greek document on the table before him.

'Are you coming?' he asked Bodley while weaving through the timeline looking for a moment when the monk had stepped out of the room.

Bodley smiled nervously and nodded his head.

46

ROYAL LIBRARY

[Alexandria. Date: 150]

They used Planudes's copy of *Geographies* to reach Ptolemy. Travelling back more than a thousand years, it was the furthest that Bodley had ever jumped and he threw up almost immediately.

Ptolemy's chambers reminded Rufius of Harrison's workshop, with experimental optical lens arrays sitting in wooden scaffolds and diagrams of various astronomical constellations pinned around the walls.

'He was something of a Da Vinci of his time,' observed Bodley when the colour had started to return to his cheeks.

'Who?'

'Fifteenth-century renaissance inventor? Painter of the Mona Lisa?'

Rufius continued to look at him with a blank expression.

'Have you had any formal schooling?'

Rufius tapped his temple. 'Dolovir gifted me some knowledge: languages and writing, but not history.'

Bodley looked a little shocked. 'Well, a historian with no

history. I take it upon myself to mentor you in the classics at least.'

He drew himself up and to his full height. 'Ptolemy was a mathematician, astronomer, philosopher, geographer, astrologer and poet. He wrote three scientific treatises that are thought to have influenced eastern and western science.' He held up the fingers of one hand. 'The first was the Almagest, an astronomical work based on his observations and those reaching back to Babylonian times, it plotted constellations and the positions of stars throughout the year.'

'Like the Babylonian astrolabe?'

'Exactly. Although it was geocentric, putting the earth at the centre of the universe.'

Rufius frowned. 'Isn't it?'

Bodley ignored him and continued. 'Second was the Geography, a compilation of the known world of the Roman Empire. It used a codified system of coordinates and a grid, with latitudes, although he used the length of the longest day instead of degrees of an arc. He put the meridian through the "Blessed Islands" which were the ones missing from the chart in the Chora monastery.'

'And the third?'

Bodley put his hand down. 'The third was Tetrabiblos, the Four Books, it's a philosophical work that helped shape the moral, religious and cosmological paradigm of Western Europe during the Medieval era.'

Rufius had no idea what that meant, but he smiled all the same. 'Sounds like a wise man. So where would he have kept the astrolabe?'

The Royal Library of Alexandria had not fared well under

Roman occupation. Its membership had dwindled, and without a royal patron, the building and its valuable collection had fallen into disrepair. Bodley explained that many of the papyrus scrolls and manuscripts had been lost in various disasters over the last four hundred years, and some of the Antiquarian curators were discussing the possibility of a mission back to save them, but nothing had been sanctioned by the grandmaster, as they were now calling Sir Robert.

'We're looking for a set of clay tablets,' whispered Bodley.

It was night, and the library was empty. Rufius followed Bodley through the corridors of Egyptian columns, the light of his small oil lamp flickering as if moved by unseen winds.

'Are you sure it's even here?'

'Ptolemy used Babylonian data. We need to find the astronomical section.'

Turning a corner into the main atrium, they heard voices and Rufius pulled Bodley back into the shadows, snuffing out the flame on his lamp.

Peering around the edge of the column, he could see two people walking into the moonlit hall from the opposite end. They were dressed in Roman robes, and one of them was carrying a kind of staff.

'Guards?' asked Bodley in a whisper.

'No,' Rufius replied.

The two figures separated and moved quietly to either side of the chamber, they were searching for something.

'It could be anywhere,' said the first to the second. 'How do you know it's still here?'

'Fortune favours the bold, Valtin. Dark relics have a certain aura,' the other man replied in a strong accent.

'Not that you have the skill to notice,' joked the first.

'They're speaking in seventeenth-century French,' whispered Bodley.

Time thieves, thought Rufius, wishing he had brought a weapon.

The man with the staff was heading in their direction. Rufius pushed Bodley back against the wall.

'I can still sniff them out!' he snapped, pulling something off the shelf. At first, Rufius thought it was a rock, but as he held it up to the moonlight, he could see it was some kind of crystal with a creature trapped inside it.

'Fossil,' whispered Bodley.

Rufius jabbed him in the ribs with his elbow to shut him up.

The one called Valtin walked over and took it out of his hand. 'That will do nicely,' he said, putting it into his sack. 'Ashmole will always pay for amber when it's got a bug in it.'

The old man tapped his staff on one of the shelves. 'Master Ashmole still hasn't paid us for the last two. What makes you think he'll cough up for that?'

Taking a clay tablet down from the shelf, the younger man inspected the writing. 'Ah, the emerald tablet if I'm not mistaken,' he said, placing the artefact into his bag, and pulling out a metallic sphere. He twisted its top half a number of turns.

'What are you going to do?'

'Nothing like a little fire to increase the price.'

'Not here?'

'No. Do you think I'm insane? I think a hundred years will do.'

He dropped the small bomb, and they both disappeared before it hit the floor.

. . .

The sphere was making a ticking sound as they approached it. A glowing ring of tiny gemstones were slowly winking out around its equator.

'What is it?' Bodley asked.

'Some kind of bomb,' Rufius said, kneeling down to inspect it.

'Don't you think we should leave?' Bodley wondered nervously.

Rufius handed him his tachyon. 'Hold this, if anything happens, click the second button.'

Bodley looked at the dials on the face of the watch, each one rotating at a different speed. His thumb hovered over the two buttons. 'What does it do?'

'The first takes you back to the college, the second rewinds back two minutes, enough time to tell me what I did wrong.'

There were only two gems left, and Rufius knew he had no time to get it out of the building. He picked up the bomb. 'How old is this place?'

Bodley hesitated, mesmerised by the dials on the tachyon. 'At least two thousand years, I think.'

Before Rufius had a chance to reply, a whirling vortex expanded out from the outer ring of the bomb and enveloped him. He began to fade.

Bodley fumbled the tachyon, trying to press the right button, but pushed the first instead of the second and disappeared.

47

ALIXIA

[Library of Alexandria. Date: 48 BC]

The blast sent Rufius flying through a stack of shelves, which collapsed on top of him, protecting him from the wall of flame that followed.

When he woke, the library was a wall of flame. The intense heat from the burning scrolls scorched the air and made it hard to breathe.

His head ached, and his vision was blurred, but he was certain there was a figure standing in the centre of the fire, her arms aflame as they held some kind of fossil high above her head. She was chanting in a language Rufius had never heard and surrounding her were the shapes of terrible monsters formed out of fire.

Her eyes were dark, and blood ran like tears down her cheeks. The flames didn't seem to affect her, even though they had burned off most of her clothes, leaving her skin the colour of ash. The woman had runes painted all over her body, like Maebh, which glowed as if she were drawing energy from the artefact. Rufius watched transfixed as the creatures solidified around her. Their bodies were a grotesque, twisted collection of bone and horn, each one more hideous than the last.

He could feel the hairs on his arms beginning to smoulder, like a thousand ants crawling across his skin, he knew he wouldn't be able to stay much longer. Reaching inside his robe, his hand searched for the tachyon before realising that he had given it to Bodley.

Then he felt a hand on his shoulder.

'I think it was time we were leaving,' whispered a soft voice.

Rufius turned to find a pale woman with long dark hair standing behind him. She was holding an unusual compass in one hand and a plant in the other. Through his bleary eyes, he thought she looked like an older version of Alixia, her mouth twisted into the same look of disbelief as the day he had dropped her precious dodo's egg.

Before he could ask what she was doing here, she took his hand and the world spun away.

[Lisbon, Portugal. Date: 1838]

'You were lucky I found you,' Alixia said, holding a glass of water.

They appeared to be in a garden. Giant ferns and exotic-looking palm trees loomed over them, creating a verdant canopy beneath a beautiful glass roof.

'I was about to go.'

She laughed. 'I doubt that. You were suffering from concussion, your burns are quite extensive.'

He looked down at his hands, they were pink and glistening, covered in some kind of salve. He couldn't remember feeling any pain.

She held up the glass so he could take a drink, the water was cool and tasted faintly of willow bark. 'What were you doing?'

'Trying to save the library from a time bomb.'

Alixia pulled a face. 'Why would someone intentionally burn the library?'

Rufius explained about the two men, and Sir Robert's theory of who was stealing his books.

'Time thieves?' she said dismissively. 'More like bandits.'

Rufius realised she hadn't mentioned the woman in the flames, and wondered whether he had imagined the whole thing.

'So you're collecting plants now?' he asked, changing the subject.

Alixia put down the cup and got to her feet, brushing down her skirts. 'All manner of extinct species actually. Seeds make for easy transportation.'

A pair of leather winged birds swooped low overheard, chasing the largest dragonfly Rufius had ever seen.

'Why?'

She sighed. 'Knowledge of course. There's only so much you can learn from books.'

'When are we?'

'1838. This is the Bemposta Palace, my father's house in Lisbon. He allows me to keep a small botanical collection.'

Rufius looked at her closely. 'You're older now. A woman.'

She blushed a little. 'It has been seven years since we last met. Much has happened after our last encounter.'

There was a squawk, and a large feathered bird burst out of the dense shrubbery.

'Maximillian!'

The bird stared at Rufius with one beady eye before turning on its heel and disappearing into the nearest bush.

'Was that?'

'The dodo, yes,' she said with a frown. 'Possibly the most ridiculous of my experiments, but I love him dearly nonetheless.'

'Didn't I drop the egg?'

She smiled benevolently. 'Luckily, I had more than one.'

His hands were badly burned. Alixia wrapped them carefully in clean bandages which she tied with a bow.

'You should avoid getting them wet for a few days. The lotion will reduce inflammation and promote the growth of new skin.'

'I need to get back to my time.'

'And where was that exactly? I've always wondered.'

'1660 or 1759.'

'Ah yes, the British Museum, you should see it now, your Antiquarians have created one of the finest collections in the world. There's even talk of a new museum dedicated to Natural History.'

'Why haven't you joined them?'

She pulled a face. 'They are too theoretical for my tastes. I prefer a more practical approach.'

'But isn't it dangerous to wander the past alone?'

'You learn to avoid certain periods.'

'Like when?'

Alixia paused as if unsure of what she should tell him.

'Before the Roman Empire, most of Northern Europe was pretty unsavoury. I would avoid the first century, the Iceni and the Druids in particular.'

Rufius thought of the Huns he had fought against at the Catalaunian Plains of Gaul. The Roman soldiers had faced a barbaric army, but there had been no sign of Druids.

Her face paled as she spoke. 'There are strange and terrible things going on back there.'

48

SHAMED

[Christ Church College, Oxford Date: 1660]

'So, the wanderer has returned,' Sir Robert exclaimed when Rufius was marched into the founder's chambers by the night watch.

'Rufius where have you been?' Dolovir asked, noting the scorching on his clothes and the burns on his arms.

'I know exactly where he's been,' gloated Ashmole, standing beside Sir Robert. 'Starting fires in Alexandria, the Great Library was the most precious collection of antiquity. Now it's a smouldering pile of ash thanks to this Viking.'

'That is a serious allegation,' the founder warned, putting down the clay tablet he'd been examining. Rufius recognised the Babylonian astrolabe immediately. 'What do you have to say for yourself, Master Westinghouse?'

Rufius could see the anger in Dee's eyes and knew that he had disappointed him once again.

'It was the time thieves,' Rufius began. 'I was searching for the astrolabe when —'

'When you burned down the greatest institution in ancient history.'

'They —'

'ENOUGH!' bellowed the founder. 'Dolovir take him down to the medica and have those burns attended to. Grandmaster, you have my permission to assemble a team and retrieve as many documents as you can from the library.'

Rufius hung his head and followed Dolovir out of the founder's chamber. There was no point in trying to argue, the founder had already made up his mind. He had seen that look before, many times on Sindri's face. There were no words that would convince him, only actions.

Doctor Crooke examined his burns carefully, his beady eyes pouring over the raw, pink skin. 'Someone has already treated these,' he observed, without looking up. Bending lower so that Rufius was staring directly at the balding circle of hair, he sniffed at the wounds. 'Smells like Aloe and honey. An interesting combination, from a herbalist perhaps? Where did you get such an ointment?'

'My grandmother taught me,' Rufius lied, 'she was a healer.'

Doctor Crooke's eyes widened slightly. 'Was she now? Aloe originates from the Arabian peninsula and can be found wild in many tropical climates. I wasn't aware that it could be found in the outer reaches of Northumbria.'

Rufius's blushes were hidden by the burns on his cheeks.

Doctor Crooke turned and went over to his vast collection of apothecary jars. 'Whoever it was, they have my gratitude, the tissue has already begun to regenerate. All I can give you is something for the pain.' He took down a mortar and pestle, filling it with dried leaves and powders.

When he turned back, Rufius was gone.

49

ASHMOLE

Ashmole sat in his study, examining the insect trapped in the blue amber with an array of magnifying lenses. It fascinated him to think that the creature could be millions of years old, and yet here it was perfectly preserved.

'Bodley, have you ever seen such a marvel?' he asked, without looking up from his work.

'No Elias.'

'This creature existed before man had taken his first step on the earth. The learned Dr Plot discovered a thigh bone of an enormous beast, I believe it to be the femur of something that once walked the earth — the fossilised remains of an ancient species. Imagine if we could travel back to witness them first hand? To walk among the giants!'

'I thought Doctor Plot considered them to be crystallisations of minerals.'

'He's a wise man, Bodley. If one were to admit the existence of ancient creatures, it could bring the estimated age of the earth into question, and we all know where that would lead.'

Bodley knew that the subject was hotly debated by many

philosophers. After Archbishop Ussher issued his chronology based on the Bible, where he had estimated the day of creation to fall on a Sunday late in October, 4004BC, any talk of finding evidence of objects that predated this was seen as heresy.

'I'm going to make him Keeper of my museum,' Ashmole announced, getting up from his chair.

'Are you sure that's wise?'

Ashmole's mouth twisted into a sneer. 'After the recent debacle with the Viking, I have been ordered to concentrate on the rare collections. The grandmaster has tasked me with recovering what we can from the Great Library, which leaves me little time for curating the Ashmolean.'

Inside his cloak pocket, Bodley's fingers stroked the watch Rufius had given him.

'And the special relics?' Bodley asked.

'The fossils are no concern of yours. Unless of course, you would like me to divulge your little secret to the founder?'

Bodley shook his head. 'No Elias.'

'Good.' Ashmole smiled. 'Then we have an understanding.'

50

THE COLOSSEUM

[Ludus Magnus, Rome. Date: 80]

The roar of the Colosseum echoed along the tunnel as a tired and wounded line of gladiators limped their way slowly back to the school. It was the end of the morning on the second day of the inaugural games and the animal entertainment had just finished. Rufius had heard one of the trainers boast that over nine thousand beasts were to be used during the festivities: elephants, rhinos, lions, bulls and bears were just some of the creatures that he had seen in the frenzied battle that had just taken place.

Alixia would have hated it. The senseless killing of so many species for the entertainment of the crowds would have made her weep.

The mauled bodies of dead men were carted away by the *Charon*, while those who could still walk made their way back along an underground passage to the Ludus Magnus, the largest gladiatorial school in Rome.

Rufius carried the weapons of Carpophorus, a skilled bestiarius who had slain over fifty animals in the last two days. He had sustained a wound from a bear and was retired from the games. The rents in his side had to be stitched closed by the medici before he bled to death. He would not be receiving the iron today, the gladiator was too valuable not to be granted *stans missus*.

A blast of trumpets broke their silent procession making the crowd roar once more. Rufius grimaced at the sound, it was midday and he knew that their cheers were for the *noxii*, criminals were being executed.

He had come to Rome on the trail of the time thieves.

After leaving Doctor Crooke's medica, he had spent days wandering through random parts of the past searching for any sign of them. Rufius knew the only way he was going to prove his innocence was to find evidence of their existence and bring it back to the founder.

It took a few fruitless days of dead ends and blind alleys before he remembered that the mercenaries in Alexandria had mentioned Ashmole by name. He was sure Bodley would know something about them.

Finding a route back to the Bodleian was difficult. Without a tachyon he resorted to scavenging random artefacts from the pawnbrokers and moneylenders of medieval Europe, moving slowly through time until he reached the Frankfurt book fair of 1455 and one of Bodley's most treasured possessions, the Gutenberg Bible.

'Bodley,' Rufius said, appearing in Bodley's private study.

The young man jumped to his feet, his faced blanching as if he had seen a ghost. His eyes darted between the door and Rufius as if trying to understand how he'd arrived.

'What are you doing here?' he stuttered, sitting down behind his desk and trying to regain his composure.

Rufius placed the Gutenberg Bible back on the shelf. 'Looking for the men that burned down the library.'

'I've no idea.' Bodley couldn't look him in the eye. Instead, he picked up a bottle and tried to pour a glass of port, but his hand was shaking and Rufius took it away from him before he spilt it.

'Oh, I think you do,' Rufius said, pouring a large, steady measure and giving it to him.

Bodley drank the whole glass in one, it seemed to relax him.

'They're mercenaries. Ashmole has been paying them to retrieve certain rare artefacts.' He blurted the words quickly as if his mouth wanted to be rid of them.

'Like dark relics?'

Bodley nodded his head. 'He is obsessed with fossils, the bones of ancient creatures. He wants to travel further back than any man has ever ventured — further even than the founder.'

'And how did he find these mercenaries?' Rufius asked, pouring a second glass of port.

Bodley seemed reluctant to say, he made weak excuses about Ashmole having nefarious acquaintances, but Rufius plied him with more liquor, and by the fourth glass the young man gave up his secret.

Holding his head in his hands, he began: 'I first encountered them while researching the libraries of Pompeii and Herculaneum before the eruption of Mount Vesuvius in 79. The volcano would engulf the surrounding cities, covering everything and everyone under a blanket of fire and ash. It was a terrible sight. Men, women and children like statues trapped in molten rock.'

Bodley went on to explain that, while the catastrophe unfolded, he had been busy in the Villa dei Papiri. It was home to the entire one hundred and forty-two volumes of Livy's History of Rome as well as Aristotle's second volume of the Poetics and a huge collection of Greek literature. He had been sent there by Sir Robert as part of an advanced recovery team, only to find he wasn't the only traveller working in that particular period. While the lava flowed down the mountain and into the streets, the thieves were plundering its treasures, unmoved by the screams of the dying echoing through the halls as they worked.

'We could have saved them,' Bodley moaned.

'It's against the rules,' replied Rufius, 'it was a natural disaster.'

Tears were streaming down Bodley's cheeks. 'What's the point of our gifts if we can't save them?'

Rufius had no answer, the founder had always told them that they couldn't change the past, that this was their burden, to know but not act. Bodley went on to describe how Ashmole reacted when he told him. The man was an opportunist, and his ambitions overcame any sense of morality.

'There is little point in ranging through time when others can do it for you,' Bodley quoted, mimicking Ashmole's arrogant tone.

It had taken them less than a week to find their base of operations, and so began the illicit collection of 'missing' artefacts. Every major find in Ashmole's glittering career as an Antiquarian was down to the work of the time thieves.

'They always insisted we met at the games,' Bodley added with a shudder. 'It was a terrible spectacle.'

Rufius took back his tachyon and assured Bodley that he

would keep the secret, at least for now. He wanted to meet these men for himself.

And so he found himself at the extravagant opening ceremony of the Flavian Amphitheatre.

The massive arena had only recently been completed and a hundred days of games were organised as a diversion for the people. Devised by Emperor Titus, whose short reign had already endured a series of disasters including the eruption of Mount Vesuvius, a fire that burned down the Temple of Jupiter and the worst outbreak of plague that the city had ever encountered.

The scale of the event was truly magnificent, and the gladiators were some of the finest fighting men that Rufius had ever seen. Bodley advised against him joining the Ludus Magnus, but Rufius ignored him, he was intrigued by the thought of gladiator training, of becoming a novicii. The thieves enjoyed the excesses of this period of the Roman Empire and spent much of their spare time sparring and drinking with the *ordinarii* — the fighting men.

As a novice, he spent his days as a glorified servant, fetching and carrying for them, a role he knew how to perform very well. Rufius quickly learned the ways of the school, there were many fighting styles to choose from as well as a whole host of weapons at their disposal: spears, nets, tridents and a wide variety of swords, but no sign of the thieves.

Until the day he got selected to fight.

A few days after Carpophorus was injured, Rufius had been woken as usual by the doctore to begin their day. The exercise yard had to be swept and the weapons cleaned before preparing breakfast for the men. It was not difficult work, and the other novices worked silently under the watchful eye of the trainer.

While the men ate, the novices were allowed to practice, and on this particular occasion, Rufius was given a weapon that came with a great deal of history. Just as with his first sword, *Gunnlogi,* he could feel the prowess of its previous owners flowing through the grip and into his mind, and he relished it.

The edge had been blunted, but nevertheless, he still managed to incapacitate three of the novices before realising what was he was doing.

Everyone had stopped eating to watch. The entire school were staring open-mouthed at his display.

'Hold!' declared the *lanista*, the owner of the school, clapping his hands and walking down the steps into the sandy arena.

They all stood to attention. Their master was still dressed in his morning robes, which were barely able to cover his bloated stomach. His head was shaven and there were dark lines around his eyes, the remnants of the make-up he had worn for the opening ceremony.

'What have we here?' he said, running his fingers over Rufius's sweating chest.

Rufius knew better than to answer. The novicii were forbidden to speak to their masters.

The lanista eyed him lasciviously, his tongue wetting his lips as if about to eat him.

'You're a fine specimen. I think Vassili will enjoy you.'

51

VASSILI

[Ludus Magnus, Rome. Date: 80]

Vassili Temperus walked along the line of candidates, his staff tapping as he counted. The master of the games was a short, barrel-chested man with thick, sinewy arms that bore the scars of many battles.

'Twelve, thirteen, fourteen, fifteen.' He counted in Latin, but with a thick Slavic accent. 'I asked for two dozen, and you give me fifteen. Hardly enough to fill one boat for the first sea battle.'

'Young talent is a rare commodity,' the lanista replied, reclining on a velvet couch whilst being fed dates by a group of boys.

'Titus wants a Naumachia, and he shall have the finest sea battle I can muster.'

He put down his staff and took off his cloak. 'You are here because Quintus believes you have promise, but he is a fat fool who idolises young men. I have no such vices, my job is to entertain the crowd. If you do well, you will be rewarded handsomely. If you do not, you will be fed to the lions.'

He took out a knife and held it out to the first in the line. 'And no, there really isn't any point in appealing to my better nature, because I don't have one. Strike me.'

Every one of them was disarmed before they could leave a mark on the man, even those whom Rufius had seen fight well in training fell before the unarmed man.

Lastly, Vassili stopped in front of Rufius, who was nearly a head taller than the games master. He stared into his eyes as if looking for any sign of weakness, before handing him the blade.

'Strike me.'

Rufius took a moment to feel the history within the knife. Its stories unwound, showing him the same test repeated many times against hundreds of different opponents. There were a few successful candidates amongst them, ones that had found his weakness — they had always gone for his left knee.

Vassili's eyes narrowed slightly as Rufius hesitated, letting his mind learn the moves that would bring the man down. In real-time, it took less than a second to process the latent memories and prepare a series of strikes.

The first was a feint, raising the dagger as if to strike then lashing out with his right foot striking the side of his opponent's left knee. As Vassili turned to protect his injured leg, Rufius jabbed his fist below his rib cage into his diaphragm, winding him. The blade flashed as it moved into his other hand and thrust forward towards the man's belly, but his opponent caught it by the wrist in mid-air and twisted it until it felt like it was about to break.

Suddenly the knife was at Rufius's throat.

'Yield!' Rufius croaked.

Vassili released his grip but kept the blade pressed against his neck. His eyes were full of questions, but there was the faintest smile beneath his grey beard.

'Impressive,' he whispered. 'You, I will keep.' Then turning to the others. 'The rest of you are bound for the galleys of Titus.'

A group of armoured men appeared from one of the side rooms. 'The Colosseum awaits you,' he said, nodding to his men.

52

BASE

Walking along the colonnaded tunnel from the school back to the Colosseum, Rufius could see that Vassili limped slightly, the pain in his knee making him wince.

He wasn't sure where they were going. The arena was quiet, a sign that the entertainment had finished for the day and Vassili had said nothing since they had left the lanista's apartments.

Vassili had given Quintus a large purse, a trade that meant Rufius was now his property; once again, he was a slave, it seemed to be his fate to be in thrall to someone.

'You fight in the Thracian style,' the trainer remarked, coming to a stop by a small wooden door. 'But your complexion speaks of Norse or Saxon blood. Where are you from boy?'

'Jorvik,' answered Rufius, unsure of whether it even existed at this point in time.

'A Dane?' Vassili said with a grunt. 'Spent a long time fighting Vikings. You're a few hundred years out of your time.'

Rufius suddenly realised that the man was the one that Bodley had told him about, the recruiter for the thieves.

The games master took the blade out of his belt and pushed Rufius against the opposite wall. 'Tell me, how does a Viking find himself in the gladiator school of a Roman Emperor?'

'I had a sword,' Rufius said quickly. 'One that showed me battles, old ones, it taught me how to fight. I followed it here.' It was a half-truth, enough to be convincing.

Vassili's eyes gleamed. 'What kind of sword?'

'A Roman one, it had writing along the blade.'

The edge of the knife glinted as the trainer brought it close to Rufius's eye.

'What kind of writing?'

Rufius blinked as the steely point touched his eyelashes.

'It was in Latin — Pulvis et umbra sumus.'

Vassili eyes glazed over for a second.

'Came upon a sword like that not so long ago. Went for a pretty penny.'

'You know where it is?'

His breath reeked of sour wine when he sighed, but the knife was lowered and the pressure released from Rufius's chest, allowing him to breathe once more.

'Sorry boy, client privilege — I have my reputation to think of.'

[Hohenzollern Castle, Württemberg. Date: 1750]

He took Rufius to a castle located on a hilltop deep within a dense pine forest, or at least that much he could tell from the scent.

Vassili had insisted on blindfolding him throughout the entire journey, leaving Rufius with no real way of knowing when or where they had travelled to get here. There had been many jumps, executed so quickly that he had no time to get his bearings before they moved on.

As he was led along the passageway, Rufius brushed his fingers across the cold stone of the wall, feeling the chisels of the master masons that carved out the blocks. The stone sang of pain and death, echoes of terrible battles that were fought against its walls vibrated through the tips of his fingers like a lute string. He could sense the hundreds of years that the building had stood against its enemies, and before that the eternity the rock had endured below the mountain.

One of Vassili's men removed the blindfold, revealing a long corridor decorated with swords, shields and vicious-looking halberds. They were arranged in elegant displays along the walls, each one a testament to a forgotten battle.

The place was a shrine to violence. The rooms they passed were filled with cabinets and racks of deadly weapons from various parts of history. These were nothing like the halls of the Museum and Rufius realised he was in the company of a very different group of travellers, ones who relished the ways of war.

Old Arnwulf would have been impressed.

He followed the guards into a large hall. It was a grand oak-beamed structure with a long table running down the centre. At the far end, a desperate-looking group of men was eating. No one bothered to greet Vassili's group, they were all too busy with their food.

Which one of you stole my sword? Rufius wondered, following Vassili to the table and sitting down where he was told. The trainer made no introductions but simply walked off to talk to one of the other men.

The mercenaries were a grim assortment of rejects; some looked as though they had been dragged out of their death beds, others were more like executioners. All of them ate with their hands, tearing at the meat like condemned men eating their last meal.

There was a surly tension between them, like a pack of wild dogs sharing a kill, tolerating each other's company for the good of the pack. Rufius noticed missing ears, lost fingers and others like Vassili limping on badly set bones.

The table was heavily laden with food: meat and bread were stacked on silver trays that had clearly been stolen from different centuries, as were the goblets that the men were drinking from.

When Rufius reached out to take a leg of pork, the man sitting beside him slapped it away.

'You have to earn your place at this table,' he said in a hoarse whisper. 'What did you do to end up here?'

Rufius glanced at the man. He was in his thirties, with black hair tied back in a ponytail. Two sharp, beady eyes sat on either side of a long nose and a scar ran down one cheek. He wore the disinterested look of a seasoned warrior, one who had fought too many battles.

'I burned down the Library of Alexandria,' Rufius said, trying to sound indifferent and hoping that this wasn't the one who had actually set the time bomb.

The scarred man narrowed his eyes. 'Did you now?'

He threw Rufius one of his mutton bones. 'Words won't get you far in this company.'

'What did you do?' Rufius asked, gnawing at the last morsels of meat on the bone, realising it had been a while since he had eaten.

'Many things,' the man replied bitterly, ripping a roast duckling in two with his hands. 'Killed a king once, not a very popular one, but nevertheless a king all the same. Ended his line and changed the fate of an entire country.'

Rufius was about to ask which one when Vassili returned.

53

DANGERFIELD

Over the next month, Rufius was kept busy with menial jobs. While the others made raids back into the distant past, he scrubbed floors and cleaned plates, waiting on them every night after they returned with their sacks filled with treasure.

While Rufius served them dinner, the king killer, whose name he eventually learned was Valtin Eckhart, the man who had set the Royal Library ablaze, told stories of how they had pillaged Druid enclaves and ancient tombs all over the last four thousand years.

It was obvious that they didn't trust him, these were men with terrible secrets who preferred their own company. Only Vassili seemed to have earned their respect, and he was not an easy man to find. He was always busy with his clients.

Rufius was no closer to finding out who had bought the sword, all he had learned was that they were raiding to order. Buyers like Ashmole were bidding for rare items, but no one talked about who they were. Vassili was careful never to mention anything about his private collectors, simply returning each time with a bag of gold and a gleam in his eye.

In the fifth week, Vassili came to visit Rufius in the kitchens.

'Everyone earns their keep,' he said, flipping a silver coin at him.

Rufius caught it and ran his thumb over the timeworn surface, instinctively searching its history. It was at least three hundred years old, part of a Spanish hoard taken during the conquest of the Americas, and the last owner was a bishop.

'We don't ask questions,' Vassili warned as Rufius opened his mouth. 'Not if we want to keep our tongue.'

Rufius nodded and put the coin away.

'I think it's time we began your training, can't have you wasting your talents washing dishes.'

He went on to explain that Rufius would need to prove himself with a sword before he could join them on a mission. He would have to defeat Vassili in single combat.

They did not return to the Ludus Magna, as Rufius assumed. The first time he took him to the dojo, Vassili made some remark about 'learning to fight, not butcher'. The castle had doors that led to other periods in time. One opened onto a Japanese fighting school in Sekiryukan where Vassili instructed him to meet every morning for his training in the art of Kenjutsu.

They would begin each day with three hours in the study of the method and technique of the sword. It was a gruelling kata, combining full contact body strikes with Shinai, bamboo weapons, that would leave Rufius bloody and bruised.

'The sword or staff is the most widely available weapon throughout history,' Vassili would remind Rufius helping him back onto his feet. 'Far more reliable than a bow or a musket, and considerably more accurate at close range.'

Rufius began to enjoy the training, his muscles hardening with the punishing routine, and as the days turned into weeks, he began to take fewer hits. Vassili was breathing harder during their sessions, and there were beads of sweat on his brow when they finished.

It took a while to grow accustomed to the time difference. No matter how long they spent inside the dojo, only a few minutes would have passed when they returned to the castle, where all his usual chores were still waiting.

After lunch, the rest of his day was spent with Dangerfield.

After Rufius, Dangerfield was the youngest member of Vassili's company. Physically he looked to be of a similar age, but in every other way, he was an old man.

Rufius learned that not everything they stole went to 'clients'. Dangerfield had persuaded Vassili to keep some of the loot for research purposes — as a potential way to track down further caches of treasure.

Dangerfield was different from the others, as he wasn't particularly interested in fieldwork or fighting. He reminded Rufius of an Antiquarian, more concerned with the cultural significance of an object rather than just its value. He was currently becoming something of an expert on the ways of pagans, studying their beliefs and rituals. Vassili had released him from his other duties and allowed Dangerfield to concentrate his efforts on learning everything he could about them.

An entire tower of the castle had been allocated to his research. Rufius had spent the last few weeks helping to convert it into a 'laboratory'. It had a library that Sir Robert would have given his right arm for; the circular staircase climbed around the inner wall lined with rare manuscripts from the last thousand years. Each of the floors was used to organise the artefacts that had been confiscated from previous raids.

One of Rufius's duties was sorting through the haul that had been deposited from the previous day. Once he had cleared away their meal and washed the eclectic collection of plates, he would climb the steps of the tower to the sorting room.

He knew there was more than enough evidence in this one room to convince the founder that these were the time bandits, but Rufius wasn't interested in proving his innocence any more. Everything had changed the moment Vassili had told him about his sword. Dangerfield had a catalogue of every item that had passed through their hands, which meant somewhere in these registers was the location of Gunnlogi. For a group that didn't follow many rules, they were very strict on keeping an audit of their ill-gotten gains.

Every day brought new and unusual finds. Rufius had catalogued all manner of things, from the skulls of ancient creatures that resembled the heads of long-dead dragons to the tools of a civilisation that carved them from flint thirty-thousand years ago. He carefully tagged each one before placing it in the relevant room.

The men would sometimes discuss their adventures over dinner. When the wine began to flow and if they'd had a particularly successful mission, their tongues would loosen, and the tales would begin. Rufius learned a great deal about the Dreadnoughts, as they called themselves. They were men who had witnessed the worst atrocities of history, who knowingly went into the dark places of the past to find the treasure and had become immune to the terrible things they saw.

It seemed that every mission started in much the same way. They would find an ancient burrow or burial site and 'tunnel' back thousands of years using the relics within.

Dangerfield's research had identified hundreds of potential locations and the Dreadnoughts had spent most of the last six months in the Neolithic plundering Druidic sites that were spread across Northern Europe — usually located near standing stones like Carnac in Gaul.

It was dangerous work. They talked of ritual summoning, of Druids using artefacts to reach gods of a 'Dark Realm'. Some of the men had reported seeing strange beasts near the sites, although none would be able to describe them in any detail. Dangerfield showed Rufius a map that he had created, plotting each incident on a timeline, with notes that classified them by beliefs and gods, as if he were looking for some kind of pattern.

Usually, when Rufius finished his cataloguing, he would take his daybook and climb the last two flights of stairs to Dangerfield's study, where he kept all the registers of finds. It was in the eaves of the tower's conical roof. A large round room with tall, thin windows that looked out over the valley.

But today was different.

. . .

Valtin's team had brought something back that Rufius knew would be far more interesting to Dangerfield than the daily inventory.

Climbing the spiral stairs, Rufius held the object carefully between a pair of thick leather gloves. Physical contact with the relics was strictly forbidden by Vassili. Apparently, the temptation to weave with something primordial was deemed to be too dangerous.

Being the cautious type, Dangerfield designed a special type of container for the more toxic relics. He had based it on Egyptian canopic jars, the kind that was used to hold the remains of a dead Pharaoh on his way to the afterlife. It looked as if it were made of clay with a seal around the animal-headed lid, but Rufius knew that internally the walls were wrapped in copper coils and lined with lead.

The outer surface was covered in spells. Archaic runes derived from Dangerfield's studies of pagan rites, which he had painted on for dramatic effect. The jars were only to be used for collecting special types of material, essentially the remains of a summoning. They were rarely ever used, no one had ever managed to capture the essence of a demon.

Until now.

Makepiece was guarding the object when Rufius stepped onto the sorting floor. The man bore a fresh set of deep cuts across his face as if he'd been raked by the claws of a bear. Rufius could see the man's teeth through his cheek, but the look of pride on his face masked any sign of pain.

'You caught one?' Rufius said, hardly able to contain his excitement.

Makepiece tried to smile and failed. 'Part of one,' he said, his voice barely above a whisper.

'When?'

'200BC, in the tomb of the first emperor of China, Qin Shi Huang.'

'He doesn't sound very pagan.'

'He isn't. We were following a new path. The emperor was obsessed with finding the elixir of life. Vassili's client had us searching for a thousand-year-old wizard by the name of Anqi Sheng when we discovered this mountain of a tomb, filled with an army of terracotta soldiers and lakes of mercury, and there in the middle of it all were these.'

He shook the jar, it rattled as if filled with coins. 'The emperor sent men to the furthest corners of his empire in search of the elixir and those that returned brought some rather interesting alchemical artefacts. Including these.'

'What are they?' Rufius asked, putting on his gloves.

Makepiece scowled. 'Talismans. They've been possessed by a djinn. Bellamir found them, and it killed him.' He sighed, handing Rufius the jar. 'If it hadn't been for Dangerfield's trap we would have all been taken.'

It was the first time Rufius had ever seen any of them show any sign of emotion. Bellamir had been with them since the beginning, he was always one of the first through the door, and the last to return.

Dangerfield's eyes widened when Rufius appeared at the door with the jar.

'Well, this is an exciting development,' he said, taking it out of Rufius's hands with a pair of metal callipers. 'Where did they find it?'

Rufius recounted the story as Makepiece had told it to

him, while Dangerfield placed the jar on a table and found a tool to peel away the lead seal.

'Bellamir was a good man,' he said solemnly. 'Let's see if we can learn something useful from his sacrifice.'

With the top loosened, he placed the jar carefully on the floor in the centre of the room and went to the fireplace, scooping out the cold embers into his hands and crushing them into a fine black powder.

'I have a theory about these creatures.'

'Djinn,' Rufius corrected him.

Dangerfield began to draw a black circle around the jar with the ash. 'An ignorant classification — one that denotes a lack of understanding. It is far easy to label something a monster than discover its true nature.'

The circle complete, he stepped inside and removed the lid of the jar.

'I've prepared a new trap,' he said, nodding to a strange-looking device on his workbench. 'If you'd be so kind.'

Rufius went over and picked up the contraption. It was a large glass tube with various copper bands wound around it.

A wisp of smoke leaked out from the jar, curling in spirals around itself until it was level with their heads and then slowly a shape began to form, expanding as if within a bubble.

'Interesting distortion,' said Dangerfield, wiping his blackened hands on his robe and going over to pick up his journal.

Rufius was about to ask him how exactly he was supposed to use the device when the tendrils solidified into a body. At first, he thought it was vaguely human, but as the shape materialised the head was too large, small eyes stared out from each side of a massive pair of jaws. Its torso was covered in leathery scales, and its two arms were small and ended in vicious-looking claws. There were no legs, just a half-body, and as the creature's features became more defined, it was clear that it was not of this world.

'Grendel!' he exclaimed.

There was no sound, but the mouth moved as if it were roaring. Rufius couldn't take his eyes from the teeth, long sharp fangs that were as thick as his forearm. Bony blades ran along the back of the creature's neck, which was a mass of straining muscle, deeply scarred with old fighting wounds.

The creature lumbered towards them, reaching the boundary of the ash and then stopped abruptly as if blocked by an invisible wall. The ring began to whiten at the point where it tried to cross.

'Temporal absorption,' noted Dangerfield, writing in his journal.

Rufius watched as the black dust transformed into grains of sparkling glass.

'Diamonds,' Dangerfield explained, making another note.

The creature's eyes burned into Rufius, who had no doubt that he would be dead the moment the ash failed. It was the stuff of nightmares, and yet Dangerfield seemed to be completely unmoved by its hideous appearance.

'I would estimate we have less than a minute before it breaks through,' he said, putting down his book and placing a small screwdriver between his teeth.

Taking the new trap from Rufius, he placed it carefully on the floor in front of them just as the air around the creature began to distort and new shapes began to form.

The line of white dust was swept away as the demon rushed forward.

Rufius frantically searched for a weapon on Dangerfield's bench and finding a hammer, he raised it to strike.

'No!' Dangerfield shouted, jamming the screwdriver into the device and levering it open.

The creature froze as the trap opened and a blast of silvery-white vapour enveloped it, transforming its body into a crystalline ice sculpture.

'What did you do?' Rufius asked, still holding the hammer over his head.

'It's a form of gas,' Dangerfield said, taking the weapon from Rufius's hand. 'I've effectively stopped time, or at least reduced the frequency of its molecules to such a level that it is impossible for the creature to function.'

Rufius walked around the translucent form. The ice revealed hidden elements that were invisible to the naked eye. Its body appeared to be trapped between two worlds, half in theirs as though it were caught emerging from a frozen lake.

'I've been studying the relics that the Druids have been using,' said Dangerfield. 'I believe these are not demons, but creatures from the distant past or perhaps even somewhere beyond our continuum. See how the body is caught between the two dimensions as if entering through a tear in the fabric of this reality.'

Rufius nodded, trying to hide the fact that he didn't understand what Dangerfield was saying. Isolde had taught him the names of the nine realms of Yggdrasil, the world tree. She called this world 'Midgard', but there were others filled with giants, elves, dwarves, gods and the dead. In his opinion, this demon was likely to be from Niflheim or Hel. His grandmother had told many tales of the ice-cold realm around the fire on long winter nights.

Dangerfield picked up one of the intricately carved

objects from a shelf. 'I've seen similar incidents with Druids, using ivory like this to summon their gods.'

'Bone conjurors?' Rufius said, remembering something that Maebh had said.

'That's one way of putting it. I believe they're creating breaches through which these creatures can enter our world.'

Rufius pointed at the jar. 'Makepiece said that Bellamir found Talismans. They sounded like metal, not bone.'

Dangerfield frowned. 'That is unusual. Perhaps the emperor found some way to bind the creature with an alloy.'

'Why?' Rufius asked.

The young man shrugged. 'Power. Knowledge. Who can say what these creatures are capable of or what laws their universe adheres to — they may not experience time in the same way as us.'

'They're dangerous.'

'Indeed they are,' Dangerfield agreed. 'But I have some ideas.' He took down one of the plans that were pinned to the wall. 'I've been tinkering with a few devices,' he said, pointing to one that looked remarkably like the incendiary bomb that had set fire to the Great Library in Alexandria.

Rufius was distracted by the sound of dripping water. He turned to find a small pool forming at the bottom of the ice sculpture. 'How long until it thaws?'

'Another hour, perhaps two.'

'And then what?'

Dangerfield looked at him blankly. 'I guess we will need to get it back in the pot.' He nodded to the empty canopic jar.

Rufius turned quickly and made for the stairs.

'Where are you going?'

'To get Makepiece.'

54

THE FIRST MISSION

[Sekiryukan, Japan. Date: 1652]

Vassili was late.

Rufius practised his kata while he waited. He was sweating, the double weave of the Keigoki and Hakama were supposed to be for winter, but he preferred the extra padding beneath the armour.

Moving through the complex fighting sequence with graceful ease. His mind still and calm, there was nothing but the moment, no past or present, just the beating of his heart and the sound of his wooden sword carving through the jasmine-scented air.

'You have become quite a swordsman,' Valtin said, appearing in the room.

'Where's Vassili?' Rufius asked, lowering his weapon.

'He's been called away. An urgent request.' Valtin picked up a wooden bokken and hefted it from one hand to the other, testing its weight. 'I was ordered to come and get you,' he added, swinging the sword clumsily.

'You don't hold it like that,' Rufius said, showing him his own grip.

Valtin moved his hands into the same position.

'So the pup has grown some claws,' he said, shifting his feet into a fighting stance. 'Let's see what you've learned.'

Rufius had never really trusted Valtin, there was always something about the man that wasn't quite right. He could never tell whether he was about to clap him on the shoulder or slit his throat.

They circled each other and Rufius quickly realised that his clumsy use of the weapon had been a diversion. He could tell from the way Valtin moved that he was well-schooled in Kenjutsu. Unlike Vassili, whom he had come to know well as a sparring partner, this man was hard to read. His movements were cryptic, and when he struck, it was with an attack that Rufius had not expected.

The blow knocked him off his feet.

'One,' Valtin counted the hit with a wry chuckle.

Rufius sprang back to his feet, sweeping the sword around at his opponent's legs, but the man leapt over the blade.

Before he had time to recover his balance, Rufius felt the blow strike his shoulder.

'Two,' came the voice from behind him.

In one fluid movement, Rufius reversed his grip and thrust his sword backwards under his arm, feeling the satisfying thud when it found Valtin's stomach.

He spun around, raising one foot, striking the man in the head and knocking him off his feet.

'Two!' said Rufius triumphantly.

Valtin's smile disappeared as he got back to his feet.

The bout settled into a dance of parries and thrusts,

both gaining the measure of their opponent with every strike.

After his initial stumble, Rufius began to fight with confidence. Twenty minutes went by in a blur as he defended himself against the masterful attacks.

Slowly he began to find his way through Valtin's defence.

He realised he had more stamina than the older man, and gradually his strikes began to find their target.

Striking Valtin's leg for the second time, he saw it weaken and took a chance, lunging forward as the man regained his balance.

Rufius executed a quick series of diagonal cuts, pushing him back until he stumbled.

And then he disappeared.

Turning around slowly, Rufius scanned the room, waiting for the next attack.

Valtin appeared a second later.

'Looks like you're ready,' he said, leaning on his sword as he got off his knees.

Sweat poured down the man's brow, and he was breathing heavily.

'Ready for what?' Rufius asked, sheathing the sword.

'Your first mission.'

55

THE BARROW

[Avebury, Wiltshire. Date: 455]

They gathered on the brow of Silbury Hill. Below them, a village nestled in the pre-dawn mist smothering the valley in a grey soup. It was nearing winter and the morning dew hung in fat drops on the long grass, soaking through Rufius's boots, chilling his toes and making him shiver.

He pulled the thick woollen cloak tighter around his body, hoping the others hadn't noticed his tremor. He moved the sword into his left hand, biting his lip as the needle-pain shot through the fingers of his right — the blade was like holding a rod of ice.

There was no sign of activity in the cottages. No smoke from the chimneys or lights in the windows of the squat little dwellings that were surrounded by a circle of giant standing stones.

'Avebury,' whispered Vassili. 'Home of the stone weavers.'

Turning to the south, their leader raised his staff and

pointed towards a long narrow mound rising out of one of the fields. 'And where there are Druids, there are always burial sites. Dangerfield estimates the barrow was built in 3600BC and used for over a thousand years before being sealed up.'

The men seemed less than impressed, their attention focused on checking their equipment.

'These tombs were more than just burial sites, they were shrines to their ancestors. I have found numerous versions of them all over this period,' he explained to Rufius on their way to the mission briefing an hour earlier.

Vassili had a slightly different take on their objective.

'The client is interested in jewellery, preferably bronze or silver. They're willing to pay a good price for torcs too, as many as we can find. A couple more decent hauls, and we'll be richer than these old kings.'

'Or just as dead,' murmured the king killer under his breath.

'Quit your whining Valtin,' warned Vassili, raising his staff. 'Dangerfield thinks the contents of this tomb could open entirely new areas of the past.'

The entrance to the barrow was barred by a 'Corpse Door', carved from large grey slabs of Sarsen stone that stood over ten feet tall.

Valtin stared at the rock for a long time before placing his hands on specific points on its weather-beaten surface and closing his eyes.

'What's he doing?' asked one of the newer recruits.

'Finding the nearest opening,' whispered Makepiece.

Rufius could see the strain on Valtin's face. Trying to weave with organic material was hard, and Harrison had told him there were only a few who could work the complex non-linear structure of stone. Rufius had tried it once, it was like trying to catch snowflakes on a dark night; the events were so random and disorganised that there was no way to know where you might end up.

'Two thousand years,' Valtin muttered through gritted teeth.

The rest of the team gathered close to him, joining hands they formed a chain with the last member, Rufius, touching Valtin's shoulder.

'Whenever you're ready,' said Vassili.

Access to the burial chamber was through a narrow corridor built from heavy stones that were carefully stacked on top of each other. It was dark, and there was an overpowering stench of damp earth and rotting vegetation.

Following the flickering light of Valtin's torch into the tomb, Rufius felt the hairs stand up on the back of his neck, reminding him that this was the home of the dead.

He had always been taught to respect his ancestors. Isolde told tales of *Draugr*, the wraiths that guarded the dead and the treasure buried with them. She would describe their re-animated corpses in grotesque detail, making the children squeal and hide beneath their furs. The *Draugr* could change their shape at will, and their deathly-blue skin was supposed to be impervious to weapons. According to his adopted grandmother, the only way to defeat one was to trap it in a grave and bind it there. She would kick off her sandals and wiggle her toes as she explained how the feet of the recently deceased would be tied together or have pins pushed into their soles to prevent them from walking. None of them would be able to sleep after a *Draugr* story, but they would always beg her to tell another a week later.

Passing the small antechambers, Rufius noticed tiny runes carved onto the stone walls; intricate spiral patterns made of small dots, which reminded him of the symbols that Maebh had drawn on her body. *Warding glyphs,* he thought to himself, *charms to protect the dead from demons.*

He stopped to look inside one alcove, which was filled with bones and small jars.

'Sacrificial offerings,' explained Valtin, making a sign with the fingers of his free hand. The others had made similar gestures when they entered the tomb as if warding off evil spirits.

Rufius kept his eyes focused on the king killer's back, watching the way his armour moved on his shoulders. He was built like a warrior, like Eric Bloodaxe or one of the fyrd. His shoulders were broad and his arms thick knots of muscle. He walked on the front of his feet, keeping his body balanced to strike as Arnwulf had spent countless sessions trying to teach Rufius — there was simple but deadly grace to his movements, like a wolf stalking its prey.

They came to the main chamber and Valtin stopped outside the stony arch. Lighting a second torch with the first, he threw it into the darkness.

The flames cast an eerie glow across a row of crude stone sarcophagi that sat in the middle of the crypt.

The rest of the squad moved swiftly into the room, eager to explore, but Valtin held back and Rufius did the same. He could hear the warrior whispering something under his breath: '*Credo in Deum Patrem omnipotentem, Creatorem caeli et terrae, et in Iesum Christum, Filium Eius unicum...*' It was the same liturgy from the gunpowder mission. Valtin had been the one who had killed James I.

'Something bothering you?' Vassili asked Valtin, following the last of the squad into the chamber.

'Neolithic,' Valtin said, touching the iron cross around his neck. 'Not my favourite period.'

Vassili sneered, snatching the torch from Valtin's hand. 'The bone conjurers should be the least of your worries right now, let's find our prize and be on our way.'

The sarcophagi were surrounded by stone weapons, flint axes and polished knives as well as carved boar tusks and deer antlers. Vassili gave the torch to Rufius and told him to hold it steady while he searched the open coffins, which seemed to be filled with nothing but dust and bone.

'Neolithic is a difficult period to work in,' Vassili explained to Rufius. 'There's very little in the way of man-made objects.' He raked his dagger through the remains of the first body. 'Tools are mostly made from flint, and jewellery tends to be shell or bone, but there is usually some silver and gold — if one was important enough.' Something metallic caught on the end of his knife and he lifted it out. A dull metal bangle slid down the blade. 'If you're lucky, one might acquire a rare trinket.'

He pulled it off his dagger and held it up to Rufius's torch. 'Silver,' he said, stroking the metal with his forefinger, 'worth at least three thousand years.'

'Close enough to reach them?' asked Valtin, still standing guard outside.

'Close enough,' Vassili agreed.

Rufius was confused. 'Reach who?'

Valtin touched the metal symbol at his neck again. 'The real prize.'

56

THE GATHERING

[Anglesey, Wales. Date: 3600 BC]

The wicker man loomed over the gathering. The crude giant fashioned from woven branches stood in the centre of a stone circle, a fire burning around its feet. Silhouetted against the shimmering orange glow, naked women were dancing, throwing their hands into the air and chanting at the moonless sky.

Deep in the shadows, beyond the edge of the firelight, Rufius crouched listening to the cries of the prisoners trapped inside the wooden effigy. He could see their arms frantically clawing for freedom between the woven stays, trying desperately to free themselves from their wooden prison.

'What are they doing?' he whispered to Dangerfield, who had appeared a few minutes after Vassili had sent someone back to fetch him.

'Sacrificing,' he replied through tight lips. 'Trying to summon their god.'

Vassili and the others were spreading out around the

circle of light, each one looking on stoically at the terrible scene. *They have seen this before*, thought Rufius.

The fire began to lick up the legs of the sculpture. Rufius turned away and put his hands over his ears as their screams grew louder, praying for the noise to stop, knowing that it would mean their deaths.

Valtin crawled over to them, never taking his eyes from the scene. 'Don't turn away, boy,' he hissed, crouching beside Rufius. 'You must learn their ways and understand their motives. Know thine enemy!'

Rufius forced himself to look, letting the terrible sight sear into his memory. Over a hundred people were trapped inside the wicker man: men, women and children sacrificed to some nameless god.

The stench of charring bodies made him retch.

Priests in long white robes walked among the standing stones, their shaven heads painted with runes of protection. The dancers bowed to them as they passed.

'Druids,' hissed Valtin.

The Druids gathered around the fire as it took hold. Chanting in unison, they held carved objects out towards the flames. Ribbons of energy unwound from the artefacts, weaving out through the spaces between the Druids until they connected with each other, creating a lattice of blue-white lines around the pyre.

The flames began to react to their influence, forming into a tortuous mass of limbs. A hideous creature writhed inside the fire, its body seemingly made from the ghosts of the sacrificed.

'Crom Cruach,' whispered Dangerfield. 'The crooked one.'

'I've seen enough,' Rufius said, turning towards Valtin. 'We have to save them.'

Valtin shook his head. 'Can't change the past.'

'Then what are we here for?'

Dangerfield was studying something in his notebook.

'Dark relics,' Valtin replied, nodding towards the objects in the Druid's hands.

'Why?' Rufius asked, watching the beast grow inside the flames.

Valtin shrugged. 'Money, why else?'

'I think they're using chaos energy,' Dangerfield interjected, tapping on a page in his book. 'From the ending of so many timelines.'

Rufius drew his sword. 'Don't you mean the deaths of so many people?'

'Now don't go trying to be a hero — shit,' Valtin swore, watching Rufius run towards the fire. Drawing his own blade, he signalled the others to follow him.

The priests were too focused on their ritual to defend themselves, but they were not unprotected. The dancing women turned on Rufius and the rest of the squad as they entered the stone circle.

It was a bloody battle. Rufius saw more than one of the Dreadnoughts fall under the knives of the priestesses. They fought like wild animals, while all the time the Druids continued their summoning. Rufius carved a path towards the wicker man, watching the flames crawl higher up the wooden structure as he fought. The women's naked bodies were slick with oil and covered in strange runes that glowed as they attacked. His blade glanced off their skin as though it were armour, *like Draugr*, Rufius thought as he parried another blow. He could see why Vassili had insisted on the training; the priestesses were deadly with a knife, as well as hand and tooth, which had been sharpened to vicious points. Even Valtin was struggling to defend himself, and it was only when Vassili finally felled one of the Druids that their powers seemed to wane.

The heat was intense when Rufius reached the base of the burning structure. The air shimmered around it, as the glowing shape of the demon coiled around the column of fire.

And there she was.

Maebh stood amid the flames naked except for her tattoos, looking at him with golden eyes and beckoning him to join her.

Entranced, Rufius started towards the fire, his body responding to her command like a puppet. He could feel the heat singeing his face as he drew closer. Suddenly, Dangerfield appeared beside him, winding up one of the firebombs he had seen in the Library in Alexandria.

'Sometimes one must fight fire with fire,' he said with a wry smile, lobbing the brass sphere into the flames and pushing Rufius to the ground.

The explosion ripped the heart out of the fire, extinguishing it instantly. The shock wave sliced through the wooden posts that held up the wicker man and it crumpled, falling on top of the stunned priests.

His ears still ringing from the percussion, Rufius ran into the embers to search for Maebh, but her body was nowhere to be found.

He helped cut the prisoners free from the toppled giant. There were more than a hundred people trapped inside, many of whom were half-dead from breathing the smoke or battered by the crush. Some were not so lucky, their blackened bodies lay curled and contorted near the base of the fire.

It was dawn by the time they had freed all of the prisoners. Rufius found Valtin and Vassili standing with what was left of the company, their armour stained black. Two Druids knelt at their feet.

Vassili held a small effigy in his free hand whilst his sword was levelled at the chest of one of the kneeling men.

He was speaking in a language that Rufius couldn't understand.

'What is he saying?' Rufius asked Dangerfield, who was sketching the runes of one of the dead priestesses into his journal.

'He's asking the Druid where he got the relic. Your heroics have forced him to reveal our existence, which may end our little sojourn into the Neolithic.'

'I couldn't let them die like that.'

Dangerfield looked up from his drawing. 'A very admirable sentiment, but our leader is a businessman first, and I doubt his clients will be too happy to learn that their source has been so abruptly curtailed.'

'Who are they?'

'The buyers? That is a closely guarded secret, but they do seem to have rather eclectic tastes and incredible wealth. My guess would be a Russian Tsar or some Ottoman Emperor. Although it would be easy to find out if one could be bothered.'

Rufius watched as Vassili swung his sword and cleaved the head of the first Druid from its shoulders. The second Druid reeled back, holding his hands in the air in an act of surrender. It was a quick death and more than they deserved.

'How?'

Dangerfield stood up and closed his notebook. 'Follow the money, of course.'

57

FINDING NORTH

[Hohenzollern Castle, Württemberg. Date: 1750]

Hardly anyone spoke to Rufius when they returned to the castle.

Vassili disappeared almost immediately, no doubt delivering the relics of the Druids to one of his private collectors. Valtin donned the armour of a gladiator and made a parting remark about going back to the Colosseum to get drunk and fight an alligator. The others followed his example, jumping back to their favourite parts of the past for some shore leave. No one wanted to hang around and discuss what had happened at the wicker man.

Dangerfield did invite Rufius to join him on a research trip to Armana in Egypt, 1824. He was going to assist the Victorian explorer Robert Hay uncover the Southern tombs, but Rufius declined, the last thing he wanted to do was spend more time with another group of tomb robbers.

He had other plans.

With everyone away, the castle was empty, providing him with the perfect opportunity to search for Gunnlogi.

. . .

After weeks of surreptitious searching through the previous ledgers, it took less than a day to find the record. The sword had been taken from the battle on the Catalaunian Plains — just as he had suspected, by Bellamir. The line was neatly written in Dangerfield's flowing copperplate:

Roman Gladius with Latin inscription. Bel. Sold to XXVII

The numerals were obviously a cypher, one which only Vassili would have the key. Whoever client twenty-seven was, they had Gunnlogi and Rufius was determined to get it back.

Scanning pages of the more recent registers, he found other references to the same client. The mysterious buyer was purchasing virtually all of the dark relics, including the most recent hoard from the wicker man on Angelsey.

Rufius went back to his room and took the tachyon from its hiding place. Unwrapping it from the cloth, he stroked the cool metal casing with his thumb, wondering if Harrison was still searching for him. He had enough evidence now to go back and clear his name. To show the founder that he could be trusted and to tell of the terrible things he had seen, but he wanted to find the sword first.

All he needed to do was find where Vassili stored his payments for client twenty-seven — except he had no idea where to start. Turning the timepiece over in his hands, he thought about what advice Harrison would have offered him in this situation.

Then he remembered the last thing his mentor had said when he gave him the watch and knew exactly where he needed to go.

[Red Lion Square, London. Date: March 23, 11.776]

The old man lay propped up in the bed, his eyes milky with cataracts, staring blindly out into the distance. Harrison's skin was pale, sallow and lined with age. Rufius hardly recognised him when he appeared at the end of his bed.

'Who's there?' he asked, tilting his head slightly and reaching out with his hand.

Walking to the side of the bed, Rufius placed the tachyon gently onto the wrinkled outstretched palm.

'The Mark II,' Harrison said proudly, rubbing the second button with his thumb. 'Is that you Rufius? After all these years, have you finally come to see me?'

'It's only been a few months,' Rufius said, sitting down and guiding the old man's other hand to his face.

The old man's fingers gently traced the contours of Rufius's face. 'So young,' he said with a sigh. 'I had nearly forgotten what you looked like.'

His death was a fixed point in Harrison's timeline, one of the only moments he knew exactly where his friend would be if he wanted to avoid going back to the University.

'And you are so old.'

Harrison chuckled. 'I have missed your frankness, my dear boy. I am dying. This is the price you pay for spending too long in linear time, but it was worth every minute.' He gave back the tachyon. 'Enough about me, tell me when have you been?'

Rufius told his mentor about the Dreadnoughts and their raids, of the creatures that Dangerfield had discovered and his ideas of other realms beyond their own.

When he finished, Harrison's eyes were closed, and Rufius thought for a moment that the old man had died.

'Did you ever see your sea witch again?' he whispered.

'No,' Rufius replied bashfully, quickly changing the subject. 'When did you leave the Order?'

Opening his rheumy eyes, Harrison patted his chest. 'I returned to my own time once Doctor Crooke had cured me. Life at the college was less eventful once you were gone. I think even the founder missed you in his own way.'

Rufius realised that this could only mean that he never returned to the University. A chill ran down his spine as if someone had walked over his grave. This was a future he hadn't considered.

'I doubt it,' he said, holding the old man's hand. 'And what of the longitude problem?'

Harrison smiled. 'As you already knew. The board finally admitted defeat and paid up, although they never formally awarded me the prize. Still, I have managed a comfortable living, two wives and three children — my son William has followed in my footsteps,' he added proudly.

'You deserved it.'

'It wouldn't have been possible without you. When I think of the things I made you do.' The old man laughed until his breathing became laboured.

Leaning forward, Harrison let Rufius adjust the mountain of pillows, making him more comfortable.

'So what brings you to my death bed?' he asked once he had recovered.

'I need your advice.'

'I thought as much. Ask away, dear boy.'

Rufius told him of his sword and the other dark relics that Vassili was selling to unknown collectors.

Harrison had closed his eyes again, his breathing shallow. Rufius wondered if he had fallen asleep this time.

'What should I do?' he asked, his voice tailing away.

'They sound like dangerous weapons in the wrong hands. I'm assuming you have a way to trace them?' Harrison replied without opening his eyes.

'If I could find where Vassili is keeping the payments — I would be able to follow them back to the buyer.'

Harrison frowned, his face folding into a hundred creases. 'Not something I would advise you to do alone. Is there no one that you trust to take with you?'

'Not since I left the Order.'

'You're a stubborn man, Rufius Westinghouse, one day that pride of yours will be your undoing,' he said with a chuckle that turned into a coughing fit. 'My advice would be to speak to the founder. He's a wise man, and this information is too important to ignore.'

It wasn't the answer that Rufius wanted to hear, but he respected his old mentor too much to argue.

'But since you probably won't do that. I have one last gift for you — the small drawer in my writing bureau, open it and bring me the box.'

Rufius did as he was told and took out the small rosewood case from the desk.

'Open it.'

Inside was a compass, similar to the one that he had used to follow Columbus.

'There are certain magnetic properties to a large quantity of metal. Assuming that the hoard is not pure gold, but rather alloy. Then it should create a strong enough field to deflect a compass needle. You should be able to use it to find his vault, just watch for any deviation from North.'

. . .

Rufius found it hard to leave his old friend, but he could see that Harrison was tiring and his breathing was becoming laboured again. He turned down the lamp and left his mentor to sleep his last night on earth.

58

THE VAULT

[Hohenzollern Castle, Württemberg. Date: 1750]

The lower levels of the castle were the most obvious place to begin his search. Built into the side of a mountain, the dungeons were tunnelled out of solid rock.

And they seemed to go on for miles.

Over the centuries, the fortress had been occupied by numerous warring factions including the House of Habsburg who controlled it during the War of Austrian Succession. Each owner had extended the network of vaults, digging deeper until they finally came upon a natural cave system deep in the heart of the mountain.

It took two days of exploring the subterranean catacombs before the needle moved. It was nothing more than a tiny deflection, but enough of a signal for Rufius to pause.

The entrance to the vault was no different from any of the other doors that he passed. A strong iron-bound portal, there was no need for a lock, it would take a hundred days of looking to find it without the compass.

Opening the door slowly, he was half-expecting Vassili

to be waiting for him inside, but instead, he was met with the glimmer of gold reflecting off the lamplight.

It was a dragon-hoard, like something from the legends of Andvari. Chests full of treasure were stacked in the centre of the chamber. Coins, plate and precious jewels had been emptied out of caskets until they spilt over onto the floor. Nestled amongst the cases was a single wooden chair, where Rufius assumed Vassili would sit and appreciate his wealth.

Waiting at their tables, he had overheard the Dreadnoughts talk of the day they would 'retire' when Vassili would finally divide up their booty, but no one knew where it was, no one had ever seen it in all its glory.

The chests were marked with numbers.

Finding one marked with XXVII, Rufius picked up a coin. It was a Spanish Doubloon. The edges were still rough from where the Sevillano coin maker had cut it to weight. He felt the age of it through his fingers, the strikes of the minters' stamp as he hammered the arms of Philip II into the soft metal. Rufius followed its chronology forward, he wasn't interested in the riches of the Spanish king. He wove through its history until just before it had arrived in the castle — when it had resided in the hands of collector twenty-seven.

In the palace of the King of Bohemia.

59

THE COLLECTOR

[Prague Castle. Date: 1591]

Rufius found himself in the North Wing of Prague castle, in a long room filled with tall glass cabinets. It was the largest collection of curiosities he had ever seen — far greater than Montagu House. There were hundreds of artefacts dating back thousands of years, according to the neatly written labels sitting under each one.

Unlike the museum of the Tradescants, the cases were not filled with the remains of animals or curious rocks, but occult objects of the arcane. Wandering along the rows of cases, it was obvious that this was one of Vassili's mysterious collectors. Druidic and Pagan objects lined the shelves, each one inscribed with similar symbols to those that Dangerfield had been copying into his journal.

Stopping in front of one particular cabinet, Rufius recognised the golden torc nestling on a velvet cushion. The runes engraved into it were still filled with the dried blood of the priest Vassili had beheaded at the wicker man. He shuddered at the memory of the screams of the sacrificed.

Lying beside it was one of the artefacts the Druid used in the summoning of Crom Cruach. Carved from the tusk of some ancient beast, the details had worn away with aeons of wear. Rufius recalled the power they conjured from it and wondered what part of pre-history it was connected to.

His reverie was broken by a low, rumbling growl from somewhere off to his right. Turning his head slowly, he glimpsed the shape of a large cat prowling between the cabinets. It was a tiger, Rufius had seen them at the Colosseum; larger than a wolf and twice as deadly. The *bestiarii* gladiators, who were trained to fight wild animals, told stories of a legendary feline from Siberia and the men who had died trying to defeat it.

Vassili's training took over. Rufius focused on his breathing, clearing his mind of the fear, allowing his muscles to relax and the adrenalin rush to dissipate. Then he looked for somewhere to hide.

The chamber was long, and the spaces between the cabinets were too small for him to fit.

Stepping out of his boots, he crept barefoot along the marble floor, searching the cases for any kind of weapon.

The tachyon was inside his tunic. He considered rewinding the last two minutes, but the tiger would still be there, and he was not afraid to face it, assuming he could find a sword.

And then he did.

The weapon hung in the centre of a tall thin box, suspended from the roof of the cabinet by a fine wire which was nearly invisible, making it appear to float.

There was no mistaking the runes along its blade, it was the Roman sword, his sword — *Gunnlogi*.

The tiger roared, and the sound of its claws raking the floor warned Rufius that the beast had caught his scent.

Without another thought, he punched the glass and ripped the sword from its mount. Turning to face the beast pounding down the hall towards him, he dropped into a low fighting stance, raising the blade.

The tiger bared its teeth, closing the distance between them in a few bounds. Rufius slowed his breathing, estimating the perfect time to strike.

'Hold!' bellowed a man's voice.

The beast stopped in his tracks, less than ten feet away.

A tall man wearing a black cap, and dark robes appeared from a side room and walked over to the snarling tiger, scratching it casually behind one ear.

'And what knight errant have you caught for us today Ferdinand?'

Rufius remained in his stance, holding the sword ready, not taking his eyes away from the big cat.

'Calm yourself, boy,' the stranger said, feeding the cat a tidbit from his hand. 'That blade would hardly be a match for six hundred pounds of tooth and claw.'

The man whispered something to the cat, and it turned and sidled off towards the exit, the end of its tail flicking from side to side with a distinct sense of displeasure.

'You're fortunate that it was I and not my master who found you. His highness takes great pleasure in watching Ferdinand at work. However, we probably should see to that wound, before you bleed all over his floor.'

It was only then that Rufius realised he had cut his hand smashing the glass. The blood was flowing down the haft of the sword and onto the tiles.

. . .

They were sitting in a small room, the stranger called it the 'alchemist laboratory' and it reminded Rufius of Doctor Crooke's sanitorium; the shelves were filled with jars full of powders.

'My name is Edward Kelly,' the man began, binding the wound on Rufius's hand with cobwebs. 'And you are John, the lost son of Robert the Bruce.'

Rufius shook his head. 'No, my name is Rufius, Rufius Westinghouse.'

Kelly smiled reassuringly. 'Yes, of course, you lost your name as well as your king.'

'You knew my father?'

He shook his head. 'No, but I have seen him.'

'Is he here?' Rufius asked, wondering if this was perhaps his father's castle.

There was a strange look in Kelly's eye, as though he were being distracted by something over Rufius's shoulder.

'No, not here. In there,' he said, pointing at the blood-stained cloth that lay on the table. 'I've seen your beginnings. How you fell through time.'

Rufius was confused, the last person to use his blood was Maebh, but she could only look into his future, not his past.

'Are you a seer?'

Kelly finished the binding and went over to a basin to wash. 'You were lucky it wasn't Mohamed, his majesty's lion. That beast is quite uncontrollable, there have been several attacks on the servants in the last few weeks. I think it's acquiring a taste for human flesh.'

'How exactly did I fall through time?' Rufius persisted as it was obvious Kelly was avoiding the question.

Kelly meticulously cleaned the blood from his hands. Rubbing the hard cake of soap against each finger. 'Fate has not been kind to you, my boy. The gift usually manifests at nine or even ten for most of us, rarely ever in an infant. Your poor mother wasn't to know that the plaything she gave you would take you away — she wept for many months — ignore me, I say too much.'

Rufius had no memory of his life before Bloodaxe's hunting party found him, all of his childish fantasies of elves and changelings were swept away in a heartbeat. 'Who was I?'

Kelly stared into the swirling bowl of water, stirring the blood into a spiral. 'Earl of Carrick, one of the heirs to the Scottish throne.' When he looked up, his eyes were like dark pools. 'But these are naught but words, do not grieve for what might have been, that path is closed now. Surely the question is, who will you become?'

His eyes cleared as he walked back to Rufius

'And who will that be?' Rufius asked, his anger rising.

The seer's fingers made strange motions in the air as if he were plucking at the strings of an invisible lute. 'A man caught between two worlds.'

Riddles thought Rufius, *the man is half-mad, these are nothing but fairy tales.* He picked up the sword and levelled it at the man's chest.

'Enough of your double-talk, warlock. What is this place, and what are you doing with all these dark relics?'

Kelly looked along the blade, studying the glyphs. 'We are but dust and shadow,' he muttered, translating the Latin as he ran his finger along the text.

'This has seen many terrible battles,' he continued, opening its timeline. 'And yet there is something else, something deeper.'

Rufius went to speak, but Kelly stopped him. His hand gripped the blade tightly as he went deeper into its past. Rufius could see the blood beginning to flow where the edges cut into the man's palm.

'Beware the ides of March! By all the gods!' he proclaimed, his free hand waving over his head. 'This blade was forged from the daggers of betrayal, the weapons that were used to murder a great man — a Caesar.'

Suddenly, his eyes snapped open, and he let go of the sword. 'Julius Caesar,' he said, staring wildly at the weapon.

'Who?'

'He was once a great general, a ruler of the Roman Republic, until his assassination in 44BC. It brought about a second civil war and eventually the fall of the republic.' Kelly explained, looking at the cuts on his hand as if they meant something.

'Why would your master want this sword?'

'It has a powerful history. Caesar was stabbed twenty-three times by the members of his senate. Marcus Antonius had their daggers melted down to forge this blade, then used it against his enemies in the war. Rudolf likes to own things that are connected to momentous events, especially ones with such dramatic consequences.'

Kelly looked him directly in the eye. 'But I think the more interesting question is: how did you come to know it? This has drifted through time for hundreds of years.'

Rufius shrugged. 'A traveller brought it to my stepfather, he was a smith. I would take it out into the woods to practice. It showed me many battles and how to fight like a warrior. I thought it was magic until I was found.'

'You were lost?'

'No. There are a group of travellers, like us, who discovered me in Jorvik and showed me how to weave through time. They're good men, they're trying to protect the future.'

'And you're not with them now?'

Rufius looked away. 'No, I had to leave. They think I started a great fire in the Library of Alexandria.'

Kelly's eyebrows raised slightly. 'So that was you.'

Rufius shook his head. 'No, it wasn't me. It was those thugs you paid to find your master's relics.'

'I doubt that,' Kelly said, scratching his beard. 'I don't think I've ever requested anything from that period. Except perhaps for Aristotle's second book of Poetics. What did you say these men were looking for?'

'An emerald tablet.'

'Ah. Yes, the fabled excerpt from the *Hermetica;* said to contain the secret of the prima materia and its transmutation. A highly valuable artefact, but not one that my master managed to acquire. There must have been a higher bidder.'

'What is prima materia?'

'The primary alchemical element, the first matter, the quintessence. His highness is a student of the occult. He's obsessed with the works of Paracelcus and his *Alkahest*. The king believes that the ancients were guardians of a secret knowledge that was lost — he wishes to commune with long-dead gods.'

'As do the Tuatha Dé.'

Kelly raised a finger, looking nervously around the room. 'That is a name I haven't heard in a very long time. I wouldn't speak it aloud, some of the artefacts have ears.'

There was a mad glint in his eye once more.

Rufius looked around the room. 'What are you doing here?'

He took out an iron coin and held it between his fingers. 'He believes I am an alchemist, that I can transmute lead into gold.' With a flick of his wrist, the coin changed colour. 'But my experiments have come to naught. So I am his prisoner, or should I say perhaps his curator.' He produced a large ring of iron keys. 'And the keeper of the keys. Come, let me show you.'

60

THE OBSIDIAN MIRROR

[Prague Castle. Date: 1591]

Inside the tall, elegantly carved cabinet hung a frame draped with a black cloth.

'No one is allowed into this room, not even his most trusted counsellors,' Kelly said furtively, taking a special key from a chain around his neck. He inserted it into the door and twisted it one way and then the other before performing a small bow to the door.

The air inside the case was stale, and there was a faint odour of decay. Kelly removed the cloth to reveal a dark mirror, a looking glass that held no reflection, it was like staring into the surface of a deep, still pond.

'This is Rudolf's most prized possession. An ancient tool of divination made from a single piece of obsidian that was born in the heart of a volcano. The Mayans believed it had rather unusual properties, it can look into the paths that have yet to be.'

The subtly shifting void beneath the surface was strangely hypnotic. Rufius could feel himself being drawn into it. Like seeing something fleetingly out of the corner of your eye, which vanishes the moment you turn to look at it.

'There are few of us who can range across the borders of time, and yet fewer still that have the power to look into the undiscovered country.'

Rufius laughed, turning away from the mirror. 'You're telling me you can use this to see into the future?'

Kelly's long fingers casually stroked his beard into a point. 'The sight is nothing but a curse. Observing the lives of others and the paths that fate may take them is a burden that can never be put down. Some seers need nothing more than a physical connection.' He grabbed Rufius's hand. 'To read another's timeline. While others require something a little more intimate.' He raised one eyebrow, letting go of his hand. It was as if he knew exactly what had passed between Rufius and Maebh.

'But to divine, the greater destiny of humanity is more challenging, it requires the use of special objects — like this scrying glass, artefacts that have been touched by catastrophe. Such talismans can aid in the navigation of the infinite.' He pointed dramatically towards the mirror. 'With this, I have seen terrible things, catastrophes, the fall of empires, the end of civilisations and the agents who brought about their downfall.'

'Agents?' Rufius asked.

'Those who seek to profit from the suffering of others.'

'Like the Dreadnoughts?'

Kelly shook his head. 'No, like the Tuatha Dé. They seem to thrive on the raw energies of chaos and disaster. I think they seek to harness this power.'

'Why?'

He shrugged. 'Why do we do anything? If not to fashion the world of our dreams? All I have learned is that they seek objects like this.' He pointed to the mirror. 'Ones that can reach into the deep past. Perhaps they wish to awaken the ancient ones that sleep there.'

Rufius remembered what Maebh had said about the creatures that slept below the ocean and the metal that had fallen from the stars.

'They can weave with the lines of natural things. I have seen one use the sea to open shadow paths.'

Kelly looked impressed. 'Indeed! I have heard reports that some can use stone and wood. Water is one of the most unstable mediums to travel through, and certainly not something I would recommend.'

'And they haven't come for the mirror?'

Kelly smiled. 'Oh, they have tried, but it is too well protected.' He pointed to the cabinet. 'This is no ordinary box. It contains the witches mark, see the wards upon its base and sides.'

It was only when Kelly pointed it out that Rufius noticed there were glyphs etched into the wood, interconnecting circles and stars carved into every internal surface.

'They cannot approach it without withering an arm. The sigils repel them.'

Kelly took the sword and stepped inside the cabinet. 'Let us see what the glass can tell us.'

Lifting the blade to the mirror, Kelly's brow furrowed deeply. His lips moving silently in prayer as he stared into the darkened glass.

Rufius heard the patter of paws on the marble floor of the corridor outside. Mohamed, the lion, padded nonchalantly into view. Kelly was in too deep a trance to notice it. The beast was less than ten feet away, and Rufius was about to take back the sword when Kelly dropped it and fell to his knees. The clatter of steel on the chamber floor sent the animal running.

Kelly's whole body seemed to be shaking when Rufius helped him to his feet.

'My gods, the stars were truly out of alignment on the day you were born.'

'What does that mean?'

'Do you know what a paradox is?'

'No.'

'Then I cannot explain what lies ahead,' he pointed to the mirror. 'Suffice to say that the Tuatha Dé seek to unleash terrible things on this world, catastrophes that would unmake this world and all who dwell within it.'

'Ragnarok?'

Kelly chuckled. 'The end of the world? Perhaps, but from what I've seen, they seek far more ancient powers that those of the Aesir, older than the time of men. This is the stuff of nightmares, giant lizards the size of ships, colossal stones falling from the sky, fires scourging the earth of every living creature.'

Rufius thought of the creatures he had seen forming in the fires of the Great Library, and at the summoning. Dangerfield had called it something.

'Like Crom Cruach?'

In a flash, Kelly clasped his hand over Rufius's mouth.

Something slithered beneath the surface of the mirror.

'Never use the name of an ancient in front of a talisman,' Kelly whispered in his ear. 'Lest you wish to meet one.' He waited until the surface calmed and then pushed Rufius towards the cabinet. 'Now, it is your turn. Tell me what you see.'

. . .

The bodies of fallen soldiers lay twisted and broken, scattered across the blasted fields. Large metal carriages crawled over the slurry, firing canons from side-turrets at troops who hid in long lines of trenches cut into the earth. Smoke and thunder filled the air, leaving a bitter taste in his mouth. Rufius watched men fall under the constant barrage of explosions that seemed to rain down from the sky.

Looking up, he could see dark shapes in the clouds. Winged machines were circling above them, dropping black cylinders onto the enemy's lines. They seemed to be filled with some kind of bad air that made men claw at their throats and fall to their knees. White froth bubbled out of their gasping mouths, and their faces turned blue as they tried to breathe.

'What madness is this?' Rufius asked, turning away from the mirror.

Tears gathered in Kelly's eyes. 'A war unlike any other.'

'When?'

'Within the next three and a half centuries.'

Rufius looked back at the mirror and his heart stopped. Maebh was staring back at him, her eyes as dark as the surface of the glass. She smiled knowingly as if she could see him.

'She's watching me,' he said under his breath.

Kelly threw the cloth over the frame and pulled Rufius out of the cabinet.

'I can feel her,' Rufius said, shivering. 'She's here.'

'I told you they have ears everywhere,' he said, looking frantically around the chamber. 'They have been using you to reach me, you have brought ruin to my door!'

The shadows began to move strangely in the room around them. Taking on a life of their own, they twisted and curled around the edges of the exhibits, putting out the lanterns as they passed over them.

Darkness crept along the hall.

'Quickly inside the box,' said Kelly, dragging Rufius back inside and shutting the door.

Rufius watched the shadows take form. Six women dressed in black approached them from different sides. As the first drew close, Rufius could see that her skin was clothed in nothing more than a swirling mass of sigils and runes.

Kelly was muttering incoherently to himself, touching each of the marks inside the box, some of them had begun to blacken and smoulder.

He heard Maebh's song from somewhere out of sight.

'I've been a wild rover for many's the year
And I've spent all me money on whiskey and beer...'

'Don't listen to the siren,' begged Kelly, his eyes wild with fear. 'It will be the end of us both.'

Rufius took out his tachyon and began to move the dials.

Kelly's eyes lit up at the sight of the device. 'And what exactly is that?'

61

THE FOUNDER

[Founders Chambers Date: 1660]

The younger version of Harrison was clearly pleased to see Rufius when he appeared in the workshop, although he kept his enthusiasm in check until he was introduced to Edward Kelly.

'Maestro,' said Kelly, bowing deeply before the watchmaker. 'Your work is sublime. In all my years I have never seen such exquisite a timepiece. You have tamed time and freed me from my prison!'

Rufius could see from Harrison's expression that there was definitely something odd about the seer. Isolde would have said he was filled with *Odr* — a kind of divine madness.

'Master Kelly, you are too kind,' Harrison replied humbly. 'I merely adapt the work of greater men such as Huygens and Galileo — those were the true geniuses.'

'Ah, the heretic astronomer.' Kelly sighed. 'I have read Galileo's *Assayer*. Cardinal Maculani and his inquisition have a lot to answer for.'

'Indeed they do,' agreed Harrison solemnly. 'Now Rufius, tell me of your travels. When have you been?'

Rufius was relieved to see his mentor as a young man again. It was hard to believe that a few days ago, he was holding the hand of his dying friend. There was nothing he wanted more than to sit by the fire and while away a few hours telling tales, but he had a more pressing task.

'I've been to Helheim and back, but those stories will have to wait. I must see the founder. Master Kelly has shown me something that Lord Dee must know.'

Dee stared out of the large round window onto Christ Church meadow. He sighed deeply, his shoulders tight and hunched, like a man leaning into a cold wind. When he turned towards them, Rufius realised quite how badly he had aged since he had last seen him.

On their way to his apartments, Harrison had warned him that the founder was constantly travelling back and forth into the past, and it had obviously taken its toll. The man had visibly withered, his skin grey and pallid, his hair whitening in places. He carried himself as if the weight of the world were on his back.

'I have missed you, boy,' the founder said with a weak smile. 'There have been times recently when I could have used your strength and relentless optimism.'

'Master,' Rufius said, bowing his head. 'May I present Edward Kelly, alchemist of Emperor Rudolf II, King of Bohemia — he's also a scryer.'

The founder studied Kelly for the longest time as if trying to remember if he had met him before. 'A scryer, you say? And what exactly have you seen with your crystal ball I wonder?'

'Many things, my lord,' Kelly answered, waving his hands in the air as he spoke. 'Seas on fire. The death of kings, even the coming of the paradox.'

The founder's eyes narrowed at the last word.

'And a terrible war,' Rufius added.

For the next hour, they sat beside the fire and Kelly told the founder how he came to be at the court of Rudolf II. He explained how the emperor's interest in the occult had grown into an obsession, imprisoning Kelly and commissioning Vassili to recover certain items, ancient ritual relics in particular.

The founder listened carefully, asking questions about the types of artefacts and the men that he had paid to recover them.

When they came to the subject of the obsidian mirror, the founder laughed.

'An artefact that can show you the future,' he said, getting to his feet, 'I have heard enough.'

Rufius glared at Lord Dee, he couldn't believe that he would refuse to listen to them. He felt the rage rising in his chest. 'Why do you never believe me? There are unthinkable things going on beyond these walls of books you surround yourself with. While you stand back and observe, others are pillaging the past. Ragnarök is coming and all you do is watch!'

The founder's expression hardened, his mouth becoming a thin, white line. 'And how, might I ask, can you be so sure it is the only future? What statistical evidence do you have to corroborate these predictions? One might just as easily say it was nothing more than a dream.'

'More like a nightmare,' Rufius bellowed taking out his tachyon. 'A war that will end all wars, millions will die.'

'May die,' the founder corrected, holding up a finger.

'He saw it too,' Rufius pointed to Kelly. 'Are you going to tell me we're both seeing things?'

The founder paused for a moment, weighing up his response. 'His real name is Edward Talbot, and he's a notorious charlatan and counterfeiter. Have you noticed his ears? How they have been cropped? He was banished from Lancaster for forgery.'

'A misunderstanding—' Kelly began, but Lord Dee continued.

'There are many with our gifts who would prey on the weak and vulnerable. Who profess to know your fortune: diviners, soothsayers and palm readers — they are nothing but a blight on the good name of the Order. Let me guess, he began by telling you he knew who your father was.'

Rufius nodded.

'And was he by any chance a king?'

Rufius nodded again, his cheeks were burning.

'Hah!' the founder said, grabbing Kelly by the arm. 'How many times have you used that particular line?'

Kelly shrugged. 'I merely say what I see.'

Rufius had heard enough, he pressed one of the buttons on his watch and disappeared.

62

TAKING A RISK

[Bodleian Library, Oxford. Date: 1660]

The tachyon had taken Rufius back to Harrison's workshop just after they had left to see the founder. It had been a mistake, he had assumed that Kelly would have been able to convince Lord Dee that there was a real danger, but instead, he had made it worse. Rufius couldn't understand why the old man was being so stubborn and why he was so against the idea of the mirror's predictions.

He sat at the watchmaker's workbench, spinning gear wheels across its polished surface and wondering who might take him seriously. Dee and Harrison were too much like Sindri, men who needed proof of something in their hands before they believed it. They had no imagination, the idea of demons, witches and premonitions were too outlandish for them.

Picking up one of the half-finished Mark IIs, Rufius thought of Drake and his Draconians, but they were too close to the founder.

The only other option was the Dreadnoughts. They had

witnessed all manner of evil acts, so the news of an impending apocalypse would be nothing unusual. Assuming they could make a profit from it, of course. The greatest problem Rufius faced would be explaining to Vassili's men why he had broken into their vault and lost them one of their best clients.

Unless of course, he could bring them something valuable.

Like whatever the witches were looking for.

Bodley was having difficulty looking Rufius in the eyes.

'Did you find the thieves?' he stuttered to his shoes. 'When the Draconians said you were lost, I assumed you had been taken.'

'Oh, I found the Dreadnoughts and learned all about their dark ways.'

'Dark ways?' Bodley asked, obviously relieved that Rufius wasn't about to punch him.

Rufius told him about the summoning of the Druids and the King of Bohemia's collection. Bodley began to shake as Rufius described the future war.

'And the founder will do nothing?'

'He thinks it's some kind of trick, that Kelly is a fraud.'

'And you do not?' Bodley said, taking a large sip of wine to steady his nerves.

'I know what I saw. That was no illusion.'

'So, how do you intend to convince him?'

'I need to find Maebh. If I can prove to him that the Tuatha Dé are real—'

'The sea witch?' Bodley scoffed, his confidence returning. 'You'll have more chance of scratching your ear with your elbow.'

'Why?'

He rolled his eyes. 'Because she'll know you're coming.'

Rufius walked over to the bookshelves, running his hands along the chains. 'Which is why I'm going to need your help.'

Bodley looked like a scared rabbit. 'Me? I don't have anything she would want.'

'I think you do,' Rufius insisted. 'Maebh said she was looking for a metal that had fallen from the stars. Do you know what that might be?'

The young curator clapped his hands. 'Indeed I do!' He ran over to one of his cabinets and pulled out a small rock and handed it to Rufius.

'A rock?'

'A meteorite. They have been falling from the heavens for millions of years. Most burn up in the atmosphere, but some are large enough to survive. That rock has travelled millions of years across the cosmos before landing here. Quite an unusual thing to imagine when you're holding it in your hand.'

'But it's a rock.'

Bodley huffed and took it back. 'They fall into three categories, this is a stony-iron meteorite made from iron-nickel and silicates, but there are others that are pure iron or pure stone.'

'Does the metal have magical properties?' Rufius asked, snatching the meteorite back and trying to open its timeline.

'I don't think so. I suppose if you discovered one large enough, you could extract the ore and create a weapon or an amulet — but its timeline would be a rather dull journey through the vacuum of space.'

Rufius gave up trying to weave with the rock, its chronology was too vast and mostly empty until it was discovered at the bottom of a well in Elbogen, Bohemia during the Thirty Years' War.

'So why would the Tuatha be so interested in them?'

'The earliest metal artefacts were made from them. Before iron was mined, it was the only source of ore. Egyptians had daggers made from them, they were supposed to never rust.'

'So they could go back to the Egyptians?'

Bodley smiled. 'Or further. Depending on when the rock fell to Earth.'

'How far?'

'Millions of years. Ashmole has been trying to use fossils to go back, but they're very unpredictable.'

Rufius thought of the blue amber that Alixia had traded with Ashmole and knew exactly who would be able to answer his next question.

63

CRETACEOUS

[Montagu House, Bloomsbury, London. Date: 1759]

It was late, and Rufius had fallen asleep against the dodo exhibit. He had waited for Alixia to appear for the last three nights, but so far she hadn't shown.

He needed to find out what the Tuatha Dé were looking for in the past, and the only person he knew who had gone further back was Alixia. In her efforts to save her menagerie of creatures, she had travelled into the deep past.

'Well, if it isn't my clumsy Viking!' Alixia's voice woke him from his nightmare.

Rufius opened his eyes to find her pale face beaming down at him, a frown creasing her forehead.

'What are you doing here? And what an earth are you wearing?'

He got to his feet and straightened the travelling robes, they made him look like a priest, but Bodley had assured him that they would be good for the trip he was about to make.

'I need your help. I want you to take me to the Cretaceous.'

Alixia looked slightly astonished. 'Even I haven't been back that far. Why on earth would you want to go there?'

'I'm looking for a rock.'

'What kind of rock?' Alixia asked.

'A meteorite.'

She laughed. 'There's no need to go back all that way. There are literally thousands scattered all over Antarctica. Why the Cretaceous?'

Rufius wasn't sure how to answer the question, he could see that she wasn't going to be satisfied with a short explanation.

'I have seen the future,' he said, walking over to one of the displays, it was filled with ancient stone axes. 'One that leads to a terrible war.'

Her smile faded as she realised he was being serious.

'When we last met, you saved me from a fire. I went back to the first century, the period you said I should avoid. There were others, like us, who could travel through time, but they were using the past for profit.'

She scowled. 'The pirates that burned down the Great Library. Why would you seek them out?'

'Because I wanted to prove myself. I was blamed for the fire, and no one would listen to me, so I went to find something that could show them I was innocent.'

'And did you find it?'

He grimaced at the memories of what he had witnessed. 'More than I was expecting. You were right when you said that was a dark period. They were collecting objects, ritual artefacts, that had been used in horrific ways, and selling them to the highest bidder.'

'Not Rudolf II by any chance?'

Rufius looked surprised. 'You know him?'

'His collection is one of my least favourite waypoints. I'd always wondered where his occult artefacts were coming from. Did you meet the tiger?'

Rufius nodded, showing her the thin white scar where he had cut himself retrieving the sword. 'I have had the pleasure.'

'And the eccentric curator, what was his name? Kelly?'

'He was the one that showed me the future — in the obsidian mirror.'

Alixia sighed. 'And you believed him?'

'Why shouldn't I?'

'Because the man is a charlatan. Did you know they cut off his earlobes as a punishment for forgery in Lancaster?'

She was the second person to tell him that Kelly shouldn't be trusted, but he couldn't forget what he had seen in the mirror. There was nothing false about his vision.

'What I saw was no trick. Death rained down from flying machines and men died from poisoned air.'

Her already pale face blanched whiter still. Rufius hadn't meant to shock her, but he was tired of people not taking him seriously.

'When is this meant to happen?'

Rufius counted silently on his fingers. 'Within the next two hundred years.'

'And who do you think is responsible?'

'The founder says it has some statistical reason.'

Alixia crossed her arms. 'He sounds like a determinist, who exactly is this founder?'

'Someone who doesn't believe you can see into the future.'

'And he doesn't believe in your war?'

'He wants proof. My word is not good enough.'

She unfolded her arms and took out her almanac and showed him pages filled with formulae. 'He sounds like a student of probability, cause and effect. I was tutored by Laplace on mathematics, it sounds as if your founder is in search of his demon.'

'A demon?' Rufius said, taking the book and leafing through it. But instead of monsters, the pages were covered in a multitude of lines weaving and branching across the paper, surrounded by notes and numbers written in a delicate hand.

'Not that kind of demon. It was the term they used for Laplace's theory of causal determinism. If one could know the location and momentum of every atom in the universe, then the past and the future would be revealed.'

Rufius closed the book and handed it back. 'I know what I saw, and it has something to do with the Tuatha Dé.'

She looked at him blankly. 'And who might they be?'

'Seers — some call them witches. They are connected somehow.'

'Witches?'

He blushed slightly. 'I met one once. She's been following me ever since, appearing at the same events. She told me they are looking for a rare metal, one that fell from the sky. I think the Tuatha will use it to summon a demon or an elder god.'

Alixia scowled. 'You realise you sound like a crazy person?'

'If I hadn't seen one, I would agree.'

She stared at him in disbelief. 'You've actually seen a demon?'

He nodded. 'There's a man called Dangerfield who studies them, he calls them the creatures of the dark realms.'

Alixia swept a loose lock of hair behind her ear and pursed her lips. Rufius had noticed she did that whenever she was mulling something over.

'Well, it strikes me that we should speak with this Dangerfield before attempting to jump back eighty-eight million years.'

'There was one slight issue.'

Rufius went on to explain how he had stolen from the Dreadnoughts and that visiting Dangerfield may be dangerous.

'This chap, Vassili, sounds like a businessman,' she said, producing a worn old coin from her purse. 'I wonder if he would be interested in learning the precise location of Montezuma's lost treasure.'

64

SCROTUM HUMANUM

[Hohenzollern Castle, Württemberg. Date: 1750]

Dangerfield was studying a large knuckle bone when they entered his laboratory.

'Megalosaurus,' Alixia observed, 'theropod of the Jurassic.'

'Great lizard, a fitting name, better than Brookes' *Scrotum Humanum*,' Dangerfield said, putting down the specimen. 'Rufius who is this enchanting palaeontologist?'

Rufius introduced Alixia and explained how they first met.

'A dodo?' He laughed. 'Why an earth would anyone want to save that fat-arsed pigeon? I would have gone for a mammoth at least. Imagine walking one of those hairy beasts through Regent's Park!'

Alixia ignored his jibe. 'Rufius tells me you have a catalogue of other-worldly creatures.'

'My bestiary,' he said, nodding to a bookshelf lined with leather-bound tomes. 'I have made quite a study of the beasts of the dark realms.'

'Dark realms?' Alixia sounded unconvinced. 'You honestly believe that there are other dimensions?'

Dangerfield nodded. 'I do, and I can prove it!'

He took down a canopic jar from one of his shelves and shook out the metal coins onto the bench. Rufius stepped back, recognising them immediately — they were the talismans of the Emperor Qin Shi Huang

'It's all right,' Dangerfield reassured Rufius waving one hand. 'I've managed to neutralise the creature.'

He handed each of them a coin. 'I have tested the metal, it's quite unique. I believe that it must originate from another reality.'

Alixia pulled off one of her gloves with her teeth and stroked the metal disc with her thumb. Her eyes widening as she opened its timeline.

'It's—' began Dangerfield

'Not another dimension,' she interrupted. 'Those are dinosaurs.'

'What?'

'This is the late Cretaceous. The beasts that you have been studying are the owners of the very bones you're examining.'

'Are you saying that those monsters used to walk the earth?' Rufius said, studying his coin closely.

Dangerfield looked confused. He picked up some of his recent sketches. They were of terrifying creatures, with armoured bodies, stunted limbs and horned skulls. 'I thought they were rejects of evolution. That somehow, their ancestors had fallen out of time and evolved in ways that even Darwin would find astonishing.'

Rufius turned to Alixia. 'How long ago?'

Alixia held up the disc. 'Over sixty-six million years ago. The metal in those coins is from a meteorite that fell to earth while these creatures still roamed the earth. The rock would have been quite a size to produce this.'

Dangerfield weighed the coins in his hand, he looked disappointed. 'Meteorites, why didn't I think of that?'

She laughed. 'Because you don't spend your days with extinct species. Their bones have lain in the ground for so long, many still don't believe they ever existed.'

'So why don't they exist now?' Rufius asked.

Alixia went over to one of Dangerfield's blackboards and wiped off his notes.

'There are a few theories about the extinction of the non-avian dinosaurs. Assuming of course that you don't adhere to Bishop Ussher's theory of the earth being created in 4004BC, or that God planted the bones of ancient creatures in the rock to test our faith.'

Rufius shrugged his shoulders, he had never heard of either.

Alixia picked up a piece of chalk and began to draw a series of parallel lines. 'There is evidence in the geologic record that shows that something very catastrophic happened over sixty-million years ago. Geologists like William Buckland have found layers of strata with little or no fossil record.' She marked the spaces above and below the lines with dashes and dots. 'Some thought it might have been Noah's great flood, which I doubt, but there is a distinct border of sediment between the Cretaceous and the Paleogene that indicates some cataclysmic event. One that may have led to the extinction of many of the land-based dinosaurs.'

'Land-based?'

'Yes, the only surviving saurians are birds.'

Dangerfield studied the board. 'So what caused this so-called extinction event?'

'That is the question that has been baffling geologists like Buckland. I think it has to have been something seismic, perhaps a huge volcanic eruption, or an external factor.'

'Like a meteorite?' Rufius suggested.

Alixia considered the idea for a moment. 'Buckland reported that there were high levels of iridium in the boundary clay. A rare metal which is abundant in meteorites, but it would have to be incredibly large, colossal, in fact, and the impact would have been enormous. No one has ever found such a crater.'

'Unless it fell into the sea,' said Rufius going over to one of Dangerfield's maps.

Alixia looked thoughtful. 'Yes, that would make sense. But awfully difficult to prove.'

Rufius tapped on the Caribbean Sea. 'I think that's why Maebh was on Morgan's ship. She was looking for something from near the site. The Tuatha are trying to summon the end of the world.'

'With what?' Dangerfield asked.

Rufius flipped the coin at him. 'A talisman made from the metal of the largest meteorite to hit the planet.'

65

TALISMAN

[Christ Church College, Oxford. Date: 1660]

Kelly was taking breakfast in the Great Hall when Rufius and Alixia found him. The seer was sitting by himself reading from a large book that had been propped up against a beer jug while devouring a plate of eggs and sausages.

'Best food in England,' he said, pushing his plate aside as they sat down.

'We have a question,' Rufius said curtly.

'Ask away, the wealth of my knowledge awaits your command.'

Alixia glanced at Rufius as if questioning the man's sanity.

'What was the oldest artefact in Rudolf's collection?'

Kelly stroked his beard while counting out various dates on the fingers of the other hand.

'I believe that would be the Löwenmensch figurine, the lion-man. It dates back to the Aurignacian culture, over thirty-five thousand years ago.'

'Upper Palaeolithic,' Alixia noted, taking out her notebook.

'What was it made from?'

'Mammoth tusk. It was found in Hohlenstein-Stadel, a cave in the Swabian Jura in Germany.' His eyes glazed over for a moment. 'Carved with a simple flint knife, it is a most wonderful piece of sculpture.'

'Not iron?' Alixia asked.

Kelly broke out of his reverie. 'No, my dear, iron was still a mystery for those cave dwellers, locked away in the rock beneath their feet.' He stamped his foot on the flagstone beneath the table.

Rufius tried again. 'What would you say was the oldest metal artefact?'

The question seemed to confuse the seer. 'Gold or Silver?'

'Iron,' snapped Alixia, raising an eyebrow at Rufius.

The man steepled his fingers over his nose and closed his eyes. 'We had a few Sumerian relics, spear tips and religious ornaments, well over four thousand years old, but not especially interesting. The iron was mostly sourced from meteorites.' He opened his eyes and held up an index finger, making circles in the air. 'It wasn't the oldest, but one of the most interesting artefacts was that of the Mayan feathered serpent, Kukulkan — that was less than two thousand years old, but the metal was truly ancient. I only ever weaved with it once, there was some great calamity in its past, it burned my hands.' He opened up his hands to show the scar of a serpent head on one of his palms.

'And this feathered serpent is still in his collection?' Alixia asked.

Kelly shook his head. 'No, his highness thought it was cursed and traded it for a sacrificial dagger from the Aztec empire of Moctezuma II. Now, that had a very different kind of history,' he said, dragging his finger up his breastbone.

'Who did he trade it with?'

'Hernán Cortés.'

'The conquistador?' Rufius exclaimed. 'The man who conquered the Aztec empire?'

66

HERNÁN CORTÉS

[Church of San Isidoro del Campo, Sevilla. Date:1550]

The mausoleum was cold and still.

A marble effigy of Cortes lay atop his tomb, carved to show him as a pious man in a simple robe, his head was propped up on a coiled serpent.

'Hard to imagine that the man who conquered the Aztecs is rotting in there,' Valtin said, taking out a crowbar.

It took both of them to move the lid. Cortes had only been dead for three years, and his semi-mummified body was still recognisable as a man. His leathery skin was nearly black, like tar, it had stretched across his bones. His mouth was gaping open as if he were about to speak. There were coins over his eyes. Spanish doubloons.

Valtin lifted his skull carefully and removed the metal serpent from beneath his head. It was covered in dust and hair, but even in the low light of their lantern, Rufius could see it was the feathered serpent of Kukulcan.

'Interesting pillow,' noted Valtin, brushing it off and

handing it to Rufius. 'I'm guessing he was trying to appease all of the gods?'

Rufius could feel the power within the iron the moment he held it. It would not be long now before Maebh would sense it too. Somehow she had found a way to connect with him. Perhaps it was to do with his blood, he didn't really care, he just knew she would come.

Alixia, on the other hand, refused to join them. She and Dangerfield were wrapped up in trying to plot the most likely time co-ordinates for the extinction of the dinosaurs.

Valtin pushed the lid back into position. 'I always imagined ending my days in the arms of a woman, preferably a large breasted whore.'

'Better to die on the battlefield with a sword in your hand,' Rufius replied, placing the statue on the floor. The sightless eyes staring blindly at him as its head rested on its coils like a snake.

'Ha.' Valtin laughed. 'You're longing for Valhalla. Not quite what I call the best choice of afterlife.'

'There are others?'

'Indeed,' Valtin nodded. 'The Egyptians believed that your heart was weighed against the feather of truth and justice, if it was found to be lighter, you could pass, but it was found to be heavier you would be devoured by the demon Ammit. The Buddhists of India, on the other hand, believe that you come back in another form — they call it reincarnation.'

'I'd come back as a wolf,' said Rufius. 'Or an eagle.'

'Hah!' scoffed Valtin. 'Are you sure? I had you down as a bull or perhaps an elephant.'

Before Rufius could reply, they heard footsteps echoing

through the vault. The slap of leather-soled boots on marble signalled someone approaching as did the dim orange glow that crept slowly along the walls.

'Here we go,' whispered Valtin, moving back into the shadows.

The stranger held a lamp ahead of them, obscuring their face. They wore a long cloak and a hat so all Rufius could see was a vague outline.

Valtin looked at Rufius, his eyes glinting in the lamp-light. 'So where's your witch?'

Rufius drew his sword.

The man was less than ten feet away now, and still, there was no sign of Maebh.

'Who goes there?' Valtin challenged the stranger, repeating it once more in Spanish.

'Hello boys,' a woman's voice said, holding the lamp up to her face and taking off her hat.

Maebh chuckled and her white teeth glowed in the light. 'You should see your faces! Two fools sitting in among the dead.' She wagged her finger like a mother chastising her children. 'Haven't been stealing from their graves have we?'

Valtin's hand went to the pommel of his sword.

'Calm yourself, soldier,' she purred. 'I isn't here to start trouble.'

Her voice was just as Rufius remembered, a mix of Jamaican patois and English with a deep, husky quality that made all the hairs on his neck stand up.

She moved towards him. 'Hello, my pretty Norseman, long time since we last met? Found yourself an older man I see.' There was something lecherous in the way her tongue ran across her teeth.

Her free hand moved towards the serpent idol. 'And you brought me a present, how kind.'

As she went to touch it, Valtin moved forward, his sword half out of its scabbard.

'Now, now.' She tutted, catching his arm and whispering something under her breath. 'That's no way to treat a lady.'

Valtin was paralysed, his eyes locked on hers.

She placed a finger in the middle of his forehead. 'Be a good bird and fly away home.'

Suddenly they were alone. Valtin had simply disappeared.

'Well now, that's better — just the two of us, all cosy.' She untied her cloak and Rufius realised she wasn't wearing anything else. Her skin was covered in runes and symbols, his eyes were drawn to her breasts and the curve of her hips. The memories of the times on the ship came flooding back.

'Magic always more powerful together,' she said, taking his hand and leading him towards the centre of the vault. 'Especially when mixed with star iron and a little fire!'

Rufius felt the connection the moment her fingers touched his, he was powerless to refuse, every fibre of his body yearned for her. He would do anything.

She put the lantern down and taking out a powder flask, drew a circle around them in gunpowder. Taking the serpent from him, she ran her fingers over its smooth surface, tracing the curves of its tail.

She smiled wickedly, holding the artefact up. 'I knew you would find it for me.'

He could already see the air distorting around the idol as it began to glow.

'Take off your clothes,' she demanded.

Unable to refuse, Rufius undressed until he was standing naked before her.

. . .

Maebh's eyes darkened and the ring of powder exploded into flames. She pushed Rufius down onto the cold ground, straddling him, then placed the idol on his chest. Chanting in an ancient tongue, her body began to move in rhythm as she wove the timeline of the ancient iron.

Phantoms took shape in the fire, the same distorted creatures that he had seen in the Great Library and in Dangerfield's study. Dragons with long leather wings, lumbering behemoths, and the vicious-toothed lizards manifested in the flames.

The fire burned with an unnatural heat, cracking the joists of the ceiling above. Rufius tried to focus on the blistering wood as waves of pleasure washed through his body.

The serpent glowed as if she were drawing all the energy from it. Her hands were blackening, but still she held onto the statue, screaming in frustration. 'More, show me more!'

He could feel the heat on his chest, burning into his skin, the pain breaking her hold on him.

He grabbed her by the hips and tried to free himself, but she was too strong.

Suddenly, the air around them went cold. Rufius's breath froze as it left his mouth and for a second he saw the faint outline of a creature's horned head surrounding hers.

'Madam!' said a man's voice, 'be so kind as to step off the boy.'

At first, Rufius thought that Valtin had returned, then he saw the gaunt face of a young man in a black suit standing just beyond the ring of fire.

He was holding something, which Rufius assumed was a weapon, but when the water hit the flames and the steam began to hiss off the hot stone floor, he realised it was a bucket.

Maebh came out of her trance, lashing out at the stranger with her long fingers and cursing him in some ancient tongue.

'Now that's quite enough of that,' he said, holding up his hand.

A small lightning bolt leapt from his fingers and struck Maebh between the eyes, she rolled off Rufius and collapsed in a heap on the floor.

The man turned away while Rufius pulled up his trousers.

'The name's Faraday,' he said, filling the awkward silence.

'Rufius.'

'Would you mind?' Faraday asked, uncoiling a length of rope. 'There is a ninety-three-point-three per cent probability that she will recover in the next two minutes. I didn't have adequate time to calculate the voltage.'

Rufius took the rope and bound Maebh's wrists behind her back, looping the remainder around her ankles so she wouldn't be able to stand.

'I'd gag her if I were you,' Rufius added.

'Good idea,' he agreed, taking out a clean, white handkerchief from his coat pocket and putting it into her mouth.

Her eyes opened a moment later, and they were full of rage. Like a trapped wild animal, she twisted and pulled at her bonds, but they didn't give. Sindri had taught Rufius to tie knots, good ones that would hold a horse still while the smith shod its feet.

Faraday opened his long coat and took a pronged metal wand from an inside pocket. Rufius could see coils of copper wire wrapped around his chest with what looked like bars of lead wedged beneath.

'Are you a warlock?' he asked.

Faraday scoffed. 'No, I'm a scientist.' He began to wind something up on the side of the wand, and Rufius noticed there were wires running from the device back into the packs on his chest.

'Electricity has a rather interesting effect on the human nervous system,' he said, pressing the Y-shaped fork into the small of Maebh's back.

Her entire body went rigid. Small arcs of blue energy rippled over her skin and she began to shake uncontrollably.

Faraday turned a dial on his chest and the shaking stopped.

'There, that should give us a little more time — at least sixteen minutes or so.'

Rufius stared at Maebh's rigid body in amazement. 'What have you done to her?'

'Physics,' said the young man, stamping out the last of the glowing embers. 'Have you never heard of Boyle? Or Galvani, Volta? Bioelectromagnetics has so many possibilities.'

'When are you from?' Rufius asked. It was obvious the man was from the frontier.

Faraday's eyes narrowed suspiciously as though he wasn't sure how much he should say. 'I think those kinds of questions can wait until we're somewhere safer. My calculations predict a seventy-six-point-five per cent chance of discovery within the next five minutes, matins is about to begin.'

Men's voices began to sing in chant somewhere above

them. 'In fact, I would say we need to leave in the next sixty seconds.'

'What about her?'

'My goal was to simply recover this,' he said, picking up the metal serpent. 'What happens beyond that has too many outcomes to be predicted accurately. Sometimes things are beyond even my capabilities.'

With that he disappeared.

Valtin returned a moment later with a squad of Dread-noughts. They all looked mystified at the trussed body of the witch.

'How?' Valtin asked, looking at her limp body.

'Not sure I can explain,' Rufius said.

Valtin picked up Gunnlogi and handed it back to Rufius. 'Take her back to Dangerfield. We'll clean up here and meet you back at the castle.'

67

WITCH

[Hohenzollern Castle, Württemberg. Date: 1750]

Maebh floated in a large glass case filled with water. Her face was covered by a mask connected to a breathing tube.

The runes on her skin were gone, washed away and her beautiful body had transformed into the shrivelled husk of an old woman. She hung suspended in the bile-green solution, her long grey hair drifting like fronds of kelp around her head — she looked like a pickled mermaid.

'It's a fixative solution,' Dangerfield explained. 'Formaldehyde and water. She's ageing so quickly I had to use preservation fluid to try and inhibit the process.'

Rufius pressed his hands against the glass. 'She can't survive in there without her hamsas. What have you done to her?'

'Ah yes, the sigils. They appeared to be a kind of glamour, retarding the signs of ageing. When I removed them, she began to return to her natural age. My best guess is that your witch is more than three hundred years old.'

'Can she hear us?'

Dangerfield pointed to a speaking tube at the end of the breathing apparatus. 'Simply speak into the funnel.'

Rufius picked up the brass cone on the end of the tube.

'Er, h-hello,' he stuttered. 'Can you hear me?'

He could hear the faint sounds of her breathing. He looked back towards Dangerfield, who simply shrugged.

'Hello, my love.' Her voice was soothing and calm, like a cool wind on a warm day. 'Have you come to save me? You know how much I detest the water.'

'Yes,' he lied, 'but first I need you to tell me something.'

'Certainly, my dear, what would you like to know? Your future? I have seen the many ways it could turn.'

'I have seen the future.' He sighed. 'I know Ragnarök is coming.'

Her laugh sounded hollow and distant through the tube. 'My, how the boy has grown! You be a man now eh? Telling Maman Brigitte the fate of the world!'

'Did you know?'

'The Tuatha know everything.'

'And you didn't want to stop it?'

'Changing destiny is not an easy thing. It requires a lot of power.'

'The kind of power you can get from the star iron?'

She paused for a moment, letting out a long slow sigh.

'You alchemists know so little of the past. You play with your machines and your science, but it blinds you to the ways of the ancients. Your ideas of order are nothing more than an illusion.'

Her fingers touched the inside of the glass and a long nail scratched a series of lines radiating like the spokes of a wheel.

'Stop that!' ordered Dangerfield.

'From chaos comes order, it is the natural cycle. The world cannot continue on this path, man's reach exceeds its grasp.'

She inscribed semi-circles on the end of each line.

'Chaos brings nothing but death, why would you seek that?' Rufius asked.

'I am of the Tuatha, we know the paths beyond this mortal realm.'

'Other realms?' Dangerfield asked, becoming more interested. 'Or other times?'

'I pity you, child. You're doomed to look into the past, never knowing the true shape of things to come.'

'Tell us!' demanded Rufius, banging his fist on the glass. 'Then they will let you go.'

She made another mark on the glass and then her breathing changed, becoming shallow and wheezy. 'My time is at an end and the crow is calling me. We are but dust and shadow.'

Maebh pulled the mask from her face. Her eyes were black; a thin smile spread over her face as she looked at Rufius and took her last breath.

'Get her out!' Rufius screamed.

Dangerfield ran to the ladder that was propped against one side of the tank, while Valtin took out his axe and began to hammer on the glass wall.

Rufius watched her, unable to act. For a second, her eyes cleared, he could see the terror growing as the last of the air left her body. She held his gaze, wanting him to witness her final sacrifice. Something passed between them and suddenly she was young again, her final gift to him. The memory of how beautiful she once was.

Valtin's blows finally cracked the pane and the force of the water did the rest. The spell was broken, and the frail body of the old woman spilled out onto the floor surrounded by shards of glass and water.

It was too late, she was gone.

Dangerfield picked up the shard that held her final symbol and studied it. 'I think this looks a little like the alchemical symbol for salt.'

'No,' Rufius said, taking it from him. 'It's Vegvisir, the Norse symbol for those who are lost in storms.'

68

PROBABILIST

[Hohenzollern Castle, Württemberg. Date: 1750]

Vassili insisted that they burn her body. Rufius carried Maebh into the courtyard and placed her gently on the pyre the Dreadnoughts had built. Fire was a fitting end for Maebh, watching the flames claim her body, he half-expected demons to form around her. Nothing appeared, and yet he couldn't leave. He stayed until there was nothing but a pile of glowing ashes.

It reminded him of Isolde's funeral. That was the first time he felt the pain of loss. Too young to mourn the parents he never met, she was the nearest he had ever come to a mother. His grief was like a bottomless well, a cold emptiness reminding him that he was alone in the universe.

He didn't feel the same way about Maebh. She had tricked him, tried to use him to find the star iron, even her beauty was a pretence.

And yet capturing her had been his only chance to prove to the founder the Tuatha were real. Without her, Lord Dee was hardly going to believe the word of a Dreadnought, assuming he could be persuaded not to lock them up and throw away the key.

The sky was darkening when Alixia appeared.

'What happened? Where is the serpent?' she asked, staring at the embers.

Rufius told her about Maebh and Faraday's intervention, leaving out the details of what exactly he was doing when the stranger saved his life.

'What are you going to do next?'

Rufius shrugged. 'Find out who this Faraday is.' He turned away from the fire and walked towards Dangerfield's tower.

Alixia lengthened her stride to keep up with him. 'You said he mentioned Boyle?'

'And Galvani and Volto.'

'Volta,' she corrected, taking out her journal. 'Alessandro Volta and Luigi Galvani. You're describing men from my era. I would say Master Faraday is from early eighteen-thirty perhaps thirty-one or two. It sounds like he was employing the latest advances in electromagnetism.'

When they reached the door Rufius turned, she could still see there were tears in his eyes and his voice was strained. 'He nearly killed her. She didn't stand a chance. He could summon lightning.' Holding out two of his fingers like prongs. 'From out of the air. What kind of magic is that?'

She took his hand gently. 'When I was a child we came to London. My father took me to a demonstration at the Royal Institute. Electrical plasma makes for an impressive display of force. Which to the uninitiated, I suppose, would look very much like magic.'

Rufius snatched his hand away. 'How did he even know we would be there?'

'Yes,' Alixia said thoughtfully. 'That is rather coincidental. You said he mentioned something about probabilities and calculations?'

Rufius nodded. 'He had a book, full of tiny numbers and lines, like yours.'

Her eyes widened a little. 'A fellow student of uncertainty, a probabilist. One who calculates the possible outcomes of events.'

'But to calculate the odds of us being there at that exact time —' Rufius protested.

'Are astronomical, even with Babbage's difference engine.'

69

ELECTRICITY

[Royal Institute, London. Date: August 29, 1831]

This was his first visit to the present. The London of 1831 had changed greatly since the time of the Gunpowder plot. The roads were packed with horse-drawn carriages, and the pavements crowded with strangely dressed people rushing along streets lined with shops selling an amazing array of treasures.

Rufius followed Alixia through the bustling crowds towards the Royal Institute. She had warned him about the smell, it was overpowering, worse than Sindri's pigsty. Sweat and sewage burned his nostrils and made his eyes water in equal measure. Streams of foul water flowed along the gutters towards the River Thames. The air was thick with the scent of coal fires, as the tall chimneys of the town-houses belched out great clouds of dark, sooty smoke, staining the sky in a sickly yellow hue.

He didn't care, *this was the present*, he reminded himself. This was the frontier that Harrison had warned him about, where every second that passed was new and untravelled, and he loved the thrill of being part of the now, the moment at which the future became real.

Alixia had told him that the presentation at the Institute was a pivotal moment in the history of electricity and it was her idea to start there. She theorised that if Rufius's rescuer was a student of Volta and Galvani, then he must be the same Faraday who was the Director of the Royal Institution.

The lecture theatre was filled to capacity. Men of all ages were crammed into the tiered rows of benches. Balding old academics with white whiskers sat begrudgingly beside eager young under-graduates with pencils and notebooks at the ready.

There were no windows and the gas lamps were turned down, leaving the murmuring audience in semi-darkness.

A row of metal spheres was arranged on stands along the long wooden desk which sat at the centre of the auditorium. Behind them stood the striking figure of Michael Faraday wearing a dark velvet jacket, wing-collared shirt and black cravat.

Alixia was wrong, this Faraday was too old.

They had arrived early so that they could observe the audience while they entered, but there was no sign of the young man that Rufius had met.

'Honoured fellows of the Royal Society,' he began, his voice reaching to the back rows with ease. 'It gives me great pleasure to demonstrate to you the wonders of a most powerful force, electromagnetism.'

With a flourish, he motioned to his assistant who began to crank furiously on a handle attached to a large copper disk. Effervescent sparks of blue-white energy began to jump between the two spheres and strange metallic smell flooded the room.

There was a unified intake of breath from the crowd and Rufius could feel the hairs on his arms stand up as the effect of the equipment reached him in the furthest seats.

'The conversion of kinetic energy to electrical energy by passing a conductor through a magnetic field, producing an electromotive force. Through the laws of induction, we may harness the limitless power of the universe.' With that Faraday held a metal gloved hand aloft and they watched in awe as he brought it close to the metal spheres and arcs leapt to his fingers.

Alixia nudged Rufius in the ribs and whispered. 'Check your watch.'

Rufius took his tachyon out of his waistcoat and found that all the dials were spinning rapidly.

'As I suspected, there's something about the electromagnetic field,' explained Alixia. 'That doesn't agree with the basics of temporal mechanics.'

Rufius quickly put the tachyon away, wondering if that could explain how it disrupted Maebh's power and made a mental note to discuss it with Harrison the next time he saw him.

He missed his mentor, but he knew he couldn't return to the Order, not until he had found the answers. With Maebh gone, he had lost the best chance of finding out what the Tuatha were planning to do.

They had come forward to the frontier in the hope of finding Faraday. Alixia believed that he had predicted where and when to find Maebh using calculus, but Rufius wasn't convinced. The man had come prepared, with a magical weapon that could overpower Maebh, one that she hadn't foreseen.

And Faraday had stolen the serpent.

The older Faraday took out a small glass globe and held it out in front of him.

A small orange glow appeared inside the glass and the crowd burst into instantaneous applause as he held the light aloft.

'More witchcraft?' Rufius whispered under his breath.

'Incandescent light,' Alixia said with a smirk. 'So begins the demise of the candlemakers.'

Faraday handed his light to an assistant and turned to another of his devices.

'Now, to demonstrate a phenomenon known as mutual induction.'

70

HOOKA SMOKING CLUB

[The Hindoostane Dinner & Hooka Smoking Club, 34 George Street, Portman Square]

After they left the Institute, Alixia insisted they dine at the most unusual establishment Rufius had ever seen.

The rooms were draped in the rich oriental silks with chairs and sofas made from bamboo canes. Dark-skinned gentlemen in black suits were smoking exotically scented concoctions from pipes whose tubes wound back into large vases of water — Alixia called them 'Hookas'.

She explained that most of the clientele were former employees of the East India Company or returned officers from the colonies. Rufius wasn't really paying much attention. The aroma of cooking wafting from the kitchen was too distracting, it was making his stomach groan.

'It was him. You're sure of it?' she asked, sipping tea from a fine bone china cup.

'An older version,' Rufius said while stuffing forkfuls of delicious curried rice into his mouth.

Ignoring his table manners, Alixia opened her almanac. 'That may prove problematic. Trying to find the exact moment in his life where he intersected with yours is not a simple calculation. We may have to work backwards using a random search pattern. What age would you estimate him to be when you met him?'

Rufius tore a naan bread in half and dipped it into one of the dishes. 'At least twenty.'

Alixia did her best not to grimace and continued. 'That would be around 1815. He was an assistant working for Humphry Davy at that time. Perhaps electricity was something of a hobby in those days.'

'Why don't we start there and move forward?' Rufius suggested, spearing an onion bhaji with his fork and eating it whole.

She chewed the end of her pencil, resisting the urge to discipline him. 'Because if we approach Faraday before he's invented the device you described we could find ourselves with a paradox — literally giving him the idea.'

'What's a paradox?' Rufius asked, remembering what Kelly had said after looking in the obsidian mirror.

'In simplest terms, a consistency paradox is when an event in the future causes something in the past, which in turn is the cause of the future event. Some refer to it as a causal loop or the grandfather paradox, where one could end one's existence by killing an ancestor. These are the consequences one must consider when travelling into the past.'

Rufius looked at her blankly and then went back to his curry.

'We need to determine when this Faraday becomes

interested in correcting history,' she continued. 'I can't sit here and watch you eat. Wait here.'

By the time Rufius had finished his meal, Alixia had tracked down the right version of Faraday. While he tucked into his curry, she flitted in and out of the restaurant returning to report small snippets of information as she visited key points in the scientist's life.

'He accompanied Davy and his wife on a visit to Paris, as his scientific assistant. Meeting André-Marie Ampère whilst visiting the Institut de France.'

Rufius made a note in his almanac. 'When was that exactly?'

'1813,' she said before disappearing once more.

A few minutes later she reappeared, quite breathless. 'Actually, he met him twice. Fascinating mathematician, very interested in Faraday's work on electromagnetism. The second time was in Florence where he and Sir Humphry successfully set fire to a diamond with the burning glass of the Grand Duke of Tuscany — to prove that was made from pure carbon.'

'When?' Rufius asked through a mouth full of food.

'That would have been late in March 1814.'

And so it went on until she had found the date.

71

THE ROYAL SOCIETY

[Royal Institute, London. Date: 1815]

The clerk cleared his throat as if to excuse the interruption. 'Master Faraday. You have visitors.'

Without waiting for a response, the old man quickly turned on his heels and left Rufius, Alixia and Dangerfield standing inside the darkened laboratory.

Faraday spoke without looking up from his experiment. 'You must excuse the darkness, but the preparation of nitrogen trichloride is a delicate procedure. It is a volatile compound that is most sensitive to light, heat and even moderate shock.'

Rufius could just make out Faraday's hands as they moved between the glass flasks.

'It once blinded my mentor, Humphry Davy, and took two fingers and an eye from the eminent French chemist, Pierre Dulong.'

There was a moment's silence while he completed his task, carefully placing the finished mixture into a metal box.

Taking off his leather gloves, Faraday turned up the

lamp on his workbench. His face was younger and more innocent than the man they had seen at the Royal Institute sixteen years later. Rufius recognised him immediately.

'How may I be of service?' he asked innocently, showing no sign of recognising Rufius.

Alixia took the lead. 'We were hoping that you may be able to help us,' she said, taking out her almanac. 'We're looking for the inventor of this device.'

She held up a sketch of the two-pronged wand that Rufius had described, along with the lead batteries and copper wire strapped around a man's chest.

Faraday placed a small pair of eyeglasses on his nose, squinted at the drawing and then looked directly at Rufius.

'Ah, yes. I hardly recognised you with your clothes on.'

'My work on electromagnetism is nothing compared to that of Galvani, Ampère or Volta,' he said humbly, walking through the basement of the Royal Institute. They descended a small wooden staircase and through the kitchens until they came to a small room with a rack of experiments wired together with copper cables. 'I'm afraid my resources are rather limited, Master Davy is very strict with his expenses.'

On one of the benches stood the device that Rufius had seen him wearing in Cortés's mausoleum, and beside it was a weapon made from a series of copper tubes.

'Interesting design,' said Dangerfield, admiring the gun, which appeared to be powered by clockwork.

'Electromagnetic energy can be a powerful deterrent,' Faraday said, picking up the gun. 'In the right hands, magnetic fields appear to interfere with temporal flux, and the shock disrupts the human nervous system entirely.

Boyle has studied the effect on superficial muscle function for many years.'

Faraday thumbed a switch on the weapon and it hummed into life. Arcs of blue-white energy coursed along the barrels. The scientist turned it on Rufius.

'Now if you would be so kind as to explain exactly why you were in the tomb of Cortés with that witch?'

Rufius let his hand hover over his waistcoat pocket where his tachyon sat on a gold chain. It would only take a moment to rewind the last two minutes, but before he could act, Alixia stepped in front of him.

'We were trying to stop the Tuatha Dé.'

Faraday's eyes narrowed. 'A noble cause, but who exactly are we?'

'We are Antiquarians from the Oblivion Order, we created the British Museum,' Rufius interrupted before Alixia had time to respond. She glared at him but said nothing.

'The librarians?'

Rufius nodded. 'Among other things.'

Faraday powered down his weapon. 'We've been watching your group for some time. You have acquired a very interesting collection.'

'Our founder believes it is the only way to save the future.'

Faraday went over to a small brass orrery that sat inconspicuously in the corner of the room. He moved the planets into a certain position and the panelled wall behind him slid aside to reveal a long, low chamber filled with men working on the most unusual contraptions and mechanical instruments.

'Welcome to Solomon's House,' he said, bowing slightly. 'Apologies for the interrogation, but the Invisible College has been a closely guarded secret since the 1660s — after the restoration. The Reverend Wilkins was a very careful man.'

Rufius recognised the name, it was the warden of Wadham College, the one who had left to go to London after Charles II returned to the throne.

Along the lines of benches, craftsmen in leather aprons were grinding lenses or winding copper coils, a pungent cloud of solder hung in clouds over their desks. The quality of their work was so exceptional that Dangerfield stopped a number of times to admire it.

'How many are there of you?' Alixia asked.

'One hundred and twenty. Mostly natural philosophers, artificers and mathematicians; all good and trusted men, devoted to the pursuit of understanding the universe and its mechanics.'

Rufius touched a dial on one of the devices. 'And time travellers?'

'Actually, we prefer the term "Historians",' he said quietly so as not to be overheard. 'The Lord moves in mysterious ways. Some of us can walk into the past, while others are happy to pursue a more academic approach to our goal.'

'Which is?' asked Alixia.

'For the betterment of mankind,' Dangerfield said with a hint of sarcasm.

Faraday smiled. 'You may think it strange, sir, but by studying the mistakes of the past, can we not learn how to avoid repeating them?'

'How have you stayed hidden all these years?' Rufius wondered aloud.

'Our members thought it wiser to improve the fate of

man through science and advancement, not by trying to alter the past.'

Rufius looked confused. 'So why take the serpent?'

'A Newtonian event,' Faraday began, his smile fading. 'Our calculations have identified a number of abnormalities in the continuum, ones that appear to be working against the best interests of the future. Sir Isaac and his mathematicians have discovered key points in history that have been adversely affected by external factors.'

'Like the Tuatha Dé,' said Rufius.

'It appears so.'

72

THE COUNCIL

[Royal Institute, London. Date: 1815]

The Invisible College was overseen by a council of twenty-one men. They gathered in the 'Star Chamber' sitting in a circle like judges around the chequered tile floor. More than half were in their dotage: white-haired and balding heads nodded graciously as Faraday introduced each of them to Rufius and his friends.

Once the introductions were over, an elderly gentleman by the name of Robert Boyle, tapped his cane twice on the floor as if to bring the meeting to order. He sat in the tallest chair with a symbol of a white shield with three red lions in one quadrant carved into the panel behind his head.

'We have always known that there would be others capable of non-linear travel. Our mathematicians calculated the likelihood of your existence many, many years ago, and until now, we have proactively avoided interaction. Master Faraday's electrical fields have helped to hide us from groups such as yours. I'm sure you can understand that we are not keen to have our work exposed.'

Rufius nodded. 'The founder believes it would undermine the purpose. To be known to exist would influence the behaviour of the subject,' he quoted directly.

Boyle glanced at one of his colleagues. 'Your founder is a wise man. I take it he was the one responsible for the formation of the libraries?'

'Yes,' Rufius replied. 'The Bodleian and the British Museum.'

A murmur of approval rippled around the room.

Boyle lifted his hand to quiet them. 'Our number total no more than a hundred and twenty, but this Institute has collected the finest minds of the age; two centuries of scientific experimentation and calculation have allowed us to develop a unique set of skills and equipment. In preparation for the catastrophes that await us in the times ahead.'

'The war?' Rufius asked, assuming they had come to the same conclusion.

Boyle nodded solemnly. 'Indeed, it seems there are certain factions for whom the gift of time presents an opportunity to change the fate of the world, generally to the detriment of others.'

'Chaos agents,' said one of the council.

'None more dangerous than the witches,' said another.

'Unforeseen factors,' corrected an old man in a long grey wig.

Boyle turned towards him. 'Master Newton, would you care to demonstrate?'

'Aye,' Newton said, standing and pulling down his waistcoat over his generous stomach. 'I have spent many years developing a computational method of infinitesimal calculus. It is one based on the theories of Kepler, Descartes and of course, Copernicus. Some have said that I merely stand upon the shoulders of giants.' He eyed the room warily as if waiting for an objection. 'But nonetheless, my fluxion methods have helped us predict the time derivative that any group might have on the future.'

He went over to a wooden panel on the wall and slid it aside. In the recess beneath was a brass winding handle which he turned slowly, opening an oculus in the domed ceiling above them. A brass sphere descended on a long metal chain. Rufius could see that its surface was covered in hundreds of small glass lenses. The ceiling of the chamber was suddenly lit with thousands of pinpricks of light.

'Behold my greatest invention — the xenoscope.'

Another man, who Rufius thought might have been called Hooke, squirmed uncomfortably in his chair as if Newton had just cursed his mother.

The window shutters were closed, and in the half-light Rufius could see there was something unusual about the machine, it revolved on more than one axis, spinning internally as if multiple spheres were encased within the outer shell.

The more Rufius stared at the globe, the dizzier he became. It was as if there was some force trapped inside the mechanism trying to get out. The sensation was hypnotic.

'Do not stare directly into the light,' warned Newton, 'it has rather interesting optical qualities that have been known to drive a man out of his mind.'

Dangerfield grabbed his arm, his eyes full of wonder. 'Optical refraction!' he declared.

'Magic,' murmured Rufius.

Newton laughed. 'No, my dear fellow, simply science. We have learned to bend light to our will.'

Rufius watched as bright lines were projected across the domed ceiling, creating an intricate map — it reminded him of Alixia's journal.

'Gentlemen,' said Newton with a theatrical flourish. 'Observe the future of mankind!' He adjusted a series of dials and the timeline began to move, tracing the various paths that led to the events surrounding 1914 and then again in 1939.

'It is not one,' Alixia gasped, 'but two world wars.'

73

IRON CHANCELLOR

[University of Göttingen, Lower Saxony, Germany. Date: 1833]

The frontier was less than a month away, and Rufius could sense the difference in the world around him. Everything felt like it was newly made, even though the university buildings around him were over five hundred years old.

'Bismarck is lodging in one of those cottages,' said Faraday, pointing towards an octagonal stone two-story building that nestled against one wall.

Above the roofs of the college, the sky was growing dark. Thunder clouds were gathering on the horizon. Rufius wondered whether the storm would affect Faraday's equipment and he was glad he wasn't the one strapped into a large metal coil.

Valtin and a squad of Dreadnoughts were loitering in the shadows awaiting their signal. It felt wrong somehow that Rufius held Bismarck's future in his hands.

'Are you sure this is the only way?' he asked Faraday,

pushing his hands into his coat pockets. 'Can't we just go back and adjust some part of his childhood?'

The scientist shook his head. 'Once we alter the time-line, the Tuatha will know we exist and they will come for us. We only have one chance to put this right.'

'But he hasn't done anything wrong.'

He pulled out a notebook. 'Not yet, but he will. Our calculations show the militarisation of a unified Germany will lead to some of the worst conflicts the world has ever seen. As Chancellor, he will inadvertently cause the deaths of millions of people.'

'One life to save a million.'

'Exactly.'

The lone figure of a student wandered out from the college and made his way towards them. He swaggered like a drunk, pulling his army coat around him as the rain began to fall. Bismarck was no older than eighteen at this point, a member of the Corps Hannovera in his second year of a law degree.

'That's him,' said Faraday, signalling to Valtin.

Dangerfield had helped to negotiate the contract between Boyle and Vassili. It was a simple business transaction, one that suited both parties: the Royal Society was not willing to kill in the name of the future and the Dreadnoughts had no such qualms.

Faraday was the only member of the invisible college that volunteered to accompany them, the others were too old or unwilling to get their hands dirty. Valtin and his team, on the other hand, were only too happy to assassinate the young noble for an extortionate fee.

The idea of executing a man before he'd actually

committed a crime did not sit well with Rufius. All the men he had killed had made their choices: the cut-throats in the alley in Jorvik; the men on the battlefield, all had chosen violence and they had died in a fair fight, not put down like a lame horse.

But Newton and his statisticians were adamant that it was the only way to avoid the war. If it hadn't been for the atrocities he had seen in the obsidian mirror, Rufius would have told them to stick their calculus where the sun never shone.

Leaving the shadows, Valtin drew a nightblade, one specially coated so as not to catch the light. The other members of his squad scattered into the dark corners of the quad.

Lightning flashed across the sky, illuminating the boiling mass of clouds for a second. The rain began to fall harder, hammering down on the slate tiled roofs, and splashing off the cobbles. Rufius counted under his breath, just as Harrison had taught him, using the speed of sound to calculate the distance to the storm.

Faraday leafed through his notebook until he found a specific page. Rufius could see there were lines and notations updating continuously across it as if someone were rewriting the page every few seconds.

'All looks in order,' Faraday murmured to himself.

Valtin stalked the drunken student like a wolf, holding the blade behind his back. *He will wait for the next thunderclap*, Rufius thought, *to mask the scream.*

When the lightning came again, it was closer, and Rufius had hardly begun to count before he heard the low rumble approaching.

Valtin quickened his step, but as he did so, there was another flash of light and a ring of warriors appeared between him and Bismarck, their weapons drawn.

Rufius recognised them immediately.

It was Drake and Selephin, Valeria and Kasia — the Draconians.

The inebriated student wandered on, unaware of the fight that had broken out behind him.

Valtin's team came to his defence, Dreadnoughts and Draconians fought hand-to-hand as the storm raged above their heads. They matched each other's skills blow for blow. Rufius had never seen fighting like it, he stood in awe as the two groups went at each other.

He turned towards Faraday only to find that the man had disappeared.

Squinting through the rain, he spotted Bismarck fumbling for his key at the door to his lodgings. Faraday was only a few feet behind him.

74

CAPTURED

[Christ Church College, Oxford. Date: 1660]

The founder sat behind the desk in his office, his head bowed studying the pages of Faraday's almanac.

'If it wasn't for young Rufius here, you would all be facing a charge of unlawful manipulation of the timeline.'

Valtin scowled, crossing his arms. 'Whose law would that be?' he asked defiantly.

Faraday stood beside Valtin, glowering at Rufius. The bruise purpling across his jaw where he had knocked him down.

'Those of our Order,' the founder declared, putting down the notebook and standing up. He seemed taller than usual as if a weight had lifted from his shoulders.

'For too long now you have abused your powers,' he said, looking directly at Valtin. 'Stealing artefacts to order, with no thought of the consequences. The past is not some storehouse for you to plunder as you see fit.'

He turned towards Faraday, holding up the notebook.

'And you sir, while your intentions are admirable, I'm afraid Newton's calculus is flawed.'

Faraday went to protest, but the founder held up his hand and continued. 'You do not have the faculties or mechanisms to calculate all the possibilities. The death of Bismarck would have led to a cascade of events that would have resulted in something far worse than the wars you were trying to avoid.'

Valtin sneered. 'So you say, but you have no proof. This is nothing but theoretical gibberish. You have no authority over the fate of mankind, you're not god.'

Drake's hand went to the hilt of his sword.

The founder nodded his head. 'That is true. I agree we are all making assumptions about the future. To consider every possibility of our actions is too great a task for one man alone. Which is why we have not chosen to act thus far, but when we do, I want to be sure we have considered every potential outcome, every possibility.'

'And the war?' Faraday asked, 'will you be able to avoid it?'

The founder sighed, turning towards the large window that looked out of Christ Church meadow. 'I'm not sure we can, but perhaps if we worked together, we might find a way.'

'Do we have a choice?' snarled Valtin.

'There are always choices,' replied the founder. 'But history shows us that those who work together are stronger. We all have unique skills, our sum would be greater than their parts.'

The manacled Dreadnought scoffed. 'You want us to join you?'

'Better that than die alone in some forgotten temple,' said Rufius.

Valtin shook his chains. 'Better to die a free man!'

The founder frowned. 'But are you truly free? From what Rufius has told me you are bound to a master.'

'One that pays,' he said, smiling.

'And where will you spend this wealth? In the pleasure gardens of Babylon? Or among the courtesans of Corinth? Hardly a legacy to be remembered for. I am offering you the chance to save the future — to leave a legacy that your children will be proud of. Come with me, I think there is something you all should see.'

75

THE ENGINE

The room was lit by a single bright object standing on a pedestal in the middle of the tiled floor. The glow from the sphere flickered and pulsed as though it were constantly renewing itself, nearing the object Rufius thought it might be full of fireflies.

'This is an Infinity Engine,' explained the founder, the light brightening as he placed his hands on each side of the ball.

Ribbons of energy began to flow from the sphere, arcing out like lightning around the chamber. Rufius looked on in awe as the room filled with stars. Each incandescent point traced lines, stretching and branching across his vision. Narrowing his eyes, he thought he could see tiny notes and symbols attached to clusters of them.

'I have designed the engine to be a computation model of our current timeline — the continuum. It uses a predictive algorithm to calculate the future based on past events.' Dee moved his hand, and the entire model turned around them. Glowing dots, like astral constellations, shifted and contracted until they could see the entire timeline, like a vast branching tree. Rufius could see the point where the future met the present, an uncountable number of branches all knitting together to form the frontier.

'With this engine, I believe we can begin to study the course of the past and make judgements on the best actions to take. Simulate the possible outcomes before we change the course of history. I believe this will be our best hope for saving humanity.'

Valtin stared into the light, trying to catch the strands with his fingers.

'What kind of witchcraft is this?'

The founder smiled. 'Not witchcraft, just a technology that you cannot comprehend.'

'And the Great War?' asked Faraday.

'There are many possibilities,' the founder said, moving his hands to change the perspective of the holographic model. It zoomed and expanded until the whole projection was focused on one particular event.

'The engine is best used to predict the effect on large populations. Here, for instance, close to 1916, is the conflict I believe you saw. A war between Germany and its allies Austria-Hungary and Italy fought against the combined armies of France, Britain and Russia. It resulted in the deaths of millions and the downfall of four monarchies as well as a revolution in Russia.'

Valtin watched the weaving strands separate and branch into each other. 'How can a machine know this?'

The founder expanded the event further until they could see that each point was made up of thousands of lines of formulae scrolling across the walls around them. 'This is the prime algorithm, the mathematical model that approximates the motivations of humanity.'

Faraday's eyes widened, pointing at various lines in the

equations. 'Yes, I can see the underlying factors. This represents the escalation in militarism as the countries try to outgun each other, while here we have the alliances between the various factions — and this branch simulates the rise of imperialism.'

'So you knew about the war?' Rufius said.

'To a certain extent, yes, but there are a number of outliers. Chaos elements that caused it to fail. They were beyond the capabilities of my algorithm.'

'The Tuatha Dé?'

The founder nodded. 'You have been my strange attractor. I needed someone to operate outside of the norms. To find my outliers and help me neutralise them.'

Rufius didn't know what to say, he stared at the dancing lines and tried to understand what was going on.

Lord Dee continued. 'Worst of all is that you couldn't know. If I had told you of my plans, then the Tuatha would have become aware of them too. Once you had met with the sea witch, your fate was sealed. Your actions had to be entirely your own.'

'You knew?' Rufius repeated, the realisation slowly sinking in. 'All this time, and you left me to fend for myself?'

'I have never been far from your side,' Dolovir said, stepping out of the shadows.

'Nor have I,' said Alixia, coming to stand next to him.

The founder took his hands away from the engine and the model disappeared. 'The Tuatha's precognitive abilities have meant we couldn't take an active part in finding them. It had to be unpredictable, a role that you have played so very well.'

'And now?'

'The Tuatha are relentless. Their plans to release the destructive power of the meteorite will put humanity back thousands of years. I have no doubt they will have found another piece of star iron to replace Cortés's Serpent. The Spanish Conquest was nothing if not efficient in the plundering of Meso-American treasure. Master Kelly has volunteered to open a sympathetic link through the talisman to locate them, and thanks to Master Faraday's galvanic weapons, we may just have a chance of defeating them and securing the future.'

76

KELLY

'How many pieces are there?' the founder asked, pointing to the serpent on his desk.

'Of this iron?' Kelly replied, his eyes closed as his fingers stroked the iron statue. 'Only five or maybe six.'

'Is it five or six?'

'Six.'

'And the Tuatha have all of the others bar this one?'

Kelly frowned as he explored the timeline. 'They have found the others, yes. This is the last piece. I can feel them searching for it.'

'Increase the current,' Lord Dee instructed Faraday.

Blue sparks leapt from Kelly's fingers as he lifted them from the statue.

'Interesting sensation,' said the alchemist, rubbing his hands. 'Not one I would care to repeat.'

'So the Tuatha are aware of its existence,' Dee said to himself.

'Can't we keep it locked away in Faraday's vault?' Rufius asked.

The founder shook his head. 'While any of these talismans exist, they will always prove to be a temptation. The power of that event is too great for them to ignore. We must end this once and for all. I need to know where and when they are?'

'But my lord!' Kelly protested. 'The Tuatha travel along the shadow paths, those ways can lead to madness.'

'You are no stranger to those paths,' Lord Dee insisted. 'Find them.'

Kelly placed his hands tentatively on the serpent once more, wincing at the shocks from the static charges.

His eyes rolled back into his head. Ribbons of energy unwound from the idol as he wove deeper into its past.

He began to mumble. Incoherently at first, the random nonsensical phrases of a madman. One hand lifted from the idol and began to swat at flies. Rufius glanced at Dolovir, who simply shrugged.

The founder seemed untroubled by the ramblings, but leant in close to Kelly's ear and asked: 'What do you see?'

'There are many ways, too many to count. I can feel their eyes upon me. They listen between the ticks of the clock.

77

FORTRESS OF SHADOWS

[Isle of Skye, Scotland. Date: 1302]

Dunscaith was a granite-walled fortress that had stood for years against the harsh storms and howling gales of Northern winters. Carved out a rocky promontory, it dominated the grey seas that surrounded it, the towers rising like talons into the storm clouds that covered the sky.

'I bloody hate Scotland,' complained Valtin, blowing into his hands and stamping his feet.

Standing on the brow of a gorse-covered hill, they felt the icy wind rise off the Loch, driving them back off the bluff.

'And what is it with these kilts?' he added, holding down the plaid skirt the Draconians had insisted they wear.

Rufius watched him walk back through the portal and into the camp beyond.

The shadow path was being held open by one of Faraday's devices: two long copper rods formed an arch which created a door into another time. It had been the only way to reach this time without alerting the witches. Dangerfield had been fascinated by it until he received a near-lethal electric shock and had to be taken to the medica.

There was a strange feeling when Rufius passed through the field as if thousands of ants were crawling over his skin. Faraday called it 'magnetic resonance', it lasted for less than the time it took to take a step, but it was still disconcerting.

They had deployed their forces over a century earlier, cloaking the entire camp with the same magnetic shielding that Faraday had used at the invisible college, and it seemed to be working. There was no sign that the Tuatha were aware of their presence. Rufius avoided the founder's tent where he knew Lord Dee and the various leaders were planning the attack.

It was summer on this side of the portal, and the sky was only just beginning to darken. A fire had been lit, and the Draconians and Dreadnoughts were gathered around drinking and swapping stories.

Kelly was sitting amongst them playing the fool. He was acting strangely, more than usual. Rufius assumed he was still affected by his time in the shadow paths. Even though he had located the Tuatha and proved his worth, his eccentric character had done little to change Dee's opinion of the alchemist, and it certainly didn't help when he claimed to be able to converse with angels.

Like a court jester, he entertained the soldiers, conjuring coins from out of thin air or from inside their ears. They all seemed to be enjoying his company and an uneasy truce had grown between the two groups. The Dreadnoughts were having a hard time coming to terms with the rules of the Order, and the Draconians had not forgotten their crimes.

. . .

'The Crow,' Kelly said, waving his fingers in front of his face like bird wings. 'Now, there is only one that goes by that name — the phantom queen, Morrígan.'

'You alchemists are all the same,' said Valtin, taking a long drink from a wineskin. 'You're all dabbling in the dark arts.'

'Do not judge us by the deeds of others,' quoted Kelly, holding up a finger.

Valtin spat into the fire, making it hiss. 'They seek the secrets of the dead.'

Kelly took something from his pocket and threw it into the flames. The fire changed colour instantly, burning a fierce blue-green. The crowd gasped in unison and sat back a little, half expecting something to leap out at them.

When it returned to normal, they clapped and asked for more.

'Witchcraft,' Valtin sneered.

Kelly opened his hand to show him a set of blue gemstones. 'Simply powder of Blue Vitriol. White Arsenic will do the same.'

As Valtin turned to respond, Selephin, who was very drunk, picked up a lute and started to sing. He was so bad that everyone quickly joined in.

Rufius continued towards Faraday's tent. He could see the blue glow of a plasma cannon shining through the seams. Pulling back the flap, he was met by the illuminated faces of a rather mystified group of Dreadnoughts all watching Faraday demonstrate its capabilities.

'Do you think this can stop them?' asked Dangerfield.

'With this weapon, we stand as good a chance as any,'

replied Faraday, handing the gun to him. 'You'll find the electromagnetic field will disrupt most, if not all, of their abilities.'

'Most?'

'In tests, it has proven to be over eighty-per-cent effective.'

'On witches.'

'On test subjects.'

Dangerfield tried to hoist it onto his shoulder but failed and nearly dropped it.

'How many witches have you tested it on?' asked one of the others.

Faraday looked directly at Rufius. 'One.'

Someone laughed, it was Valtin. He was standing at the back of the tent and Rufius realised that he must have followed him. He walked over to Dangerfield and took hold of the device. It was a complex set of tubes and wires, made from components that would travel safely back through time without degrading.

'What's the range?'

'Thirty feet,' answered Faraday. 'Longer if you lower the voltage. It's exponential.'

Valtin weighed it in his hands. 'Too heavy,' he said, throwing it back to Dangerfield and drawing his sword. 'This is the only weapon I trust, can you get me close enough to use it?'

'I'm not sure a blade will have any effect,' Faraday said nervously, moving the point away from his chest. 'But I may be able to adapt it if you wouldn't mind.' He put out his hand to take the weapon.

The Dreadnought laughed, sheathed his sword and walked out of the tent.

Rufius could hear him muttering as he passed.

'Don't trust them. They hide their technology away from the world like a miser and his gold.'

Later that night, Rufius was helping Harrison to hand out tachyons to the men when Kelly came skipping out of the shadows, the collar around his neck glowing in the darkness.

'What say you, good people? Shall we ride down the moonbeams and dance on their graves?'

The others looked at him as if he were insane. Rufius had noticed there were moments when he would say the oddest things. Dolovir's implanted memories recognised a few of the phrases from the works of a sixteenth-century playwright by the name of William Shakespeare, but others were totally obscure.

The founder appeared at the door to his tent. Vassili, Drake and Boyle followed, and each went their own way without another word. Boyle opened his tent, and Rufius could see the interior of the Royal Institute. Newton was waiting on the other side and behind him were the rest of the council. Drake went over to join the men at the fire and Vassili simply disappeared.

Lord Dee motioned for him and Harrison to enter, and Kelly trailed in behind.

The interior of the founder's quarters was far larger than they appeared. It seemed as if they were standing in a grand drawing-room. A long mahogany table ran down the centre of the room, and the Infinity Engine sat on a pedestal in the centre.

'We have come to an agreement with Boyle, though I'm not sure Newton will concur,' he said, looking over his shoulder to check they were alone. 'The man is quite insufferable. It's obvious that most of the xenoscope was the work of Master Hooke.'

'Electricians,' said Kelly, as if it were a curse.

'Master Kelly,' the founder said, his eyes widening at the glowing collar. 'What on earth are you wearing?'

Kelly took off the glowing torc and the blue field faded. 'An energy field of sorts, Lord. Master Faraday believes it will protect from the worst of the witches powers. It's rather a strange sensation as if one is wearing a suit of feathers. Quite exhilarating. Would you like to try?'

'No, thank you,' replied the founder, shaking his head.

'The Dreadnoughts have something that may prove more useful,' the founder said, pouring himself a large glass of brandy. Kelly helped himself.

'Are we sure this is the only way?' Harrison asked.

The founder sighed, picking up the now inert golden sphere. 'I have studied this scenario for countless days and nights. The Tuatha are too chaotic, too dangerous to be allowed access to such power. They cannot be reasoned with, the future is at great risk while they still live.'

'But sire, they have so much potential, surely their ability to look into the future could be harnessed?' pleaded Harrison.

'The future cannot be known, only predicted. How are we to be sure that the path they see is the true one? As I'm sure Master Kelly will agree, there is never one single path.'

'Too many to count,' agreed Kelly, holding up his fingers.

'The destruction from an extinction-level event would throw the earth back into another ice age, setting humanity back thousands if not millions of years. I'm not sure we would even survive it. It is hardly a rational alternative.'

'And the wars?'

'Millions will die, yes. But we will endure it.'

'A terrible price to pay,' reflected Harrison.

78

BATTLE

In the gloom of pre-dawn, they moved in silence across the dewy grass. A hundred men or more, each one covered in a subtle shimmering field of blue energy, crept quietly towards the fortress of shadows.

Rufius had been ordered to stay at the back with Faraday's engineers and help carry the spare batteries. He had hoped to join the vanguard along with a hand-picked team of Dreadnoughts and Draconians, but both Dolovir and the founder had refused. He was still a boy in their eyes, and it was only after Faraday requested his assistance that he was allowed to join the attack at all.

The heavy battery packs weighed him down, making his temporal armour chafe against his skin. Its leather seams were stiff and inflexible, and even though they had been training in them for weeks, they still showed no sign of give. Threaded through the outer layers was a fine copper matrix of wires. An electrical grid that Faraday assured him would hide them from the witches' prescience as well as dealing a shock to anyone who struck him with metal. They called them 'static suits', because of the discharge they gave off whenever two of them came too close to each other. It had been a novelty at first, to zap one another with blue lightning, and more than one Dreadnought found themselves in the infirmary with strangely ornate-looking burns.

In the distance, Rufius could make out the glimmer of the stasis field. Faraday had taken a team of electricians out in the middle of the previous night, to install a string of temporal beacons beneath the formidable walls of the castle. They returned spooling long cables behind them and attached them to Faraday's 'Leyden piles', which were huge stacks of lead and other metals that had been sunk into a nearby bog.

The air around the beacons distorted and rippled, the energy making the hairs on their arms stand up as they approached. Faraday had tried to explain to Rufius about how his beacons would prevent the witches from leaving this area of time, effectively trapping them in a loop of one day. He had made a joke about how it was going to be like 'catching fish in a barrel,' but Rufius wasn't convinced it was going to be that easy.

A volley of huge blue fireballs roared over their heads and the men instinctively ducked as the first artillery barrage was launched. This signalled the beginning of the assault. Designed to neutralise the watchmen on the battlements, the enormous spheres of energy exploded against the granite walls of the castle and released a charge that made every one of the guards' bodies dance like a children's marionette.

. . .

Time seemed to accelerate as Rufius was pulled along in the rush towards the castle walls. More plasma bombs raced through the cloudless sky above them. The men around him were breathing heavily as they ran down the slope and ahead of them he could see Vassili's Dreadnoughts climbing the slick stone walls, ropes trailing behind them as they hoisted themselves over the top.

Faraday called his team to a halt. They were less than ten yards from the 'killing zone,' just out of range of any of the enemy's weapons. He ordered his team to make ready and everyone set about unbuckling their loads. Shirking off the lead pack, Rufius felt like he was floating. His shoulders ached where the straps had bitten into the muscle and he was happy to be free of the burden.

They were the rearguard. Men opened long wooden boxes and began to construct their 'Long' guns which were mostly composed of thin copper tubes with intricate arrays of ringed coils along their length. Once mounted onto a tripod, the long gun would require three men to operate: one took charge of the firing, the other two maintained the batteries, each of their backpacks was nothing more than miniature Leyden pile.

While Faraday was distracted with organising the cannons, Rufius found himself free to join the main attack. The second wave was heading for the rope ladders, which were being lowered down from the top of the wall by the vanguard. By the time anyone noticed he was gone, Rufius was climbing over the crenellations.

The courtyard was a sea of swords.

Vassili and the first wave were fighting hand-to-hand against the remaining guards. They were fierce warriors who wore no armour, their skin painted blue like that of the *Draugr*, which the sharpest weapons failed to penetrate. Rufius watched Valtin cleave at the head of one giant, only for his sword to bounce off the man's skull. Faraday was right; steel alone was not effective against the power of the Tuatha. The guard reminded him of the *jotun* he had slain at the battle on the Catalaunian Plain, and a chill ran down his spine when he realised the Tuatha were able to raise the dead.

Rufius drew Gunnlogi, feeling the force of its history running through its grip. Faraday had offered to enhance his sword, but like Valtin, he had refused. Gunnlogi had enchantments of its own, but he wasn't about to waste them on the ground troops. Instead, he focused his efforts on reaching the inner keep. He had to find the Tuatha before they invoked Ragnarök.

Moving swiftly between the warriors, Rufius ducked and weaved through the melee. The *Draugr* were unnaturally strong. Parrying a blow from a heavy iron club, Rufius felt his hand go numb as the shock rippled up his arm. A wall of undead surrounded the keep, and he lost sight of it as they flooded into the yard.

His foot caught on the shield of a dead Dreadnought, and he fell.

Crawling across a floor littered with bodies and discarded armour, he scrambled over the pallid corpse of a decapitated guard and found himself back where he started. It was clear that the vanguard was never going to break through their defence, all the Draugr simply had to do was hold them back long enough for the Tuatha to summon the extinction event, and it would be over.

Rufius watched as a beast of a man, standing nearly seven feet tall and half as broad, grabbed Valtin by the neck, lifting him off his feet. The ghoul's eyes were hollow, empty sockets and a black liquid drooled from his lips as he shook the Dreadnought like a rag doll.

Rufius slowed his breathing, just as Vassili has taught him. He cleared his mind and opening the sword's timeline. He could sense every blow it had ever struck, every wound it had ever inflicted. He sought out one specific event, finding the dagger blows that had ended Caesar, and he focused on them. Time slowed as he leapt into the air, his sword arm became a blur as he executed twenty-three near-instant attacks on the jotun.

The man dropped Valtin and toppled over like a stone statue.

'What the devil do you call that?' Valtin said as Rufius helped him out from under the corpse.

'The death of Caesar,' Rufius said with a wry smile.

Valtin looked slightly confused but nodded his thanks.

'We need to rethink our attack,' said Rufius.

'The weapons are useless against the undead, we're not going to last much longer,' Valtin said, picking up a second sword and grimacing. 'No large-breasted whore for me.'

'I have an idea,' said Rufius, looking up at the menacing keep looming over them like a dark monolith.

Valtin followed his gaze.

'You're not thinking of going in there alone?'

'The Tuatha have brought these men back from the dead.' He began to unbuckle his chest plate. 'Until we kill them, they won't stop.'

. . .

Valtin helped him out of his armour. Rufius needed to be fast and agile, and the heavy leather was more of a hindrance. Free of the protective plasma field he could feel the chill of the dawn through the rough cotton tunic.

Picking up his discarded belt, he sheathed his sword and strapped it over his shoulder. There was a cry from above as men from the second wave came over the wall. The remaining members of the vanguard cheered, but it would be short-lived if Rufius couldn't reach the keep.

'Take this,' Valtin said, handing him one of Dangerfield's time bombs.

Rufius weighed the device in his hand. It was similar to the one in the library, but with only three jewels around its equator.

'No safety margin,' Valtin noted. 'No chance of escape.'

Staying in the shadow of the curtain wall, he moved away from the second wave as they descended into the fight.

The first rays of dawn hit the top of the tower, painting it gold, as he searched the walls for any sign of an entrance, but there was no obvious way in. It was the perfect stronghold, one that could only be entered from underground.

The tower was over a hundred feet tall, made from smooth stone with little in the way of handholds. Dead bodies of men from the first wave lay crumpled around him. The ropes, grappling hooks and the pitons they had used to scale the outer walls still wrapped around them.

Rufius carefully removed a set of spiked boots, climbing gloves and a line and hook from one of the men and made his way back up the battlements.

He would need height, the grappling iron would have to

reach the roof of the keep if he was going to have any chance of getting any purchase.

The parapet was clear, everyone had come over the wall. Rufius could see Faraday's men protecting the escape route, their cannon bursts holding back wave after wave of undead that rose out of the moor.

They hadn't known what the Tuatha would use as a defence, but they had planned for some kind of reinforcements — Vassili had assumed it would be Druids, but Drake had disagreed, Faraday had told Rufius that the Dragon had warned them how many battles had been fought here. Long dead warriors were being summoned from the bogs and unmarked graves in their hundreds. Faraday's orders were to keep them away from the castle long enough for them to get inside the keep.

Rufius turned his back on the battlefield and lifted the hook. Swinging it over his head, he slowly let out more line until it was less than twenty feet from the keep and angled its arc up and into the darkening sky.

The hook disappeared over the top of the keep and Rufius held his breath, feeling the rope slip quickly through his gloved hand.

A flash of lightning lit up the sky, illuminating a swarm of clouds that were fast approaching from the sea. Harsh winds swept over him, bringing with them the smell of rain. The line went slack and the hook fell back down to earth. He knew he had one more chance before the storm would be on them.

Gathering up the hook once more, he swung the line harder and faster than before, this time loosing it just before it reached the stone of the keep. Lightning fractured the sky, allowing Rufius to watch the trajectory of his throw as it sailed over the top of the tower.

This time it caught. He pulled down on the rope and felt the iron hook bite into the granite.

Twisting the rope around his arm, he leapt out in the air, feeling the first drops of rain on his face as he jumped.

Time slowed as he crossed the space, the stone wall turned slick with water as he flew towards it. He bent his legs to take the impact, feeling the spikes of his boots skitter on the hard, wet stone. He looked up the slippery wall above him, letting the cool rain wet his face. *This was no ordinary storm*, he thought. He could sense it, there was something unnatural about the way the clouds were moving.

Gripping the knotted rope with both hands, he began to climb.

79

RITUAL

The rain made it hard going, and it took him half of an hour to scale the wall. By the time Rufius reached the roof, his arms felt like lead, and his hands were blistered and sore despite the gloves. He wasn't going to be able to hold a sword, let alone fight someone with it.

The fighting below was relentless. Rufius could hear the cries of the wounded as he climbed — it had given him the strength to keep going, knowing the sooner he reached his goal, the sooner they could be saved.

The roof had four small turrets at each corner. There were doors in the west and east towers, and Rufius headed for the nearest.

Taking off his boots and gloves, he started down the winding stairs into the keep. His bare feet making no sound on the smooth stone steps, he descended silently through the floors until he reached the second storey.

The sounds of chanting rose up to meet him. A chorus of incantations echoed across the chamber. Singing in an ancient tongue, the voices rose and fell as if trying to find the right pitch or frequency to harmonise with the relics.

Rufius kept his back to the wall until he reached an arched doorway. Peering around the edge, he saw the Tuatha sitting around a fire. In the centre of the round chamber was a large brazier full of glowing coals, surrounded by seven throne-like chairs. Metal cages hung from the ceiling, the emaciated bodies of half-dead prisoners lay slumped within.

Each of the witches held an iron idol, some were crude pagan designs while others were intricately carved like the feathered serpent.

One chair was empty. *Maebh's seat*, thought Rufius.

The air above the fire began to distort, blistering like a bubble as their chanting found its resonance. Rufius could see the outlines of terrible creatures come and go in the flames, he could feel the chaos energy flowing as they reached into the extinction event.

The fire took on a new lease of life, and the heat became so intense that Rufius could see the skin of the Tuatha begin to blacken, yet none cried out or dropped their artefact, nor did they take their eyes away from the portal that was expanding above the fire.

A vision of a comet streaking across the night sky appeared at the centre of the distortion. An enormous glowing ball of rock, it tumbled end-over-end towards the earth, its rocky surface turning to molten glass as it entered the atmosphere.

The artefacts they held began to glow with the same intensity, smoke rising from their hands. Suddenly, one of the witches burst into flame, her body flaring like a human torch. She screamed as the flames engulfed her and Rufius watched as the tail of the comet was drawn out of the swirling vortex, fiery tentacles reaching out to embrace her.

The body of the first witch was changing, its charred husk suspended in mid-air, smoke pouring out of the hollow sockets of its skull.

Two more witches followed, and then a third.

The room began to lose its shape as the aperture grew in size. The chaos energy distorted the floor, the boards buckled, and the walls seem to twist in on themselves.

Rufius took out Dangerfield's device and primed it. Holding it close to his chest, he edged into the room, feeling the super-heated stone against his back. There were only two priestesses remaining, and he knew he had to detonate the device before the last of them joined the maelstrom of ash and smoke in the centre of the ritual.

The room began to shake violently, making his teeth rattle. The comet was nearing land, he could see the vague outline of a coast. Rufius recognised it from Morgan's charts, it was over the Caribbean and heading for the Gulf of Mexico. An island nestled in the glittering blue sea off the Yucatan peninsula and the meteorite was heading directly for it.

Another witch caught fire. Her screams snapping Rufius out of his reverie.

With only seconds before the impact, he threw Dangerfield's device into the centre of the room just as the last of the Tuatha ignited.

The device exploded like a star, bright white light filled the room and for a second, time seemed to stop altogether.

He felt the force of the blast wave hit his chest, pushing him back through the wall as if it were made of paper, and out into the cold night air.

Falling backwards towards the ground, he watched the keep crumble and fold in on itself as if some god were unmaking it.

80

MORRÍGAN

Rufius woke to find himself in the courtyard surrounded by dead bodies. The lifeless corpses of *Draugr* lay entangled with the fallen Dreadnoughts and Draconians, their blue skin turning black after the bomb had ended the Tuatha's control.

The ruins of the keep smouldered into the cloudless sky, a serene silence lay over the scene, nothing moved, and for a moment Rufius wondered if anyone else had survived.

He tried to lift his head, but the effort made him dizzy. His chest felt as he had just gone ten rounds with Hagar.

Staring up into the dawn, he listened for any sign of movement, keeping his breathing shallow, his ears strained for the smallest sound.

Minutes passed like hours before he heard the scraping of armour on stone. Out of the corner of his eye, he could see men getting to their feet like drunks after a heavy night in the mead hall. Dazed and confused, the remnants of the army shook off the dead weight of the enemies and rose.

Rufius forced himself to sit up. The pains in his hands and arms reassuring him that he was still alive.

He recognised a few of those nearest to him, they stared at the inert Draugr with disbelief, poking them with the ends of their swords to make sure it wasn't some kind of trick.

Slowly the realisation sank in, and smiles broke out across their faces. Then they were cheering, raising their weapons and hollering at their hard-won victory.

Faraday and Dangerfield found him and helped him to his feet. Both were battered and bruised, but still in better condition than Rufius. As was Valtin when he was found trapped under a heap of bodies.

'What happened to you?' Dangerfield asked, looking at Rufius.

Rufius looked at his hands, they were blackened with soot and he assumed so was his face. He was about to explain when he noticed the smoke from the smouldering keep was acting strangely.

It curled in unusual patterns, creating swirls and eddies like the wake of a boat.

Something was still alive in there, he thought, *one of the Tuatha has survived.*

His mouth was dry, and his voice hoarse when he cried out a warning.

She rose from the ashes like a black Valkyrie. Her raven-like wings shaking off the rubble and dust.

Emerging from the ruins, Morrígan's eyes burned red with rage. She raised one of her hands, and every man in the courtyard froze. Held like statues, Dreadnoughts and Draconians stood hopelessly enthralled by the Phantom Queen.

She moved among them like a wraith, drifting through the air, slicing their throats open and drinking their blood.

'You men, always needing to know how things work!' she ranted. 'As if the universe were some kind of clock to be dismantled. You toy with powers that you cannot begin to understand.'

She stopped when she reached Rufius.

It seemed as if her eyes were full of stars. Dark orbs of oily black that swirled with pinpricks of light.

'You have condemned mankind to a terrible fate,' she hissed, her sharp fingernails leaving traces of blood along his cheek. 'A thousand years of war and suffering await them.'

Rufius couldn't speak. Every muscle strained to be free of her spell, but she had bound him with an incantation that left him paralysed, his body refusing to respond to his will.

Morrígan leaned in towards him, so close that he could smell her charred skin. Beneath the burns, he could see a dense pattern of runes, newly etched glyphs were glowing, healing her damaged body. When she spoke, he could smell the blood on her breath, see the dark red stain on her lips.

Her nose twitched as she sniffed at his skin, and she recoiled. 'I smell Maebh on you man-child. You reek of her.' Her lips twisted into a snarl, exposing long pointed teeth. 'Did you end my sister?'

There was something in the way she spoke that compelled Rufius to tell her, to move his lips and make sounds, even though the answer would lead to his death.

'Your words are too clumsy,' she stopped him, wrapping her long fingers around his neck and pressing one of the sharp nails into his vein. Rufius felt the blood pulse as she stooped to drink from the wound.

Her mind entered his like a cold shard of ice, slipping between the layers of his consciousness, she began to sift through his memories.

Diving deeper into his timeline, he felt her opening his past. She raced through the last few weeks, searching for the moment of Maebh's death. She screamed at the sight of her sister's withered body in the water tank, sharing the pain and grief of her loss with him until he wept.

But she didn't stop — she went further back, finding their time together on the ship, the moments of passion that they had shared on the ship. Experiencing it through her eyes, he realised that the lovemaking had been nothing more than a way to keep Maebh young, she had drawn on his energy — replenishing herself.

'You have hidden talents. Where did you come by these?' Morrígan whispered into his ear.

Digging deeper into his past, to the time before the founder, he found himself back in the village working as Sindri's apprentice.

Further still, until the day that Eric Bloodaxe found him in the wood, wrapped in a small bundle of rags.

81

MOTHER

[Dunfermline Palace, Fife. Date: 1325]

They appeared in the chamber of a castle. Two infant boys lay coddled among furs in a wooden cot, tiny fingers reaching out for a small metal cross that dangled above their bed.

Morrígan's head slowly twisted around, scanning the nursery. 'Where is she?' she hissed, 'where is that whore of a mother who bore you?'

Rufius stared down at the children, they were identical, he realised that he must have a twin.

'Morrígan, I should have known,' said a woman, stepping out from the shadows. She was dressed in a long courtly gown, her hair pinned with pearls, but there was something hard behind her eyes.

'Praetorian,' Morrígan hissed.

'Kindly move away from my sons,' the woman said in a strong Irish accent, drawing a dagger from her belt. Rufius noticed the symbols etched along its blade which looked similar to the ones on Gunnlogi.

The blade disturbed Morrígan, she shrank away from the cot. 'How long do you intend to bind me here?'

The woman laughed. 'Until the ninth wave,' she said, tapping on a symbol on the wall. Rufius noticed that the same mark had been drawn on every flagstone on the floor.

The Phantom Queen sneered, her hands moving in strange circles, drawing invisible signs in the air as if she were trying to cast a spell.

'You sacrificed your own child to lure me here?'

'He was protected,' the woman said, holding out one hand towards Rufius. 'His destiny is a strong one.'

Rufius took her hand. Something about her smile was familiar, he felt a connection to the stranger.

The old witch laughed, a dry cackle, like wind in old leaves. 'So you married the man you were sworn to protect and gave him twins. How does your king think the boy dies?'

The woman raised the dagger. 'That is none of your concern. Your time in this world is at an end.'

Morrígan laughed, raising herself to her full height and extending her black wings. 'We do not end. We are eternal.'

'Your kind are nothing more than ghosts of a dead race.'

Morrígan lashed out with her talons, snatching one of the children from the cot. 'All paths lead to chaos. You still believe that these fools deserve to forge their own destiny?'

'I do. The wars to come will serve as a terrible lesson, but they will endure.'

His mother changed her grip on the knife. Rufius could tell she was preparing to strike.

Morrígan threw head back and laughed. 'Hah! They're naught but children playing with deadly toys.'

'As is their right.'

She held up the baby and stared into its eyes. 'They have no idea of the things that are to come.'

The witch's nails dug into its soft skin, and the child began to cry.

'Put my son down,' his mother said through gritted teeth.

'You're all fools. The alchemists will ruin this world —'

In one swift movement, his mother pushed Rufius behind her and leapt into the air. Her body seemed to blink out of existence for a second before reappearing behind the phantom queen and thrusting the dagger into her back until the point of the silver blade burst through the centre of her chest.

Morrígan stared down in disbelief at the blade, clawing at it with her fingers as her body turned to ash.

Rufius caught the baby as the queen disintegrated.

'Who are you?' Rufius asked, handing back the child.

She placed her son gently beside his sleeping brother. 'My name is Elizabeth De Burg, daughter of the second Earl of Ulster, wife of Robert the Bruce and I'm your mother.'

She wiped the blood from the baby's neck, a small crescent-shaped wound bled from where Morrígan's talons had cut him. Rufius felt a twinge in his neck and felt for a scar beneath his ear, but the skin was unblemished.

'And you are like me? A traveller?'

'Among other things,' she nodded. 'I was sent here to protect your father.'

'From what?'

Elizabeth came over to him, placing a tender hand on his cheek. 'There are so many things you've yet to learn. So many questions I cannot answer.'

Rufius stared into her eyes, trying to understand what he had just witnessed.

'Was she telling the truth? Was this a trap? Did you use me as bait?'

She picked up her knife and examined the blade. 'I had no choice. The Aeons are a threat that requires extreme measures.'

'Aeons?'

'One of the oldest races. They're a parasite, one that survives by moving from host to host, extending the life of the ones they possess. Morrígan and her Tuatha are one of many infestations that we have had to deal with.'

Rufius remembered how Maebh's body had aged when she died. 'There are more of them?'

'Many more, as you will soon discover.' His mother handed him the dagger.

'Me?'

Her expression hardened. 'My mission will end in less than two years. I will die falling from a horse during a royal visit,' she said, taking the iron cross from the baby's cot. 'I sent you away so that you could be prepared. I never thought I would ever see you grow to be a man.'

Walking towards him, he could see there were tears in her eyes. 'Where did you go?'

'Jorvik, 954.'

She frowned, holding up the metal charm. 'The tinker that I bought it from assured me it was only a few hundred years old. Who raised you?'

'A blacksmith and his family,' Rufius said. 'They were good people.'

His mother turned to the ashes of the dead queen. 'I wish there had been another way, but we are so few.'

'What is a Praetorian?'

'Royal bodyguards, protecting key figures in history.'

'From Aeons?'

She nodded. 'We need to keep them out of positions of power.'

Rufius looked down at the blade. 'We are but dust and shadow.'

'Our motto — did the blacksmith teach you Latin too?'

'No,' he said, shaking his head. 'I've seen this before.' He reached for Gunnlogi, but it was missing. 'On a sword.'

His mother looked confused. 'What kind of sword?'

'Roman. A gladius, someone told me it was made from the daggers that killed Caesar.'

'And how did you come by such a weapon?'

'It was left by an old man, for sharpening.'

She laughed. 'Did he have a limp?'

'I never really met him.'

'Oh you will. He's an interfering old goat. When the time is right, he will find you.'

One of the children began to cry, and she went over to the crib to calm it.

'You will need to leave soon.'

'But—'

'It is not safe to be near yourself,' she said, looking down at her babies. 'The continuum doesn't take too kindly to closed loops.'

She came over and hugged him, he buried his face in her hair, feeling the warmth of her breath on his neck.

'Be safe,' she whispered.

82

INAUGURATION

[Isle of Skye, Scotland. Date: 1302]

The Draconians found over thirty prisoners in the dungeons of the castle. Most had suffered too badly at the hands of the Tuatha to ever make a useful contribution to the Order. Some spent the next few weeks in the care of Doctor Crooke, trying to rehabilitate the least affected, but those that had lost all hope were made comfortable in a wing at Bedlam and left to their demons.

Rufius had returned to a hero's welcome, the entire Order was present at his inauguration. They used the Royal Institute — filling every seat with the most eccentric collection of people. Members from the last six hundred years attended. The front rows of the ranked benches were filled with familiar faces: Harrison, who still looked deathly pale but beamed with pride at him, Bodley sat next to Alixia who waved awkwardly and Dolovir nodded with fatherly pride.

Rufius stood beside the founder on the small dais, his hands folded behind his long black robes. The blisters on his palms had healed quickly, thanks to Alixia's medicine garden.

'There were times when I thought this day would never come,' began the founder, as the audience settled. 'Defeating the Tuatha Dé has proved that we all have a common goal — the preservation of the future.' He turned towards Rufius. 'This young man has shown us all that one selfless act can change the destiny of mankind. For too long some of us have used our powers for our own ends, whether that be for personal gain or altruistic reasons,' he said, staring directly at Vassili and the other members of the Dreadnoughts. 'But we have proven that when we work together, there is nothing that we cannot achieve. I propose that from this day forward, we come together as one, creating an order dedicated to protecting the future, whose sole ambition is to preserve the past and ensure the best possible future for humanity. I invite all of you to join us.'

The founder turned and placed a golden chain over Rufius's head. Hanging from the chain was a symbol, a snake eating its tail.

'May I present the first member of the Oblivion Order.'

Most of the audience rose to their feet as one, cheering and applauding. Vassili and Valtin were slow in rising and only did so when Dangerfield chided them.

Harrison came over to congratulate Rufius, slapping him on the shoulder and shaking his hand. 'The first member,' he said with a knowing grin. 'How does it feel?'

Rufius examined the medallion. 'Why the snake?'

'It's the Ouroboros, an Egyptian symbol of renewal.'

'Like Jörmungandr, the Midgard Serpent?'

'Let's hope he never lets go of his tail,' Harrison said with a wry chuckle that quickly developed into a hacking cough.

'Oh dear, think it's time for me to return to the infirmary,' he said, once he'd recovered.

Rufius watched him go.

'He will recover,' said the founder catching his eye. 'Doctor Crooke has been talking to Boyle from the Institute, they have a new form of vapour that should alleviate his condition.'

Kelly approached them and went down on one knee to present Rufius with the handle of the sword of daggers. 'Your blade, Sire.'

Rufius thought he saw something in Kelly's eye, a knowing glint.

'It has served you well,' said the founder.

'Indeed it has,' Kelly said, getting to his feet.

As he walked away, Rufius noticed he had a slight limp. 'You exceeded my expectations — eventually.'

83

FATHER

[Battle of Bannockburn, Scotland. Date: June 24, 1314]

It was the second day of the battle. Rufius and Bodley stood on Gillies Hill watching the Scottish attack the English army of Edward II.

To his left was Stirling Castle, the royal fortress, occupied by the English and Edward had sent a considerable army to reinforce it, but Robert the Bruce had been waiting for them and the first day had ended with the invaders being turned back.

Rufius had watched his father cleave open the head of Henry de Bohun with an axe on the first day. His troops went on to push two English cavalry units over the river and into the trees. It had made him feel proud to see him fight so bravely against the greater numbers of the English.

'Edward will retreat soon,' he said to Bodley, watching the king's forces begin to lose formation.

'How many times have you visited this battle?'

Rufius couldn't tell him, he had lost count. It had been nearly a month since he had met his mother and since then he had spent most of it here, observing the conflict from every angle, studying every moment of one of Scotland's greatest victories.

'Giles d'Argentan is about to take the reins of Edward's horse. Once that happens, it's over.'

They watched as the king was led from the battlefield, accompanied by hundreds of mounted bodyguards.

'Impressive,' agreed Bodley, 'but why exactly did you bring me here?'

'I wanted you to help me find my father's heart.'

'Your father?' Bodley said with a tone of disbelief.

'Robert the Bruce,' Rufius nodded towards the man leading the charge. 'Fifteen years from now, when he dies, one of his Lords, Sir James Douglas, has his heart removed from his body and placed in a silver casket so it could be worn around his neck. Douglas was killed in the siege of Teba in Andalusia, 1330 — the casket and heart were lost.

'How do you know The Bruce was your father?'

'Kelly told me.'

'And Kelly knows this for sure?'

'I've always known I was different, not a Dane nor a Saxon,' he scratched at the beard that had grown longer over the last few weeks.

'But how did you lose four hundred years?'

Rufius thought of his mother but stopped himself from telling Bodley the truth. 'Kelly thinks my gift came early, that somehow I displaced while I was still in swaddling clothes.'

Bodley looked impressed. 'That would be a significant leap for one so young. I've never heard of anyone showing signs at such a young age.'

'Perhaps they don't survive. If it wasn't for Bloodaxe's

hunting party finding me, I would have been eaten by wolves.' Rufius laughed.

'Not exactly a laughing matter.'

'It's not that,' he replied. 'I used to think that I was a *vixlingr*.'

Bodley smiled. 'A changeling.'

'And that my mother was one of the fairy folk.'

They both began to laugh. Watching the Scottish pikeman form a shield wall as they pushed into the English ranks.

ALSO BY ANDREW HASTIE

Follow more of Rufius's adventures in Anachronist

Buy now on Amazon

ACKNOWLEDGMENTS

Thanks to everyone who continues to support me – you're all amazing. To Simon and Karen for their editorial scrutiny, and my beta-readers for all of their comments!

This was the most difficult book to write. The Colonel is a complex and well-loved character, creating his early life took a great deal of work.

I hope you enjoyed it.

Andy x

ABOUT THE AUTHOR

For more information about The Infinity Engines series and other Here Be Dragons books please visit: www.infinityengines.com

Please don't forget to leave a review!
Thank you!
Andy x

Printed in Dunstable, United Kingdom

76777342R00221